Also by Marie Still:

We're All Lying

Beverly Bonnefinche is Dead (as Kristen Seeley)

Upcoming:

Bad Things Happened in this Room (2025)

Lucketts (2026)

Such a Pretty Thing (2026)

My Darlings

Marie Still

Text copyright © 2024 by Marie Still

All rights reserved. For information regarding reproduction in total or in part, contact Rising Action Publishing Co. at http://www.risingactionpublishingco.com

Cover Illustration © Nat Mack
Distributed by Simon & Schuster

ISBN: 978-1-998076-40-6
Ebook: 978-1-998076-42-0

FIC031080 FICTION / Thrillers / Psychological
FIC031010 FICTION / Thrillers / Crime
FIC031100 FICTION / Thrillers / Domestic

#MyDarlings

Follow Rising Action on our socials!
Twitter: @RAPubCollective
Instagram: @risingactionpublishingco
Tiktok: @risingactionpublishingco

For Lyric, Braelynn, Blakely, and Austin, it could be worse, at least I'm not a serial killer.

And for my baby sister, Laura, who is becoming a new mom the same year this book is published, she is also not a serial killer (or she's really good and hasn't been caught yet).

My Darlings

Chapter 1

MELISSA

I never understood why people say things like, "She died doing what she loved." I died doing what I loved, and it didn't make my death any less tragic. I guess if it makes them feel better, they can go ahead and spout that contrived line from an uninspired obituary. However, despite the unfortunate situation of being dead, I'd much prefer they'd dig a bit deeper, try a bit harder. You do only die once, after all.

"Such a shame. So young. But hey, she died doing what she loved!"

Nope. Still awful, still terrible, still dead.

My Nikes pounded rhythmically on the leaf-covered path, each step creating a satisfying *crunch*. I didn't listen to music when I ran in the woods on those early mornings. Instead, I preferred the measured sound of my even breaths and the steady increase of my heartbeat as my footfalls connected with the winding trail.

The forest was most alive on fall mornings. The crisp air bent the tree's branches, making their leaves quiver and the speckled light dance on the trail. These sights, sounds, and smells, all so rich and overwhelming, faded the faster I ran, until it was just my body and me.

On these mornings, running in the woods, I experienced pure, unadulterated bliss. The stress of my business, the worries of never finding the right man to marry and dying alone, and my regrets of past decisions all melted away. Turns out one fear was worth fearing. The dying alone part. But I wasn't alone, not in the literal sense. She was there.

Morning after morning, I woke up, put on my leggings and tank top, slipped into my running shoes, and lost myself in the forest.

I always knew the risks, all women runners do, especially here in DC. Years ago, the infamous Chandra Levy case consumed every media outlet. You couldn't watch TV or read the newspaper without hearing about it. The rumors of her affair with a senator made the story so tantalizing, that the entire nation tuned in. Eventually, a man already serving time for attacking two female joggers in Rock Creek Park was convicted of Levy's murder. Her remains decomposed for almost a year before they found her body on a trail not more than ten miles from the one that I was running on that morning. Even with the statistics and constant coverage of attacks on women doing exactly what I was doing every morning, I never felt afraid in those woods. I should have. Maybe I'd still be alive.

She seemed so normal, so safe, at first. Just a woman, around mid-forties, in need of help. That is until I drew close. Her eyes were the last thing I remembered. Irises as green as winding ivy surrounded by dark, full lashes. I looked into those eyes and thought *They're so beautiful*. I'd never seen eyes that color before. But they weren't human eyes. Human eyes have compassion. These eyes held no love, they had no soul.

When you're dying, time doesn't work the way it normally does. Those green eyes became a green sea with white-capped waves fierce enough to swallow a massive ship whole. As the angry water pulled me deeper and the green water turned black, I couldn't help but wonder how many people those beautiful eyes had fooled. How many people those pupils had burrowed beneath—people who looked back without fear, too mesmerized by their beauty. They saw no storm and instead gazed into sea glass and emeralds.

The problem was, you had to look, really *look*.

The burning in my lungs cooled, and I became sure no one had looked hard enough.

For the ones who had—the others like me—it was too late.

She stole our voices, and we couldn't warn anyone.

Chapter 2

Eloise

The news anchor laughs at something her co-anchor says. She then turns to the camera and covers her big white teeth with a red frown. "A body found on a popular hiking trail in Great Falls Park has been identified as prominent local business owner, thirty-six-year-old Melissa Goodwin. Tom is reporting live from Great Falls, Virginia. Tom, what can you tell us?" She shuffles her papers, revealing chipped nail polish on the middle finger of her left hand. One should be more prepared when they are reporting on such a paramount discovery.

The camera cuts to Tom. He grips his microphone; his thin lips plunge in an exaggerated frown. He's trying his best to look solemn, but I don't miss that twinkle in his eyes. It's an excitement brought on by murder, as long as that murder isn't yours or someone you love. He, like his viewers, yearns to know more. He's placed himself strategically in front of the plethora of fussing police, the angle perfect so we gawkers can witness the activity behind him from the comfort—and perceived safety—of our living rooms. The bright yellow tape screams 'a terrible crime has been committed' with its bold black lettering announcing *Police Line Do Not Cross*.

Another woman killed. That makes six in the last twelve months; a serial killer is amongst us. How appalling, how alarming. I clutch my pearls and gasp at the TV while hiding my smirk.

"Robert!" I cry to my husband. He grunts his acknowledgement. "Robert, do you hear this, love? Another woman murdered. And found so close." I tsk, tsk, tsk. My head shake, shake, shakes.

I am Eloise Williams. PTO president, stay-at-home mom, HOA treasurer, respected local philanthropist who sits on the boards of many distinguished charities, doting wife, and serial killer. And tonight, they have found another one of My Darlings.

I abhor that name, though—serial killer. I am an artist creating masterpieces. Pure, poetic magic. When My Darlings' souls leave their bodies, their eyes ignite with fear, then glaze over with a milky film. A delicate puff of air escapes their lips. To observe this moment is to be connected to them in a way very few people have experienced. I become them while my veins pulsate from the power of it all.

Cancer, fatal car accident, murder. People gorge themselves on the misery of others while assuring themselves these things happen to other people and that it's nothing they need to fret over. But it *can* happen to them. Terrible, life-destroying things can happen to anyone. Every second of every day, we are potentially breathing our last breath. Would people live their lives differently if they were more conscious of this fact?

Bryony, my daughter, is tap, tap, scrolling on her phone. I refrain from huffing in annoyance. Robert's gaze is on the TV, but he's tuning it out, looking through it, thinking of his latest case most likely. My husband is a prestigious attorney. His field is corporate law, so of no use to me should I ever find myself in need of criminal defense. Not that I would. I'm very good at what I do. They'll never catch me. Robert works for a large company. He does a lot of mergers, a lot of acquisitions, a lot of business things requiring him to be on the road, out of town and out of my hair. In addition to his constant absence, he earns a generous salary with annual bonuses. When I decided I was ready to marry, this was the most important quality I sought in a mate. I love money as much as I love My Darlings. With my looks, talent, and body, I could have had any man I wanted. Beautiful men require too much work. Their egos are too large, always in need of stroking and complimenting. What I required was someone average-looking but wealthy, interested but distant, someone like Robert. He is the perfect companion. While an ugly husband was perfectly fine with me, I realized after-the-fact that ugly children wouldn't do. Thankfully, Bryony takes after me in looks. She is stunning, perfect. I'm obsessed with her. My gaze travels to her, and I study my perfect specimen. My doll. My pet. My favorite possession. She senses me looking, and her eyes leave her phone and look up. I smile my sweetest smile, the one I've ritualistically practiced every night in the mirror. I'm sure I've mastered it; Bryony and Robert could lick their lips and taste honey if they really concentrated.

"You look lovely tonight, Bryony. Is that sweater new? That shade truly is your color."

"Thanks, Mom. It's the one you bought."

I don't need her to tell me this. She never did thank me for it, though. "Ah, yes. I must have forgotten. Did you see?" I ask, ensuring I don't sound too eager. The perfect fusion of concern and shock. "They found another dead woman."

"Mhm," she replies, eyes back on her phone, not even looking. I resist the urge to cluck my tongue. Melissa was some of my finest work and the two people who are supposed to be my biggest supporters sit there ignoring the big reveal. Well, I may have a headache the next time either of them requires my presence to celebrate a victory or accomplishment of theirs.

"Eloise," Robert says. "Would you mind grabbing me another beer?"

I would mind. But instead, I say, "Of course, dear." I take the empty beer from his outstretched hand and narrow my eyes at the wet circle imprinted on the side table next to his chair. When I come back with a fresh beer, I make it a point to wipe the wet mess with a paper towel, slide a coaster over the empty spot, and place the beer on top of it. It's insufferable he insists on drinking his beer straight from the bottle but then to ruin my snakewood end table in the process? Really.

My house, like me, is beautiful. Enviable. I prefer it that way, for friends and strangers to covet my possessions and life. Most of the homes in Northern Virginia are cookie-cutter versions of their neighbors, Mc-Mansions, they call them. Highly unacceptable. I demand different, special. We purchased our land on the outskirts of DC—where my husband commutes to daily—and custom-built our home. My design aesthetic ranges from modern to classic, with a hint of southern charm derived from my Mississippi roots. A handcrafted, wrought-iron gate opens to a brick driveway lined with red maples. In the fall, when their leaves turn, a river of blood leads to my home.

Every room features carefully selected materials and details, from the imported, Italian white marble flooring in the two-story entryway to the contrasting African Blackwood floors throughout the rest of the home. I spent over a year visiting foreign lands and inspecting the finest furnishings and art available. I painstakingly curated each item and each architectural nuance. My home is so exquisite several local and national magazines have featured it.

The news anchors have moved on to other less appalling features: the weekend's upcoming farmers' market and craft fair, the weather report, and a local scam targeting the elderly. My moment has passed with little fanfare. I turn off the television and announce that I'm going to bed. Robert heaves himself from his chair, muttering something about work, and plods off to his study.

My tongue traces my teeth, counting—molars, canines, incisors—this keeps my inside thoughts from oozing through my lips.

Bryony—eyes and fingers still glued to her phone—stands and departs without so much as a goodnight.

I tidy the room, put everything back in proper order, and glide up the winding staircase to our bedroom. Even with no audience, I ensure every move I make is as elegant as a ballerina's. Robert and I have separate walk-in closets, another feature I insisted on. I take two steps into mine and inhale the musky notes of vanilla, sandalwood, and mandarin orange, a bespoke detail courtesy of a master perfumer in Paris. Robert always insists on scrunching his nose and complaining of the smell being too strong. According to several studies, sociopaths have shown to have an impaired sense of smell. However, in this case, I'm sure it's simply his lack of taste, and he'd be better off staying out of my things anyway.

I step out of my nude Jimmy Choo kitten heels before unzipping my A-line, short-sleeved, belted, black Prada dress and placing it in the concealed hamper. Melanie, our house manager, will empty the hamper on Wednesday for laundering. I slide open a drawer and select a pajama set. Once dressed, I release the pin holding my hair in its chignon and let my long, silky, black waves cascade down my back. Not a single gray in sight. Lorna, my hair stylist, always compliments me on this fact when she sees me every Tuesday for my weekly appointment. I step up to my vanity and walk through my nightly skincare routine. Wash, skin serum, moisturizer, eye cream, lash serum, lip mask. I'm a big proponent of leveraging science where nature has disappointed. A good skincare regimen makes a world of difference in the amount of Botox units one needs every six weeks. With my skin glowing and the light reflecting in my lips, I begin: smile, frown, smile but sympathetic, laugh, smile again. With a curt nod, I internally compliment myself on how well I've done.

After fluffing the down-filled pillow on my bed and sitting with my back supported, I grab my readers and book from the nightstand. I read a single chapter, then slide between Egyptian Giza sheets. Their soft, luxurious embrace doesn't distract me from the itch, the one which accompanies the announcement a Darling has been found.

The excitement is over.

It's time to find the next

Chapter 3

BEATRIX

I'm not sure whether it's Melissa being the same age as me or because of the striking similarities we share, but the news of her murder has stitched a constant sense of unease to my ribcage. I didn't know her, never met her once, yet as I flip through the articles on my phone, zooming in on each image of this smiling stranger, I realize I've never felt so connected to someone I've never met.

After finding her social media pages, I spent hours scrolling through pictures and posts. She no longer feels like a stranger, more like a sister or an old roommate. With each new piece of information I devour, grief blooms in my heart. Our hair is—or in her case was—the same chestnut brown, both cut in the same style and length, layers to frame our face, falling just below our shoulders. Our eyes are the same pale shade of blue, closer to gray, really. There were differences, of course; her nose was slightly larger, a bit pointier, her face a little rounder. But the longer

I looked, the more similarities I found, and the more I missed her—this woman I'd never met.

A cool shudder vibrates through me. I exit out of the article and trade my phone for the glass of wine on my nightstand. A smooth merlot. It's risky, I know, to sit with my legs crisscrossed while drinking red wine over our white comforter. But David, my husband, is sleeping at the hospital tonight after a long surgery, and I'm too, something—nervous, uneasy—to be downstairs by myself.

My fingers tap on my bottom lip. Despite the empty wine bottles sitting on my nightstand, the last one just opened an hour ago; I'm wide awake. If I close my eyes, it's Melissa's face I'll see, and she'll haunt my dreams. I could call Poppy, Suzanne, or even Eloise. Hearing another voice would bring comfort, I'm sure of it. I can't bring myself to do it. I've been pulling away from them, all my friends, lately. Spending more time at home alone, drinking. I still show up to the brunches, dinner parties, and events. But that's simply to keep up appearances. My secrets have grown like ivy, imprisoning me. I've no one to blame but myself, which makes it all the more lonesome.

Chapter 4

Eloise

B eatrix leans forward with her gray eyes wide, making her look more insect-like than usual. "Did you hear? They found another woman." A full circle of white shows around her irises. It's unbecoming.

I do sit up straighter, though. Finally, this conversation has taken a more intriguing turn. We are on Tuscarora Mill's back patio. A brunch meeting to discuss our upcoming Gatsby-themed dinner event. "Revamps and Champs," is the name the ladies have chosen for this brunch. Not the actual event. We are gathered at the event—if one could call a brunch an event—to plan the event. They name everything, usually with rhymes. I suppose that's what you do when you have nothing but time on your hands and your husband's money in your designer purse. In reality, Revamps and Champs is a get-together to plan the Night of the Restoration. Working name, of course, it doesn't rhyme, so we can't have that. And if these ladies were being honest with themselves—which they never are—Revamps and Champs is just an excuse to day-drink. Because drinking is okay if it's champagne and orange juice and in the name of charity. It's sophisticated, even.

I'm enjoying my virgin juice. Alcohol causes bloating, and while I'll enjoy a glass of wine on occasion, I prefer to abstain in the early afternoon of a weekday. I also prefer a sharp mind, especially when Beatrix, Suzanne, and Poppy are in attendance. My best friends and all that. If only I could flick my wrist to demonstrate how I truly feel. They are neither friends nor the best of anything. I smile and nod and frown and shake my head in all the right places. No sense in alerting them to the fact that I'm in my head thinking, scheming, only partially paying attention to their yapping and droning on about whatever it is they are droning on about.

The lattice of the metal chair is carving its pattern into my thighs, and I shift in my seat. Fidgeting isn't something I'm prone to, but I prefer my porcelain skin to remain unmarred, and some sacrifices just need to be made.

"Horrific, just horrific," Suzanne says. I like horrific. It snaps me from my thoughts. She places her right hand across her heart as if she is feigning the horror she's reacting to. A diamond tennis bracelet dangles around her wrist, catching the sun.

"Oh, Suz." Poppy gasps. "It's gorge!" She grabs Suzanne's wrist and twists it, inspecting the diamonds.

"Isn't it? Tobin bought it for me." She smiles and smooths her hair with her free hand as if even the slightest strand would be out of place. When you've let yourself go as she has, it's natural for one to attempt to maintain control over the things still within your control. In Suzanne's case, that includes her hair and makeup, but sadly, not much else. Desperate really. Pathetic mostly. I do, however, silently curse myself for changing my hair appointment to Friday when I knew we'd be meeting t oday.

"What's the occasion?" I ask, smiling over my champagne flute of OJ. She flashes me a look and juts her chin slightly. "No special occasion. He came home with it last night. A 'just because' gift, he said." Turning her attention back to the group, she beams, holding out her wrist and twisting it to bring out the diamond's sparkle.

Beatrix chokes on her mimosa.

"Something wrong, Beatrix?" Suzanne turns pointedly, not dropping her hand.

"No." Beatrix chortles. "You know what they say about random gifts, though." It's almost a song, these words dancing from her lips.

Suzanne drops her hand to her lap, her eyes narrowing. "I do not. Why don't you enlighten us?"

"That it's the first sign of a cheater." Beatrix grins at Suzanne, but it doesn't meet her eyes. I could teach her a thing or two. She continues, "I'm sure that's not the case with Tobin."

Suzanne's glare melts into a too-sweet smile. "Tobin would never cheat. I'm not worried about that." She flicks her other unadorned wrist to demonstrate how unconcerned she is. The one with the bracelet is now hidden away below the table.

"Of course, he wouldn't," I say, patting her arm. "What a ridiculous thing to suggest, Beatrix. Really."

Beatrix's grin doesn't leave her face, clearly unfazed by my judgment. Suzanne seems to have disappeared into her head, searching for clues she may have missed, no doubt.

I slice through the silence to bring the ladies back to the more important topic. "Did anyone know her?" I ask.

"Who?" Poppy asks.

I stomp down the flash of annoyance that sparks in my chest. "The woman they found. The dead one."

Poppy rolls her eyes. "Oh, duh, silly me. I didn't." She lowers her voice and leans in as if she's about to deliver a secret. I can't help myself and lean in to scoop it up. "Did y'all notice how much she looked like Beatrix?"

"She did not," Beatrix snaps, loud enough to catch the attention of the other diners. "Why would you say that Poppy?"

"Sorry," Poppy says, patting her mouth with her napkin to hide her flushed face. She looks from Suzanne to me. "You two see it though, don't you? The hair, the eyes..."

"Now that you mention it—" Suzanne says. I can't tell if she actually agrees with Poppy, or if this is her revenge for the cheating comment.

Beatrix's hands are clenched in fists on the table, and she looks like she may jump it and wrap them around Poppy's neck. Her reaction fascinates me. "Enough. Shut up, both of you."

"Now, ladies, this conversation is clearly upsetting Beatrix," I interject. "Why don't we move on?"

There's an awkward silence, and everyone except me avoids glancing in Beatrix's direction. She almost looks on the verge of tears. How strange.

"Well, I, for one, will not be doing any running or anything else alone," Suzanne says, pursing her pink lips.

Beatrix stifles a laugh behind her champagne glass, apparently fully over her earlier outburst. We all know Suzanne hasn't run a day in her life. Her loose blouses do nothing to hide the extra forty pounds she's carrying around. She tosses her blonde hair over her shoulder and looks away from the group. I suck in a breath of anticipation, wondering if anyone will point this out and make her blue irises swim beneath tears.

"Me either," Poppy exclaims. I deflate internally.

"I'm most worried about my Bryony," I say. "Teenagers can be so brazen, never taking these things seriously."

Three heads bob up and down in unison.

The server approaches and asks if he can bring us anything else. Both Poppy and Suzanne ask for mimosa refills. Poppy is on number two, Suzanne three, and Beatrix is working through her fourth. They will all get in their luxury SUVs and drive home, potentially killing themselves and any number of innocent drivers or pedestrians on the roads. And yet, I'm the evil one. If I could roll my eyes without raising eyebrows, I wo uld.

We finish our meals—the ladies finish their drinks—and we make our way to the parking lot. Beatrix has already sped off, and as I walk away, I hear Suzanne say to Poppy, "You don't think it's true, do you?"

I pause and pretend to be in search of something deep in the recesses of my purse.

"Don't think what's true?" Poppy asks.

"What Beatrix said about Tobin and the cheating. Eloise, have you lost something?"

Both Poppy and Suzanne are staring at me. I can't decipher if they're attempting to be helpful or prying. I open my mouth to say my keys but stop. Not one of us drives a car that requires a key to unlock our vehicles or even turn our cars on.

I smile. "I thought I left my phone at the table." I hold it up. They return my smile.

Poppy turns back to Suzanne. "No, 'course not. Tobin adores you. You know how Beatrix is, always trying to get you all riled up. If you let her, she wins."

I make a humming sound. Their attention is back on me. Waiting. I let the moment drag on a few beats to raise Suzanne's blood pressure a tick.

"It's just," I say, tapping a finger on my lips. "While Beatrix's delivery might have been a tad crass, she makes a good point, don't you think?"

Suzanne's jaw seemingly unhinges, and her mandible drops. That is the lower part of the jaw. I'm well-versed in human anatomy.

Her mouth clamps shut, recovering herself quickly. "Beatrix doesn't know what the hell she's talking about. Look at what she did earlier, throwing an absolute fit over a dead girl."

Poppy's head bobs. "It *was* weird. Such an overreaction, especially since they look like they could be sisters, twins, even. Don't you agree, Eloise?"

I want them to stop talking about Melissa. She's mine. At the same time, I want them to go on forever. I shrug and turn my back to them, continuing to my car.

I spend the drive home wondering if Suzanne's drama could make for a nice distraction while I find my next Darling. Suzanne has never been the most stable of our group. A few little taps to the chest. It wouldn't take much to push her off the edge she's already teetering on.

Chapter 5

THE WATCHER

S he's having lunch with her friends today. Or brunch, I suppose they would call it, thinking they are fancy. Her friends are as awful as she is, but I'm sure she realizes this. She doesn't care about them, and they don't care about her. They all deserve each other. Eloise has surrounded herself with a circle of vapid women for as long as I've known her. Well, that's not exactly fair. They weren't all terrible people, not before meeting her. She changes people, warps them, and draws out their faults. She's like a virus, spreading her sickness to anyone she breathes o n.

I've been watching her for so long that I fear I'm becoming desensitized to her or even becoming her. I used to wail and vomit and scream after each murder, wishing I had stepped in, wanting to do more, knowing I couldn't. I tried once. It didn't work. Nothing ever does when Eloise is involved.

I do none of that now. I simply bear witness, go home.

"Ma'am?"

I peek over my large sunglasses at the server, unsure how long she's been standing there.

"I'm sorry, what?"

"I asked if everything came out alright." Our gazes fall to my untouched food.

"Oh yes, great. Thanks." My smile is pinched.

She looks doubtful. I take a bite to reassure her.

"Mhm," I exclaim through a mouthful.

Eloise's head turns our way. Always the careful observer. Probably considering whether I'm a worthy victim. I raise my glass and smile at her and wonder if some instinctual alarm bell rings in her mind, alerting her to the fact that she knows me from somewhere. She'd never recognize me. I look so different from the last time we saw each other. And the time before as well. She nods curtly and focuses her attention back on her friends.

I pop a green grape in my mouth. My teeth break the skin, and I enjoy the sweet juice bathing my tongue. Beatrix has said something to upset Suzanne. There's always one, a woman who wants to be her more so than the rest. That woman in this circle is Beatrix. At one point, she even dyed her light brown hair black and wore green contacts. I can only assume by how quickly her look changed back that one of the other women, or even Eloise herself, commented on these changes in a very public and humiliating way. This all occurred at the beginning of their friendship. Once Beatrix realized she could never be Eloise or even a poor copy of her, her infatuation turned to hate. Thinly veiled, but even to the far away observer, it's obvious.

Poppy is my favorite. Maybe it's the sprinkling of freckles splashed across her nose. They remind me of my cousin Layla. I was always jealous of Layla's freckles, especially when our grandpa would tell her every freckle was a new kiss from an angel. I wanted angel kisses too. One day, I took a brown marker and dotted it across my nose and cheeks. Layla pointed and laughed, sending me running to the bathroom to scrub my skin until it was red and raw. I know where Grandpa is now, six feet below the earth. His death wasn't long after my 'incident.' I'm sure my mother blamed me for the heart attack that killed him. I wish I knew where Layla was. I miss her something fierce. I hope she is living an amazing life with a husband who's sweet to her, one or maybe two kids, and a house with a picket fence.

I look at my lap. My fists are squeezed, knuckles white.

The face with the constellations painted on it flickers behind my eyes. An old movie, I can practically hear the film clicking and crackling.

I watch from the sidewalk, standing behind that white picket fence. The front door opens. She lifts her hand in a wave, her image juddering and disappearing along with Layla's imaginary life and imaginary family.

I blink and stare at Poppy's freckles.

Maybe one day I'll find Layla and tell her I'm sorry for the lost time. If I ever get the chance to start over.

I throw a hundred-dollar bill on the table. I'm done with Eloise for the day.

Chapter 6

Eloise

The news got a few things right. Melissa Walters was thirty-six and she did own a business. But prominent? Quite the stretch. Melissa's florist shop catered to small weddings and Hallmark-manufactured holidays. Washington, DC, isn't short of rich and powerful people—politicians, celebrities, athletes. Maybe if her client list included any of these well-respected figures, she would be considered 'prominent,' but no, before her death, she was just an average woman living a boring and monotonous life. I made her special. I made her prominent. Something she should be thankful for.

Melissa, being a nonentity, was the precise reason I chose her. I spend a good deal of time selecting My Darlings according to specific criteria: unmarried with no children. This has nothing to do with me possessing a conscience of any sort. There is no bit of heart or some kernel of goodness inside that would prevent me from ripping a mother from her young children's lives. It's nothing like that. It's simply self-preservation. Husbands and children are emotionally attached to their wives and mothers, which increases my chances of getting caught. You can't hunt and kill from jail, which would bring my fun to an end.

I plucked Melissa from this world as easily as the flowers adorning her shop were plucked from the soil. When I first laid eyes on her mousey brown hair, pulled on top of her head in a messy bun, and saw her crooked smile, I knew she was the one. I never finalize my choice right away. There is always more research, but my initial instincts have never been wrong. She was wearing a black apron draped over a T-shirt and what they refer to as 'boyfriend jeans,' but which are simply ill-fitting, baggy pants. These pants give the impression the wearer is clueless that an entire profession of tailors exists to customize clothing to fit and flatter. Her small shop was in one of the many pockets of historical downtown areas speckled around Northern Virginia on a cobbled street in Alexandria. The downtown area is preserved to retain Virginia's roots and differentiate us from other suburban areas. To prove we're more cultured due to our history and whatnot.

Alexandria is also known for its haunted history. An ice cream shop shares its space with the spirit of Laura Schafer, who burned to death the night before her wedding in the 1800s. The Devil-Bat occupies the old clock tower, keeping watch over the town and its people. The Female Stranger, a nameless ghost, still wanders the tavern she died in. I often wonder if Melissa somehow made it back to her shop when her spirit left her body and if she'll become a legend as well. While I'm not sure I believe in any of that nonsense, I do find the stories to be quite entertaining.

Bryony and I were doing some Saturday shopping when we came upon Blooms of Happy.

"Let's pop in and buy fresh lilies for the entryway," I said.

She read the shop's name and rolled her eyes, only expressing what I was thinking: a terrible name, so trite. Bryony and I, we're so alike.

"Fine, but can we go home after? I'm sick of walking."

"Of course, dear. Do you have plans tonight?"

"Yes, Mother, just a few girlfriends watching a movie at Olivia's house."

A lie. Bryony thinks she's the most capable liar, but what she doesn't realize is I'm the best liar of all. No one can fool me, especially not her. I had no desire for a debate to unfurl in front of Blooms of Happy, so I let this lie slide.

We stepped through the door into a room filled with every color nature could produce. I pretended to breathe in the mixture of perfumes emanating from the flowers stuffed into every corner, commenting on how lovely it smelled. Melissa greeted us with a toothy grin, giving her a horse-like expression, and provided exemplary customer service while she explained the home delivery service she offered. A chatty one, she also divulged a significant chunk of her life story while Bryony stood off in a corner absorbed by her phone. Confident I'd gathered the information I needed, I cut her off, accepting a business card in exchange for a promise I'd be in touch. The less Bryony remembered, the better. None of my personal details or credit card were provided. My connection to Melissa was severed almost as quickly as it had formed.

With my new Darling selected, the arduous pre-murder process began. The first phase is always research. I start with online—social media, public records, and the like. While the internet has made getting to know My Darlings much easier, it is also traceable. For this reason, I utilize VPN access to hide my search and browsing history. Another connection snipped away, like pruning shears snipping through weeds.

My investigation confirmed Melissa Walters was the perfect selection. She lived in a row house in Georgetown with no roommates save for a black tabby named Shadow. Her father died of colon cancer ten years prior. Her mother—bless her heart—was living in a home, suffering from dementia. No siblings. No close family. She did, however, have a good many friends. But Melissa was independent, often going days or weeks with no social obligations. She ran in Great Falls Park, usually in the very early mornings before opening Blooms of Happy for patrons.

I have been waking up at five to run each morning for the entirety of my marriage. In keeping this regimented schedule, when I move from the research to the stalking phase of hunting my prey, my family is none the wiser. They think I'm just out for my daily jogs. When more bodies began turning up, Robert casually mentioned I should consider joining a gym. Safer, he said. At least until they catch the creep.

I've become hungrier lately, killing more frequently, and that's the only reason the media or he took notice. DC has plenty of murders, almost two a week, to be exact. But when those murders aren't gang members and drug dealers and are instead pretty, young women, people start to pay attention.

The morning of Melissa's last breath was a crisp September day. The air was tinged with the scent of fire, nature's whisper alerting us colder weather is on its way. She came up the path, and I hobbled from the tree line in front of her.

"Dear, do you mind helping me?" I moaned.

"Oh my gosh," she said. "What happened?"

I reached out a hand, showing her the empty dog leash. "I'm afraid my Rex got excited by a squirrel. He ran into the woods, and I twisted my ankle chasing after him. I hate to bother you, but I could use some assistance finding him." I frowned and took a limping step for emphasis.

"Of course. Which way did he run? What kind of dog?"

"German Shepherd. He's quite old, so I don't suspect he's gotten very far. He went off that way." I pointed deeper into the woods. Melissa followed obediently like Rex would have if he had been real. Both of us called Rex's name. I rested on a tree, rubbing my ankle, and let her get a few steps ahead before limping behind her. Once far enough from the path, out of sight, I slipped on a pair of leather gloves, pulled a black ski mask over my head, and retrieved the syringe from my pocket. Jamming the needle into her neck, I pierced her skin and released the poison into her blood. She turned, eyes wide. But I had the shock of it all working for me. Her lips parted, preparing to scream, and I slammed her head into a tree next to us. She collapsed to the leaf-covered ground, still fighting, still thinking she'd live through this. I had time before the drugs would do more damage than simply soften her senses, so I straddled her, fighting through her grasping hands and kicking feet, and used her attempts at sitting up to slip the garrote fashioned from piano wire behind her head. She was young, healthy, and full of vitality, but I was practiced, precise, and too fast. I crossed the garrote across her throat, switched hands, and pulled. When her hands lowered and stopped scratching at my face, I pushed the mask up, re-revealing my face. You see, the mask isn't to conceal my identity. What would be the point when she saw my face and dead mouths don't speak? Facial injuries, however, do. They can be hard to explain away, especially claw marks from a Darling not ready to die. The mask keeps fingernails from scratching my skin.

Leaning down, I looked into her panicked eyes, trying to drink her thoughts. They rolled into the back of her head, and her convulsing lessened. Sitting back, I twirled a strand of her brown hair around my finger and shushed her while running my fingers down her cheek. I wish I could have stayed longer, the two of us, enjoying this moment. Too risky.

My face tilted to the sky. The hum of the woods seemed to grow louder, almost deafening. I sucked in a deep breath, and with closed eyes, laughed. My entire body ignited. Pricks of ecstasy danced across my skin. Orgasmic, but more intense.

I opened my eyes and looked down at her, still alive, but barely. I picked up the garotte's handles and pulled, finishing the task.

Melissa's jerking settled, her death mask resting permanently on her face. I stood, brushed the dirt from my clothes, placed the garrote and syringe in my jacket pockets, and retrieved a compact. After a quick smoothing of my hair and fixing of my face, I filled my chest with the fire-scented air and sauntered away from her body.

Chapter 7

Eloise

A few days after brunch with the ladies, I stand with Bryony in our entryway.

"Bryony, that just won't do. This is an important night. First impressions are crucial. Go back upstairs and put on the dress I had Melanie lay out for you."

Her mouth opens. I cross my arms and dare her with my eyes to defy me. She makes the right decision and turns around without a word, heading up the stairs and into her room. She emerges at the top of the stairs a few minutes later and, much improved, adorned in the long-sleeved, boat-neck black dress that falls an inch above her knees. Her hair is in a bun circled at its base by a thick braid. A simple pearl necklace with matching pearl earrings are her only accessories. This is more acceptable. Elegant and beautiful, complementing the notes from her violin rather than distracting the audience from them.

"Better, Mother?" she asks, once again joining me in the entryway.

I give her a curt nod. "Is your father almost ready?"

She shrugs and digs her phone from her clutch. The room turns crimson, and my hand twitches with the desire to smack the dreaded device from her palm. To calm my temper, I close my eyes and picture the custom invitations I sent a few weeks earlier. Gold foil lettering embossed on thick cream paper had been received by scouting agents for the most prestigious programs for young classical musicians from all over the world. I included the event details in a loopy script and tucked a photo of Bryony and a short bio neatly inside the thick envelopes. All but three responded positively, with those three not able to make the trip due to scheduling conflicts. I considered offering accommodations and flights as part of the invitation but didn't want to be perceived as desperate. They needed to crave Bryony, not the other way around. The positive response rate improved from the last concert. Word of her talent must be making its way around the right circles.

Robert comes pounding down the stairs with his elephant-like steps. "Bryony, my love, you look so grown, so beautiful. How about a twirl for your old dad?"

Bryony's face lights up as if her father has flipped up some invisible switch on the side of her neck. He grabs her hand and holds it above her head while she spins in circles, head thrown back, laughing.

"Stop that right now! She'll be disheveled before we get there."

I can sense the look exchanged behind my back while I walk to the front door. I mentally note the time, so later, when they are both in bed, I can scroll through the security footage and observe their exchange for myself.

We drive to the theater, listening to the compilation of Bryony's past mistakes, a 'symphony of failure' I called it when I played it the first time.

There is to be no talking during this drive. Bryony knows she's expected to study every missed note, every faltered timing. Listening and learning. A reminder that the only acceptable outcome for tonight is perfection.

⎯⎯◆⎯⎯

Annabelle, Bryony's best friend, and her mother, Grace, are in the parking lot when we arrive. Annabelle spots us and waves. They stop walking and wait for us while Robert pulls the car into an empty spot. I practice in my head. A smile not forced. A greeting not grating.

We exit the vehicle and make our way to them. Bryony and I exchange cheek kisses with the mother and daughter, and Robert and Terrence shake hands. Our husbands are both rich and lawyers, but that's where the similarities end. Despite being the same age, Terrence looks ten years younger. He's tall and fit, with dark skin and a smile that sets fire to his entire face. Grace is elegant and beautiful herself, but marrying such a handsome man was a mistake. I see the way the other moms drink him in with their eyes, as if he was the only glass of Sauvignon Blanc at a dinner party. Only a few inches shorter than her husband, Grace resembles a model who has just stepped off the runway. Tonight, her fitted column dress hugs her body like it was made for her, which it probably was. The hues of her rich brown skin against the emerald-green dress have an enchanting effect. I wonder if she designed the dress for this occasion. I consider my own Armani and wonder if I should have gone Couture instead. Grace's fashion brand is iconic, especially in the DC area. She's dressed women from First Ladies to movie stars. Annabelle, on the other hand, looks inappropriate for the event. Her own black dress's neckline plunges too low. Her natural curls, usually thick and lovely, have been ironed flat and blunt bangs slice a sharp line across her forehead.

"The girls have worked so hard for tonight. It should be a wonderful show," Grace says. "I swear Annabelle hasn't left the piano bench for months." She chuckles.

"I'm sure your performance will be splendid, Annabelle," I say, offering her a quick smile. "Bryony hasn't really changed much in the way of her practice schedule. No extra sessions. If only she could be so dedicated."

"A natural talent," Grace says, offering Bryony her own smile. I study the angle of her lips and how the expression changes her eyes. Grace probably assumes I'm suggesting Bryony should practice more. I know what's said behind my back, how much I push her. But what I'm implying is that my Bryony does not need extra practice. Grace, always the picture of class, sidestepped the hidden insult. The other ladies are more fun. They take my bait. Killing Grace would be a delight, but I'd have to break so many rules to do so, including the most important one: No killing anyone whom I'm personally connected to.

We walk into the theater and the girls leave us to head backstage. Two other mothers join Grace and me, and the fathers walk to the bar.

"What do you think about the ... murders?" one of the moms, shorter and rounder than the other, asks. She lowers her voice while saying 'murder,' as if speaking the word will cause her to drop dead in front of us.

"It's just so awful," her friend says. Her features don't fit properly on her face, all small and pinched, like a Fernando Botero painting come to life.

"Eloise, what are your thoughts? Do you think they're related?" Grace asks.

I sniff. "I try not to pay much attention to those types of things. It's too depressing and stressful. Robert and I are keeping a closer eye on Bryony these days, though."

It would be just like Robert to choose this moment to appear behind me and take an interest in our conversation, mentioning that I was in fact quite interested in Melissa's demise based on my reaction to the news report. I glance over my shoulder; he's deep in conversation with Terrance and not paying a lick of attention to us. My annoyance goes from his possible injection to him talking, unaware that I am looking at him and could possibly require his focus.

The three moms nod in unison. I spot a recruiter for a New York-based program, a known feeder for the New York Philharmonic, and excuse myself to pick my way through the crowd and make my introductions. Robert joins us as we are chatting and places a hand on my lower back. I introduce them, then it is time to take our seats for the concert. All perfectly timed, giving Robert no time to open his mouth and undo my work with some silly statement about letting kids be kids or that Bryony plays music for fun, or who knows what else. I haven't spotted any of the other recruiters amongst the parents, but they are here, I have no doubt. Once we have found our seats, I'll be able to scan the crowd more easily.

Annabelle performs before Bryony, who always closes the show. She is a decent technical pianist, but her performances lack heart. Her musical career will end when high school does. I escape into my head and re-watch Melissa's murder like a favorite movie. Her smile, so open and trusting, so willing to help. Her body writhing and convulsing while the wire compressed around her throat, stealing her final breath. Finally, it's my Bryony's turn. She walks to the center of the stage, and a single spotlight illuminates only her. She lifts the violin and places it under her chin, dragging out the start, making the audience sit forward in anticipation. This is all part of the show. I close my eyes, ready to be taken away by Bach's Partita No. 2. She begins to play, and my eyes pop open.

"What is this?" I hiss to Robert, keeping the pleasant smile on my face and gaze locked on the stage.

"I believe that would be Radiohead, Eloise."

"Radio-what?" Unable to control the volume of my voice, a few heads swivel in our direction. I return their glares with my own until the last head swivels back to Bryony.

"Radiohead is a band, and 'Creep' is the name of the song, if I'm remembering correctly." He chuckles.

I sit still for the remainder of her performance as if a steel rod has replaced my spine. I'm confident our important guests are as appalled as I am. The last note echoes through the auditorium. Bryony lowers her bow and violin to her side. The silence has thickened the air. I refuse to lift my clasped hands to wipe the sweat beading my face.

After a few pounding heartbeats, someone whistles. The entire crowd follows suit and Bryony receives a standing ovation. I'm the only one still seated.

In the car on the way home, Robert showers Bryony with compliments. I twist in my seat and wipe that proud look from her face with one look.

"The crowd seemed to enjoy her performance. Don't you agree, Eloise?" Robert says. There's an edge to his voice. Is that a threat, I sense?

Silence is such a powerful weapon. I ignore his threat and continue to stare silently.

I smile because if you smile when you speak, it makes your words seem softer, kinder. A smile is also a powerful weapon. "Yes," I agree. "Wonderful indeed."

The sweet smell of fear seeps from Bryony's pores. I wonder if Robert, with his keen olfactory system, picks up on it.

We arrive home, and Robert announces he has some emails to respond to. When I'm sure he's safely tucked away in his office, I step toward Bryony and lower my face inches from hers. "Go to your room and play Bach's Partita No. 2 until I'm asleep."

"How am I supposed to know when you fall asl—"

My palm connects with her cheek, and she hunches over, cradling the side of her face with a hand.

"Figure it out," I snap on my way up the stairs.

Chapter 8

THE WATCHER

I was the first one on my feet after Bryony's brilliant cover of "Creep." I didn't think she would dare go against her mother so brazenly, but she surprised me. Eloise's pouting had me absolutely tickled. The way she was sitting there, her entire body frozen. I wonder if she felt embarrassment for the first time in her life.

I also wonder if she's starting to sense my presence. All predators possess an instinct to alert them when danger is near when it's creeping in.

Bryony and I have been online friends for about three years now. She believes I'm an eighteen-year-old girl from California who also plays the violin. I added her on Instagram, not sure if it would work. But teens these days have no sense of privacy or personal safety, and she returned my follow within seconds. After a private message exclaiming how much we had in common, I was in. I moved slowly at first. A few comments and likes on photos. A private response to a story here and there. Soon, our friendship blossomed. Every once in a while, she would complain about her mom. This isn't unusual for teens; however, Bryony feared her mother. She'd never admit to it, but I could tell. Teens aren't as sly as they believe themselves to be. I blame it on the raging hormones.

I use her occasionally when shadowing Eloise becomes too dull. Like when Bryony told me about her upcoming concert, how her mother had embarrassingly sent custom invitations to music program scouts, and how she was so sick of Bach she wanted to break her bow and stab herself with it. A few days later and a YouTube link sent with a certain violin cover, I'd planted the seed; it didn't even require watering to grow.

BryLove: They loved it.

CaliViolinGrl: Oooo you did it?

BryLove: Yep. Didn't tell anyone, just walked out and played Creep. Standing ovation.

CaliViolinGrl: Even your mom? (laughing face emoji)

BryLove: No. She was pissed.

CaliViolinGrl: What happened?

BryLove: I dunno, gotta go. Talk later, k?

CaliViolinGrl: K, later (kissy face emoji)

I knew better than to push too far. I could fill in the blanks myself. My heart aches for Bryony. There must be a way to save her from her mother. At first, my catfishing scheme was a method to find out more about Eloise. I'm probably too close now, my emotions too wrapped up. I love Bryony. Eloise doesn't deserve her. She doesn't deserve anything good that she has. The unfairness of it all is enough to drive a person mad. And maybe it has.

With Melissa dead and buried, Eloise must be getting to work on another victim. I've noticed the time between her killings has shortened.

She used to go months, even years, without killing. Not anymore. I did some research and found this is typical behavior for serial killers. She's not the typical profile, though, so I have to fill in the blanks with my own assumptions and knowledge of her.

Eloise is the mycelium beneath our feet. The gravity pulling us down. She is the carbon monoxide filling a house while its victims breathe in the poison unaware. She is there, but she is not. Her curated life is the perfect disguise.

The scariest monsters are those hiding in plain sight.

She has no reason for being the way she is. She was born evil, nature's flaw. A beautiful flower that kills without mercy. Protection from natural selection. But this type of evil, this type of species, has no place among humankind.

Chapter 9

Eloise

"Eloise. Eloise, my darling, where are you?"

It was the summer of 1971, and the air was bloated with heat and moisture. Everything and everyone always moved a bit slower during those summer months. Mother hollered my name from our wraparound front porch while I hid with the grasshoppers in the fields of our sprawling property. They rubbed their legs and fluttered their wings. Together, the humming and buzzing created the song of a Mississippi summer. I dropped the magnifying glass I'd been holding over the anthill and stood on my tiptoes to peek over the tall wheatgrass. I looked down at the massacre. Red bodies lay burned and scattered around the mound of dirt that served as the entrance to their underground home.

"That'll teach you to bite me," I said to their fire ants' corpses before running toward the sound of Mother's voice.

"There you are, my sweet." She greeted me with a smile as bright as the summer sun. I walked past her, my own face impassive. "I've made a pitcher of lemonade and key lime pie. Come on in, and let's get your belly filled."

She followed me inside. From the corner of my eye, I saw her hand reach out to pet my head, so I sped up to avoid her touch. I stomped over the wooden planks—an original feature of the home's 1901 construction—through the lavender-scented entryway, past the sitting room whose stone-surround fireplace stood proudly in the center of the room, down the hall past the locked door of my father's study, and into the large bright kitchen, whose yellow walls and white cabinets added to its cheery demeanor. After climbing onto the wicker stool, I silently waited with my fingers intertwined on the counter and my legs crossed at the ankles for my mother to serve me.

She placed a small plate with a slice of pie and a glass filled to the brim with lemonade in front of me. "What adventures has my Eloise been on today?" Her hand went to smooth my hair, but she quickly dropped it, realizing her mistake.

I took a bite of pie and swallowed it down with a small sip of lemonade before answering. Even back then, I knew how improper it was to speak with one's mouth full. "I killed those ants that bit me."

Her smile faltered. "Eloise. Those ants were just being ants. I know you didn't like the bites, and they hurt very bad, but killing them wasn't making a good decision. Or a nice one. Remember we talked about this?"

I shrugged and took another swallow of the homemade, freshly squeezed lemonade. The sweetness from the sugar hurt my teeth, and I winced. She was always putting in too much sugar. The pie was delicious, though; at least she managed to get that right.

"Don't worry. We'll work on making better choices. You don't have to get upset."

I cocked my head to the side, unsure where she conjured up such an impression. I wasn't upset. I also had no plans of taking her unsolicited, and frankly, bad advice. She sat on the stool next to me and placed her chin in her hand. Her other hand thrummed its fingers on the counter.

"Your ninth birthday is coming up soon. Have you thought about what you'd like for your party?"

"I don't want a party."

"Why ever not? It's a big day, *your* big day. We could make a cake and have ice cream and invite all your friends from school—"

"I don't have any friends."

Her smile dropped into an exaggerated frown. "That's not true. You have lots of little friends. What about Emily? Don't you think she'd be upset to not be invited to your party?"

"Well, there isn't a party for her to be upset about, and I bit her hand for trying to steal my favorite pen, so she's not my friend anymore."

Mother sighed, pushed herself up, and walked to the sink, busying herself rewashing the dishes from the dish dryer. If I walked over, I'd probably see her crying again. She was always doing that. Something was probably wrong with her eyes, they were always doing that. Or maybe it was inside her head that was the issue.

"Love you, Eloise," she called to my back.

I sped up my steps and pretended not to hear.

Chapter 10

Eloise

I am restless. My skin grows tighter with each day, and if I wait too long, it will rip apart. I try my hardest to maintain my composure, but the color drains from every face my gaze falls upon. Their lips turn blue. Their eyes glaze over. My imagination sprints away from me, picturing their flesh flaking from their skull. Their bodies discarded beneath the dirt. The worms wiggling through their rotting corpses. Furthermore, I have Bryony's sudden insubordination to deal with. Tonight, however, I have other pressing matters to attend to. I've called an emergency PTA meeting. The mommies are anxious. A serial killer lurks in their town, ready to snatch their babies at any moment. I'll feed on their fear from my podium with a smile on my face and reassuring words. The fear that I hope will satiate my hunger a bit longer. They won't realize the smile isn't to help calm their worries, but rather for a meal they're unintentionally serving.

"Parents, welcome," I announce from the front of the room. We're arranged in the cafeteria, with me and the other PTA members seated behind a long table, on a raised platform brought in for the occasion. The rest of the parents sit in rows of chairs lined up in front of us. There are a more dads in attendance than usual. Serial killers are more interesting than book fairs, bake sales, and teacher appreciation planning.

A mom in the front row stands. Wringing her hands, she cries, "What is the school doing to protect our children?"

"If I could get everyone to take their seats, all your questions will be answered." My voice, assisted by the microphone, carries over the din of the room. A silence eventually replaces the rustling of clothes, the scraping of chairs on linoleum, and the hushed whispers. I continue, "Wonderful. Thank you all for coming. I assume you are all aware of the terror plaguing our community. We felt it important to meet so we could alleviate any concerns you may have for your children's safety." I pause for effect, glancing around the room at the mixture of pursed lips, slack jaws, and wide eyes. "Principal Michaels will review the extra precautions the school has taken to ensure the safety of all students during school hours, and the chief of police is here to share some tips to assist us with how to handle this awful situation at home." I take my seat and Principal Michaels replaces me behind the microphone.

The fear crackles in the air, so palpable it raises the hairs covering my body. I shift in my chair, a dulled version of the familiar static tingles beneath my skin teasing me in the most pleasing way.

Principal Michaels explains how they have increased on-campus security and blah, blah, blah. Inside I'm cackling. This entire room is so sure their boogeyman is right outside the gate, lurking in the streets. If they only knew. The monster was already inside, and she was leading them.

PTA meeting attendance is required. Our children have the luxury of attending a prestigious private school. Parental involvement is imperative. It fosters a community of learning and ensures our children will thrive. At least, that's what the document we all signed declares. Usually, parents grab their belongings and sprint to the door after each required meeting. The parking lot becomes a tangled mess. No one wants to get caught in the line of cars exiting the parking lot, not after suffering through an hour of content they only pretend to care about.

This evening, there are very few sprinters. They feign concern, but are too afraid, or not self-aware enough to admit the other reason for their increased attentiveness. The entire situation excites them. Parents stand in clumps around the room, discussing. I work the room, playing the part of a soothing yet equally scared mother.

"Great meeting, Eloise," Grace says. I don't understand why she feels the need to tell me something I already know. It's as if she believes I require her validation.

Of all the years I've known Grace, I'm still unsure if her compliments are sincere or if she's just as good as me at hiding her true feelings. Perhaps she's a murderess as well.

I remember to blink. "It is an unprecedented time. I just hope the content was helpful and the children will be safe."

"They'll catch him soon. These criminals always mess up, eventually," she says with more confidence than she should have.

"It may not be a he, you know," I reply.

Grace's head tilts to one side. "Of course, it's a he. Why would a woman be killing other women? Female killers are never so random."

"You're right. They usually kill their children or husbands."

Grace's perfectly manicured hand meets her chest. I imagine the heart beating beneath it and what it would feel like to cut it out. "This is all too ghastly. I can't think about it anymore. I'm already having nightmares."

I place a comforting hand on her shoulder. "I'm sure he'll be apprehended soon enough, and life will return to normal." I offer her a smile.

"Yes, we just have to believe that, don't we," she whispers. I nod encouragingly.

After an hour, the mommies and daddies begin trickling out the door.

"I think that went as well as can be expected," Principal Michaels says to me.

I contemplate his words while I watch the last parent pass through the door. "Yes. I suppose so. I don't believe this is the last time we'll have to talk about it. I have a feeling this isn't the last murder. These types never really stop, do they?"

"Not until they're caught, I'm afraid."

"Oh, I don't think this one will be caught. Call it intuition."

"I hope you're wrong." He shakes his head. "I'm starting to worry that may be the case, though."

I retrieve my purse and walk toward the door, my back to him so he can't see my face. My chin a little higher, my lips tugging up at the sides. *Yes, it will be the case; they'll never catch me.* I lift my hands to the glass door to push it open when Principal Michael's reflection catches my attention. His gaze is on my back, a quizzical look on his face. I quickly adjust my own expression and resist the urge to glance back at him over my shoulder. My footsteps quicken, bringing me to my car as quickly as possible. Once safely hidden behind my window's tint, I reach over and open the glovebox. I keep a small knife hidden here for emergencies. With the knife laid on a towel spread across my lap, I unbutton the wrist of my blouse and roll up my sleeve. A small trail of blood beads on my skin in the wake of the knife's tip. Only an inch. I don't like scarring myself, but there are times when I need to be punished. Discipline demands harsh lessons. It's what I'm always telling Bryony. Tonight, I let my guard down; the glass window may as well have been a mirror. The knife goes back into the glovebox, and I hold the towel around my wound.

With my eyes staring through the windshield, the curiosity of getting caught infiltrates my thoughts. It would be exciting. There's no doubt my face would be on every TV, my name in every newspaper. A full trial would give me a much larger platform. The entire world would become my puppets. How fun.

Now is not the time for that. I'm much too busy, and that would be entirely too inconvenient.

Chapter 11

Eloise

It's just Bryony and I for dinner. Robert is out of town on business, so we've foregone the formal dining room and instead sit in our in-kitchen dining nook. Our formal dining room has a solid mahogany table that seats twelve. When we eat as a family, Robert sits on one end, I sit on the other, and Bryony sits to her father's left. Each meal, I have Melanie light fresh candles in candelabras lining the center. With the gilt-bronze, cut-glass chandelier dimmed, the candlelight provides a lovely flickering light.

"There's so many new rules. It's excessive," Bryony complains over her almond-crusted salmon drizzled in a lemon butter sauce served over rice.

"Everyone is concerned, Bryony. The school is simply doing what they can to ensure you're all safe."

"You mean avoid a lawsuit."

We both laugh, knowing she's absolutely correct. The school doesn't care about the safety of its students any more than I do. They care about the large checks each family writes at the beginning of the year and their reputation, which keeps those checks coming from the next generation of students.

"There's a bonfire tonight. I'm going to sleep at Annabelle's after."

"Are you sure that's a good idea?" I remember to look worried.

She rolls her eyes. "The guy isn't even killing kids, just old ladies. We'll be fine."

"Melissa was hardly what I'd consider an old lady."

"You know what I mean. And you talk about her like you knew her or something. The news said she owned a flower shop; remember we went in there once? Kind of creepy that we talked to a dead lady."

My hand tightens on my fork. This I was not expecting. "Did we now?" I ask, looking off to the side as if I'm attempting to remember. "I guess this old lady is finding these types of things harder to remember."

"Yeah, I can't believe you forgot. I recognized her almost immediately."

"Well, it's best to keep this to ourselves. It's not like we have any information pertinent to the case, and all it would do is get us pulled into some ghastly police station for hours, answering questions for no good reason."

"Umm, yeah, of course."

"Melanie has really outdone herself with this meal, hasn't she? I'll have to tell her to add this to our favorites so she can prepare it again."

"Yeah, it's good."

"The polite thing to do would be to thank her yourself and with more eloquence."

"Yes, ma'am. May I be excused?"

"You may. I would like to see your outfit before you leave. No need to parade around in front of a group of horny teenage boys looking like a whore. And we don't need a repeat of the last time you tried to leave this house looking like that, now do we?" I narrow my eyes over my crystal glass.

Bryony's back straightens, and her silverware clatters to her plate. Her jaw flexes, biting back the argument she's manufacturing in her head. The post-concert slap is likely still fresh in her memories. She nods curtly and retreats to her room. I'd prefer her to stay in with me tonight and every night, really, but I have work to do and having an empty house to do it in is most convenient. An hour later, a car horn sounds from our driveway and Bryony runs down the stairs and out the front door, yelling her goodbyes. This time, my jaw is the one clenching and my words are being swallowed back.

Before I get my laptop out, I head to Bryony's room. With her gone for the evening, I'll have the opportunity to have a look through her things. I start with her computer. I have the passwords to her electronics; she knows this, as I've confronted her many times about things I've found. The one thing I've never understood is why she doesn't delete anything or tries to hide things from me. I almost wonder if she enjoys the confrontations. It's as if she leaves certain items on purpose, knowing I'll find them. I've always assumed she is her father's daughter, but times like those make me wonder if she has more of me in her than I realize.

Chapter 12

BRYONY

I slide into the front seat of Annabelle's candy apple red BMW.

"You look gorge, B," she gushes.

"Thanks, babe. You too."

Annabelle's hair is loose, wild, and free. This adds to my happiness at escaping my house. I hate it when she flat-irons it. Annabelle drives around the looped driveway to take me far away from my prison and my mother, at least for the night.

"And how is Queen Eloise tonight?"

"Perched on her throne of thorns and loneliness," I say, and we both laugh. "Mind if I take a hit? I need to de-stress."

"Only if you share," Annabelle says, winking.

I pull a joint from my purse and puff on one end while holding the lighter to the other until it sparks to life. I inhale the skunky smoke and hold it in my lungs until they beg for mercy. While blowing the smoke out the window, I pass the joint to Annabelle.

"Is she being all weird about this whole killer-on-the-loose thing? Grace is totally extra. Made me turn on the location tracking on my phone. She's like fucking Big Brother now. Constantly texting me and asking why I'm here or there. Wish she'd just fuck off."

"She says she's all worried and concerned, but I think she's full of shit. She just likes the extra attention she's getting with the dumbass PTA. 'Oh, Eloise, save our children, protect us.' She's so fake it's nauseating."

"Ugh, mothers. When we have kids, we'll be way more chill. Nothing like them."

"Screw that. I'm not having kids." I make a gagging noise.

She passes the joint back to me and I swipe my hand at the falling ash before it can burn my jeans or the car. "Speaking of, I heard Collin will be there tonight."

"What the hell does Collin have to do with kids?" I ask, choking on my hit.

"Kids come from sex, duh." She waggles her eyebrows at me.

"Oh my God. But also, ohhh yeah? Maybe I can do some baby-making tonight, minus the baby."

"Yas, I love it."

From the number of cars lining the side of the road, the party is already packed.

"How's my face?" Annabelle asks after she parks. She twists in her seat to face me.

"Besides your bloodshot eyes? Perfection."

"Shit, do you have any Visine?" she asks, digging in her clutch.

I shrug. "No, but fuck it, who cares?"

"You're right, let's go." We unbutton our cardigans, throw them in the back seat, and pull our non-existent boobs up as high as they will go in our crop tops, then saunter toward the bonfire.

Several stale beers, a few bong hits, and a Z-bar later, I'm properly numbed. Collin is here, but he's making out with some freshman slut. Screw him, he's not that cute anyway. I lost Annabelle what feels like hours ago, but time has slowed along with my mind. I stumble around the party, looking for my next bit of fun.

"Whoa, you okay there?"

"Who the hell are you?" I ask the boy gripping my elbow. In the dim light, I can see tattoos covering his arms. His dark hair falls in his face, and I squint to bring his features into focus.

"Damon, how about you?"

"None of your fucking business," I retort, but the last two words are a combined half-audible word.

He throws his head back and laughs. I rip my elbow from his grip, stumbling backward.

"You don't look so good. Why don't you let me help you sit for a bit? There's a big log over there." He points to a spot that appears miles away. The entire scene around me starts spinning and I suddenly want nothing more than to be sitting on that very far away fallen tree. I nod and let him lead me there.

"Alright, sit before you fall." He doesn't have to push my shoulders hard to force me down.

"I think I need water," I mutter, putting my elbows on my knees and my face in my hands. I squeeze my eyes shut to stop the spinning.

"Give me a minute, I'll go find some. Don't move."

I moan in response. Everything goes black.

When I come to again, a crowd of kids tower over me. Tattoo boy is off to the side, gripping his hand. I think I hear him say something about being bitten by something, a person, maybe an animal. How'd an animal get here with all these people around? The faces come in and out of focus, and I lean over and puke between my knees.

"Get out of here, move, go away." Annabelle elbows her way through my audience and grabs me by the chin. "Dude, what the hell did you take?" Her words sound garbled like she has marbles in her mouth, or she's underwater, or maybe I am.

She stands and walks to the boy who was bitten by an animal. It dawns on me that he was supposed to get me water. I'm about to ask him where it is, when my head lolls to the side, and I see the bottle sitting next to my foot. Only a small splatter of puke on it. I rub it against my jeans and unscrew the cap before drinking half of it in three large gulps.

Annabelle is pulling me up by my elbow, and the sudden change of position makes me lose my bearings. She grips my arm and starts dragging me away from the whispering crowd. With my arm thrown around her shoulders, and my weight mostly supported by her and not my wobbly legs, she somehow drags me to the car.

After tossing me into the passenger seat and getting in the car, she cranks the A/C, and I hold my face directly in front of the vent. The fog begins to lift.

"You fucking bit that dude," Annabelle says, laughing.

"Huh?"

"He said he handed you water, and you chomped his hand like a freaking rabid dog. Broke the skin too. Sweet Jesus, what are you on? He could have like AIDs or something."

MY DARLINGS

I notice the metallic taste in my mouth and lick my lips before leaning my head back against the headrest and passing out.

Chapter 13

Eloise

Bryony consumes my thoughts while I get ready for my morning run. I sense her becoming braver, and I don't care for it one bit. I blame myself for this. I'm not paying close enough attention. I've allowed myself to be too easily distracted. There haven't been enough teaching moments, and this is my fault. Her growing independence is also something to consider. She seems to be finding her voice, and with it, her fear of me lessens each day. This won't do. There are things that must never be said, not to her father and most certainly not to her friends. But what am I to do about it? My family has always been my greatest disguise; however, the usefulness of this façade may have run its course.

Beatrix calls while I'm on my morning run. She's very distraught that we haven't secured a location for our Gatsby event.

"Not even a proper name, Eloise," she cries into the phone. As if a name and location for an event that will accomplish nothing more than a few useless trees and flowers planted in a rundown area is of the utmost importance. Foliage that will be forgotten as soon as it is put in the ground, only to be dead within months, weeks potentially.

"It is dreadful," I agree. "We must not let ourselves be further distracted. We have duties, responsibilities, and our guests to think of."

She concurs wholeheartedly and says she will meet me at my house in two hours. If the rest of the ladies couldn't take this seriously, it's up to the two of us to do so. She knew I would understand.

I turn around to head back home and am about to put my earbuds back in when I hear a branch snap. With my hands frozen midway to my ears, I listen. Another snap is followed by the rustling of leaves and the distinctive sounds of steps.

"Who's there? I can hear you. Come out immediately," I demand into the tree line. I don't have any of my usual tools, but still, I'm unafraid. A figure dressed in a black hoodie and black jeans emerges from behind a tree too far for me to make out their face shadowed by the hood. Neither of us moves. The person is so still that for a moment, I think I'm imagining them.

I laugh. How unlucky of them to choose me for whatever deviant crime they plan on committing.

"It's so lovely of you to join me on my morning run, but the polite thing to do when meeting a stranger is to introduce yourself, darling. Why don't you remove your hood, and let's get better acquainted?" I have to raise my voice for them to hear me, something I don't particularly enjoy. They continue to stand, to stare, to remain as still as the trees surrounding them.

A deer bounds out from behind the brush. My eyes leave the figure for no longer than a second. I curse myself when I look back, and they are gone. My hands clench and unclench at my sides. My eyes squint, scanning, trying to find where they've disappeared to.

I take several steps toward the spot they previously occupied.

A mass slams into me, smashing my face into the rough bark of a tree before I fall to my hands and knees. Dazed, I look up only to see their retreating form. Not running, not even walking very fast, just casually strolling deeper into the woods as if they hadn't just attacked me. What a curious thing to have happened. This is personal, planned. I sit back on my legs and tentatively touch the side of my face. My hand shakes as I bring it away. Blood covers my fingers.

I stare at the bright red liquid, and an unfamiliar noise, like the chaos of wind and ocean waves, roars within my ears. I watch the retreating figure, and the noises are gone. This stranger has taken me by surprise; they've inflicted pain. I'm equally fascinated, impressed, and rage-filled.

I stand, and my obsession with this mysterious figure grows, knowing they'll be stealing my thoughts for weeks to come.

I won't run after them, no. Not this time. I will find them though, yes. They must be shown who is in control.

A thought hits me. I can report this attack to the authorities. Not only will everyone assume this is the killer they have been searching for, and thus proving said killer is not me, a convenience if I ever find myself in need of having that fact proven. It will also give the police, Bryony, Robert, and my friends the opportunity to demonstrate how important I am to them. They will shower me with gifts and attention, two things I do very much like.

However, my name would be linked to the case, a potential victim, the one who got away. Do the benefits outweigh the risks?

I pull out my phone. "Yes, hello, this is Eloise Williams; I was just attacked. Please send help immediately."

"Are you in a safe place, ma'am?"

"I don't know." I force my voice to wobble. "He ran away. I'm still here, on a path near my home."

"How far away are you from your house? Can you get there?"

"Maybe half a mile, probably less. Yes, I'm a tad scratched up, but I can walk."

"Okay, give me your address, and I'll put the call in. Stay on the phone with me."

I give the sympathetic emergency operator my address. She is forced to listen to my heavy breathing and the crunching of my feet on dead leaves while I quickly walk home. The police are pulling up to the gate when I arrive.

I wave my arms above my head and run down the driveway to meet them. "I'm Eloise Williams; I was attacked."

After the gate opens, the officer folds me into the front of his cruiser, assuring me that I'm safe. I give instructions on how to operate the gate so he can leave it open for the paramedics, who are already on their way. Not far behind, according to the kind officer. We slowly make our way down the winding driveway, and then he assists me into my house, where I am gently placed on my custom cream B&B Italia sofa in the sitting room. I would prefer not to bleed on the fabric, but I believe if I say as much, they may question the seriousness of the situation.

I answer all his questions and provide my account of the attack, including my unhelpful description of the suspect with their average height and average build. No, I didn't see their face, or their race, or really anything other than a black hoodie and black jeans. The officer's shoulders slump, as the chance of him being the hero who uncovers the first solid lead on the infamous serial killer disappears. If this poor boy only knew how close he really is. The paramedics come in, and they take my vital signs, clean the wound on my face, and treat it with a very large bandage. No hospital visit needed. A trip to the plastic surgeon and dermatologist will be absolutely necessary, though. I refuse to have my perfect face marred by some criminal.

"Eloise!" Beatrix screeches from the hallway, hands covering her mouth, eyes wide with terror. "What is all this? What happened?" Beatrix the actress has arrived. Today's role, the doting best friend. She would be just as excited to be standing by my grave, playing the grieving best friend. That would garner a much brighter spotlight.

I shoo the paramedics away and stand. They go to help me, and I reprimand them with a look.

"I was attacked on my run. Can you believe it?" I reach my hands out to her. She clasps them, and we kiss the air on either side of the other's cheeks. I'm also a very adept actress.

"My word, how horrific. Do they think it's—"

"It may be. It's just so scary to think about how close I came to being murdered and so close to home." I wipe a tear from beneath my eye, imagining how lovely the green must look with the extra sparkle from the salty water.

"Are you all done here?" Beatrix says, turning her attention to the uniformed men and women filling my sitting room.

"Yes. Here's my card. I've written the report number down for you," the officer who helped me into the house says. "You can have Mrs. Williams call us if she remembers anything else. However, we may be in touch if we have further questions. You ladies be safe." He tips his head at us, and they begin packing up and take their leave.

"Do you need tea? Coffee?" Beatrix asks.

"Are they not going to search the scene of the crime?" I ask after the thudding of the front door signifies the last of them have left.

Beatrix's eyes widen. "I should go stop them—"

With a hand held up, I shake my head. "No, I'm sure they have their reasons. Coffee would be lovely." She hooks her arm in mine, and we walk to the kitchen, my face not revealing my utter shock at the police's incompetence. This is why I truly am the only person qualified and capable of managing any situations pertaining to my life.

I sit at the table, and Beatrix inspects the complicated coffee machine only Melanie knows how to operate.

"Are there instructions for this thing? I've never seen so many buttons."

"Melanie won't be here for another hour, but a glass of ice water will be fine. You weren't supposed to be here this early," I say, keeping my tone light and breezy.

"I was on Park and saw the ambulance fly by with its lights on, so my curiosity got the best of me." She giggles uncomfortably. "I figured it wouldn't hurt anyone if I followed. I thought they may have found another body. When I saw it turn into your driveway, I was beside myself with worry."

I drink my water. Her timeline doesn't exactly add up, but as much as I'd love to question her until she trips over the lies she's spewing, it's better to file this interesting tidbit away for later.

"Did he hit your face?" She points to the area on her face where mine has been injured.

"No. Pushed me into a tree then ran away. Not very serial killer like, if you ask me. Maybe he was just a creeper, or some crackhead I happened upon. Who knows?" I shrug. "I need some time to get ready. Do you mind if I—"

"Eloise," she exclaims. "I wouldn't dream of expecting you to still tour locations with me, not after the morning you've had."

"Don't be dramatic, Beatrix. I'm fine. I just need to shower and change. Can you entertain yourself? Bryony may be home soon. She stayed the night at a friend's place. Don't be alarmed if you hear someone come in."

"Yes, okay. No problem. Maybe I can find a YouTube video and figure out how this contraption works." She walks over to the coffeemaker and returns her attention to the various buttons and levers.

After a quick shower, with my hair knotted at the back of my neck and a cashmere sweater and dark jeans on, I lean toward the mirror to get a closer look at my damaged face. I don't want to disturb the fresh bandage, but I worry over the lasting effects. I'll leave a note for Melanie to make an appointment with my dermatologist and potentially with a plastic surgeon as well. I finish my makeup and am making my way down the spiral staircase with careful steps when Bryony comes walking through the front door. I purse my lips at her disheveled appearance. We meet at the bottom of the stairs.

"No lecture, Mother, please. I'm sick enough as it is. I promise you this is far worse than any punishment you could give me."

Her bloodshot eyes rise to my face, and her eyebrows follow suit. "What happened to your cheek?"

I gingerly brush the bandage with my fingertips. "You missed quite the morning. I was attacked on my run. Thrown right into a tree. Almost killed, in fact."

"Jesus Christ, Mom. Are you okay?"

"Yes, yes. I'll be fine." I wave a hand as if to dismiss the incident entirely.

"Did you call the police?"

"They've come and gone, along with the paramedics. All happening while you slept your hangover away, apparently."

I walk around her toward the kitchen. "Beatrix is here, but we'll be heading out soon. Important errands. Unlike most people, I am not easily distracted from my responsibilities. Now get upstairs and out of sight. I won't have my friends seeing you like this."

Beatrix is still fiddling with the coffee machine when I rejoin her in the kitchen.

"I give up. This thing would take an engineer to figure out."

"Or a Melanie. Let's go. We can stop at the coffee shop on the way."

Later that evening, I'm once again dining with Bryony.

"Did you tell Dad about this morning?" Bryony is looking much better. Freshly showered, which means she's spent the entire day lying around in her own filth.

I set my utensils next to my dinner plate. "Your father is very busy with work. I didn't think it necessary to bother him."

"He's gonna be mad if he finds out from someone else and you didn't tell him."

"The word is 'going,' not 'gonna.' He's going to be mad, is how we say that. However, it's of no concern to me if he's more upset by his lack of knowledge than my injuries."

Bryony stops chewing and narrows her eyes. "That's not what I meant. He'll be worried, is all."

I stare back, unblinking, until she breaks eye contact and continues eating.

We finish our dinner in silence, and I send Bryony to her room for homework and violin practice. I could call Robert and tell him about the attack, but I can't think of any good reason to do so. I'd be stuck on the phone answering questions, letting him console me when I don't need consoling. Just the thought of the conversation exhausts me. I choose instead to run myself a bath. A drum beats in my ears with every heartbeat. Being a victim, thrown to the ground like a piece of trash, has my normally methodical mind ignited in chaos. I need to quiet it, to think, to find a way to feed this insatiable desire for revenge. If I don't, I'll act too quickly, too irresponsibly. I can't have that.

Chapter 14

BEATRIX

I've always been a curious person. Nosey would probably be the more appropriate description, but it sounds harsher than I believe is necessary. It wasn't a complete lie, the reason I gave for being at Eloise's so early, but it wasn't the complete truth either. And after what happened, it's a good thing I was there. She needed me. Fate put me there, and that's all that matters.

I've dropped Eloise off a home and am now sitting in my living room enjoying the glass of wine I've been craving all day. I could have made myself one at her house when she left me on my own to get changed, but I held back. My hands shook, trying to figure out the damn coffee machine—shaking hands, maybe it's time to admit I may have a problem. Eloise is too observant; even if I had hidden the evidence, she would have known, and she would have judged. The thought was enough to ignore the craving. Besides, I needed a clear mind. I had been determined to complete our mission. Finalizing our location was important.

The time on my phone reads 7:30; David was supposed to be home thirty minutes ago. The dinner I've prepared has gone cold. I can reheat it, but it won't be the same, will it? Not that he will care. He'll come in, all apologies and excuses. Patients, surgery, paperwork, whatever. I've heard it all. At least his tardiness usually makes him feel guilty enough not to question how much I've had to drink.

"Well, David, if you'd have been home on time, I wouldn't have had time to crack open this second bottle now, would I?" I say to the empty room. Then laugh at myself as if what I've said is absolutely hilarious. I should slow down. I shrug and haul myself up from the couch to refill.

I stand in the kitchen and take a long pull straight from the bottle. The meal I've carefully prepared shames me from the dishes on the island.

An hour later, another bottle gone.

I grab a trash bag and sweep the entire contents, serving dishes and all, into it with the empty merlot bottle thrown on top.

Time moves in jagged leaps. I'm upstairs in my bed in sweats and a T-shirt, but I don't remember how I got here. My eyelids are heavy. I vaguely remember a phone conversation with Suzanne, or did I fall asleep, and that was just a dream. Something about Tobin. Her telling me I'm drunk. Both of us laughing about something. No, I was the only one laughing. She was mad. Or was I mad? I decide it doesn't matter and let myself drift off to sleep. Right before the nightmares overtake me, I tell myself not to forget this. I should start hiding my phone when I'm drinking. There's no telling what secrets I'll reveal.

Chapter 15

Eloise

P oppy and I have been called to Suzanne's house. Supposedly, it's an emergency. I find Beatrix's absence peculiar, but I'm sure I'll find out soon enough why the invite was only extended to the two of us.

Poppy and I arrive at the same time and meet on Suzanne's porch.

"What happened to your face?" Poppy asks.

Before I can answer, Suzanne flings the door open, an ugly scowl twisting her sallow face.

Her blonde hair halos around her head in a frizzy mess, and her round face is more swollen than usual. I try to hide my disgust. She looks like a sick lion. She isn't the prettiest of my friends, but her personal care is usually at a much higher standard. Without a word, she turns around and walks away from us, rudely leaving Poppy and I confused on her front porch. We look at each other, and Poppy shrugs. I assume Suzanne means for us to follow her. A formal invitation to enter would be appropriate. I consider leaving to demonstrate that her lack of manners will not be tolerated, but curiosity is a magnet that pulls me into Suzanne's home in Poppy's wake.

We find her pacing the living room. It's extremely obnoxious. I wish she'd sit the fuck down. I sit on the couch and cross my legs. Poppy joins me.

"Tobin is cheating on me," Suzanne finally blurts out. Her chin wobbles, and here come the tears. Not dainty ones either, but snot-dripping-down-the-face, ugly sobs.

"If you think he is, you're probably right. Our instincts are usually correct in these cases," I say. I'm not in the mood to play make-believe today.

Poppy's head whips in my direction, and I can feel the knives she's shooting from her eyes. I smile and wipe an imaginary piece of lint from my arm, refusing to comply. Poppy can give me all the looks she wants, but her brackish roots are showing, making her blonde bob look utterly middle-class. I will not be admonished by a woman so unkempt. These women have nothing but money and time, so there really is no excuse for them to be letting themselves go like this. I may need a new circle of friends.

Poppy turns her attention back to Suzanne. "What makes you think that?" Her eyebrows knot in concern.

I consider killing Suzanne, putting her out of her misery. It would be a mercy kill, really. She should be thankful to have a friend as empathetic as me.

"I don't know what you find so amusing, Eloise," Suzanne says. The waver in her tone has gone, and they are both staring at me, looking less than pleased. I've forgotten to control my face. I hate it when that happens.

"Oh darling," I say, sprinkling sugar on my words. "I just don't see how your Tobin would cheat on you. He adores you. It's just the two of you; you're all he's got."

"I have proof," Suzanne says, collapsing into the armchair.

Poppy gasps, and I lean forward.

"You remember what Beatrix said the other day at brunch about the bracelet being a sign of cheating?" She shakes her head and covers her mouth with her hand, looking off to the side. My Lord, if she can't control herself, we'll be here for days listening to this blubbering. After a dramatic sigh, she continues, "I just couldn't stop thinking about it. Tobin has been coming home late a lot more, blaming work, and traveling quite a bit."

Poppy stands and walks to her, squatting and placing a hand on top of Suzanne's. "That could mean a million things other than cheating. Maybe he's just really busy with work stuff. You know how our husbands are, all workaholics."

I nod. Yes, that's why we've married them. Their money and their absence. It's a lovely life. Suzanne should be more appreciative. It's not as if she's anything special.

"That's not all. I tore this house apart today. His office, closet, anywhere I could think of." Another exaggerated quivering breath. "I found receipts. Jewelry, dinners at romantic restaurants, hotels here in DC, all on days he was supposed to be out of town on business trips. There's no other explanation why he'd have a receipt for a local hotel, especially on a week he was supposed to be in California." She buries her face in her hands, and her shoulders heave with sobs.

Poppy drapes her arm across Suzanne's convulsing shoulders. "Oh, sweetie, I'm so sorry."

"You should kill him. And the woman. It's what they deserve," I say.

Suzanne chortles, a disgusting sound that bubbles in her throat. "I wish. I don't even know who she is." This answer piques my interest. I've never had the opportunity to push someone else to murder.

We move on from Suzanne's decomposing marriage, and I fill them in on our tours of the locations. We've decided on a spot and signed the contract. Suzanne would normally bristle at not being involved in the final decision, but she's too distracted to be bothered. Poppy, on the other hand, looks ready to cry. I can't take any more outbursts, so I tell them the story of my attack.

"Why wouldn't you call me?" Poppy practically shouts. "You must have been terrified."

"Yes, it was traumatizing. But it's fine. I'm fine." I say this, but I look off to the side to make myself look very much not fine.

Suzanne mutters her sympathies, and Poppy looks even more distraught now that there are two crises we've filled her head with.

I'm bored with the whole ordeal and suggest we leave. Suzanne bolts from her seat and I can't tell if she's happy to be rid of us or upset we're leaving. The more likely answer is she's probably upset I've stolen her sympathy.

Regardless of her feelings, she's remembered her manners and escorts us to the door, muttering her goodbyes.

"Terrible, isn't it?" Poppy says when we reach our cars in the driveway.

"I can't imagine." I shake my head, a hand clutching at my pearls.

"Want to go to the club and play a quick round of tennis?"

"Sounds lovely. I'll go home and grab my bag and meet you there."

Suzanne

I stare at my closed front door for a long time after Poppy and Eloise have left. Something isn't sitting right. My emotions have been on a roller coaster for the last twenty-four hours—one minute, my stomach is flying into my throat, and the next it's plummeting to my toes. Eloise was saying all the right things and playing the part of the caring friend, but everything about her told a different story. She was practically dancing with delight, energy leaping off her. Yet, from the neck up, she was a robot. Her head barely moving, her eyes barely blinking.

Was she the one sleeping with Tobin? I shake my head and slowly shuffle back into my living room. I sit, rocking, chewing my thumb's cuticle. Finally, I get up and grab my laptop from the coffee table and Google *gun shop near me*. There's only so much a woman can take. I've been putting up with far too much for far too long.

Chapter 16

Eloise

The summer after the fire ants summer was just as hot and humid. Ten-year-old me was sick of the heat and tired of Mother fussing over me all the time.

I was minding my own business on our front porch, curled up in one of the white rocking chairs, reading *Lord of the Flies*. Footfalls pounded up the old wooden steps, and my name was sung in an exaggerated southern drawl. The voice's owner was Christie Lee, but everyone called her Cricket. She was older than me by one year, but you'd think by how she acted, she'd been alive nearly a decade longer. She somehow got it in her head that those twelve months earned her a crown—queen of Mississippi, possibly the entire south. She was bossy and spoiled. The same could have been said about me, but I was much less obvious about it all.

"It's too hot to be sitting 'round; come to the creek with me," she demanded, hands on her hips. We lived next door to each other, and times were different then. Children were allowed to roam free, and that's exactly what we did. I wasn't in the mood to listen to Cricket blabber on about herself for the remainder of the afternoon, and I hadn't even gotten to the part where they killed Piggy yet, but the creek's cool bubbling water did sound refreshing, and I was baking like a biscuit, so I agreed to go.

I followed Cricket through the field of tall wheatgrass, both of us swatting at mosquitos and wiping the sweat from our foreheads that dripped down our faces and stung our eyes. At the end of the field, there was a path cut through the forest. The trees provided some relief from the scorching sun. Finally, the woods cleared, and we stepped onto the sandy bank of the creek. Lined with large boulders, it was wide enough and deep enough to swim in if you were in the middle, or you could sit on a rock with your feet dangling in the cool water. Hot from our trek, we waded into the swirling water, our feet sinking into the muddy bottom.

"Ma says she's buying me a pony in a few weeks. Bet you wish you had a pony, don't you Eloise? I'll let you come pet him. But he probably won't like you much."

I waded back to the bank, picked up a stick and started poking at a school of fish, pretending I didn't hear her. The pony was probably a lie. She was always fibbing or exaggerating. A liar can always spot a liar. She took my silence as interest and droned on about her family's upcoming trip to Gulfport, how her dad took her shopping and let her pick out five new dresses, and her mom said they could go out to any restaurant Cricket wanted for dinner that weekend, even a fancy place if that's what she chose. I plopped down on a rock and kicked my toes in the water. The ripples dancing across it were much more interesting than Cricket's bragging.

"Who's there?" Cricket yelled toward the woods.

"What're you talkin' about, Cricket?" I asked, twisting around in the direction she was looking.

"Didn't you hear that? Someone's coming. It sounds like boys, ugh." She scrambled up the bank and stood facing the racket with her arms crossed, hip jutted to one side.

Brian was the first to arrive, fishing poles thrown over one shoulder and a tackle box in the other hand. He was followed closely by Justin, then Billy, who scrambled after the older boys. Brian and Justin were Cricket's age, and Billy was Justin's younger brother, who was a year behind me in school.

"Ach, not you," Brian said to Cricket.

"Feeling's mutual," Cricket huffed.

"Hey, Eloise." Justin waved.

I waved back and smiled sweetly, enjoying the red blooms the interaction brought to Cricket's cheeks. She dropped her arms by her sides, her hands squeezed in tight fists.

"Have you seen any frogs today?" Billy asked. He had a bucket in one hand and a net in the other.

"Not yet, but I'm sure there's some around here," I replied.

"Why don't y'all go find somewhere else to be annoying?" Cricket said.

"Last time I checked, this was a free country, and you don't own the creek, so stuff it," Brian said.

Cricket started tapping her foot, glaring at the boys. She wasn't used to not getting her way. They ignored her and started wading into the water. Billy made his way carefully over the slippery rocks to where I was sitting so he could start his hunt for frogs.

"Come on, Eloise. Let's go do something else," Cricket called over her shoulder, walking toward the forest path. When she realized I wasn't following her, she stopped and turned around. "I said, come on." The tone of her voice set my chest on fire. A small stone was inches from my hand—*I could pick it up and throw it at her.* I almost did, but she was pretty far away, and I didn't want to be embarrassed if I missed.

"I'm going to stay here. It's too hot to be doing anything else today." I turned back toward the spaces between the mossy rocks to continue helping Billy on his hunt for critters. "Find any yet?"

He shook his head, his determined stare not leaving the water.

I peeked over my shoulder. Cricket stomped her foot, her fisted hands pumped up and down with her leg. "Fine, y'all are just stupid kids anyway." She marched off and disappeared into the woods. The boys and I all looked at each other before doubling over in laughter.

"Good riddance!" Brian called.

The older boys fished while Billy and I filled his bucket with frogs and bugs. The afternoon dragged on as summer afternoons do. Finally, Justin announced he was bored and not catching anything.

"Come on, y'all. Let's go get a snack at my house," Brian said.

"Yeah, I'm sick of this. Billy, let all those animals go, and come on, we're heading back."

"I don't want to go to Brian's," Billy whined.

"Well, you don't have a choice. Move it," Justin said.

My head swiveled between the two boys. I chewed on the inside of my cheek. I really wanted to go home and get back to my book, but I was also having fun and didn't want to leave. If I could get rid of the older boys, Billy and I could have even more fun without the two of them breathing down our necks.

"I'll stay with him," I volunteered.

Justin looked at me with his eyes narrowed. "Fine, but bring him back home before dinner. Otherwise, our ma's gonna make him pick a switch."

Billy's eyes widened.

"We'll only stay a bit longer," I promised. "I'll walk him all the way home."

Justin's head swiveled back and forth between Billy and me. "Fine. Whatever," he finally said, and the two older boys took off into the woods.

As soon as the sound of the older boys' footsteps and chatter faded, I turned to Billy. "Let's have some real fun now. Have you ever seen the inside of a frog?"

He shook his head. His big blue eyes looked scared, but I didn't care.

I grabbed the bucket from his hand and started making my way to the bank. "Well, come on. It will be fun, I promise. Don't be scared."

I squatted over the bucket, deciding which one we would dissect first. Two still had dreams of escape, slipping and sliding on top of each other trying to make it to the bucket's lip. One sat still on the bottom, having given up. We needed something sharp to cut it open, but we'd have to kill it first, otherwise it would just jump away. I didn't trust Billy to hang on to its slippery skin while I sliced its belly open. I could already tell he was nothing but a big scaredy cat. I reached down and grabbed hold of the fattest one and held it out in front of his face. "This is the one we'll start with. Do you wanna give him a name first?"

"Not really," he whispered.

"Fine. We won't name him. We need a sharp stick and a rock. You go find a stick; it must be thick enough not to break, okay?" I put the fat frog back in the bucket and walked around, looking for the perfect smashing rock. Right when I found a rock that fit perfectly in my hand, I saw Billy approach in the corner of my vision. Before I could stop him, he grabbed the bucket and ran toward the creek.

"Stop! What are you doing?" I cried.

"I'm letting them—" Before he could answer, his foot slipped on the mossy part of a rock. His arms pinwheeled for a few moments until his feet flew up, and he landed on his back on those very same rocks. His head smashed against the stone with a loud crack. The bucket plopped into the water, its prisoners escaping. I ran over and tried to gather them back, but it was too late.

"Look what you did!" I yelled. But Billy didn't seem too concerned with all our hard work being wasted. He was sprawled on the rocks, one leg dangling in the water. "Stop messing around, Billy; they all got out because of you." He didn't move. *Stupid faker,* I thought, *afraid of getting yelled at.* Well, he should have been afraid, as I was right mad. We'd have to start all over with our collecting. I walked over and kicked his side. "Get up, dummy. Come help me find more frogs." That's when I noticed the red seeping from his head onto the rock and trailing into the water. I bent down and dipped my fingers in the line of red. When I brought them up to my face, the wet blood glistened. It was the prettiest shade of red I'd ever seen. Red has always been my favorite color.

I gave his side a few more shoves with my toe. "Stop messing around, Billy, it's not funny." He didn't move. I stood over him, waiting, watching. Finally, I stepped over his body and bent down, and with both hands on his side, I gave him a good shove. He was small for his age, and he rolled right into the water, landing face down. His blond hair was a deep maroon where the rock had cracked his head open, and the rest of his hair a light pink. I slipped into the water and got as close as I could to inspect the wound. My chest felt as if my heart had grown ten times its normal size. It was then, at that very moment, I discovered dead people are so much more exquisite than dead animals.

The blood from his skull mixed with the water his face was floating in. I stuck my fingers in the cool creek and spun it around with my finger. The blood swirled round and round, making pretty patterns. I tried to turn Billy over, so curious to see the change to his face, but the water weighed him down and my weak arms couldn't get him flipped over. Even my young mind knew I couldn't get caught sitting here playing with Billy's dead body, so—much to my disappointment—I decided it was time to go tell someone what happened. I didn't get to read about Piggy dying on that hot July day, but watching Billy die was worth it.

Chapter 17

Suzanne

I take another baby carrot from the bag and bite down on it with a crunch. I've let myself go and put on a few extra pounds, but I spend hours every week on my appearance—getting my hair done, facials, Botox, and waxing every hair from my body. I wake up every damn day and spend at least two hours getting my makeup just right, dressing to accentuate my new body, cleaning, cooking, and I do it all for Tobin. To keep him happy, to keep him from fucking other women. All a waste of time.

I pick up the carrots and throw them in the trash, then walk to the freezer and grab a pint of cookie dough ice cream. Sitting back at the table, I shovel the ice cream in my mouth, anger growing with each bite. Eloise, of all people. I spent last night staring at my darkened ceiling listening to Tobin's snoring and wondering why her. She's a cold bitch. Everyone loves *Eloise*. She does *so* much for the school and the community. She's so selfless, so put together, so reliable. She's an absolute fake.

How is it my fault she married a balding dud of a man? No, that's not nice. Robert is kind and successful. He's just as much of a victim as I am.

I pause with a spoon of ice cream halfway to my mouth. *Victim.* That's exactly what I am. And Tobin may be exactly what Eloise deserves.

I've been searching for an escape for so long. Here it is. My freedom. My ticket. Why am I fighting it?

I used to think so much better of myself. I didn't need a man to validate my self-worth.

I know how it all got to this point. How I became this shell of a human. A helpless *victim* fighting for a man she doesn't even want.

I look at my phone. Maybe I should call Robert, tell him exactly the type of person his perfect wife is. Being with Tobin isn't enough punishment. I need to destroy everything she cares about. Steal it from her and leave her and Tobin to rot.

I'll need proof before I do that. Robert will never believe me if I call with nothing but a hunch. I drum my fingers on the table and pick up my phone. I don't have any concrete proof, but I know it's her. It took me a while to understand her strange behavior. Now I understand. Poppy had responded to the news like a friend, like a caring person. Not Eloise. There was only one possible explanation: she was the one sleeping with my husband.

"Beatrix, hi. It's Suzanne. Are you busy? No? Wonderful. Mind if I pop by?"

Beatrix sounded a bit frazzled on the phone, but I can't worry myself over putting other people out right now. My husband is a cheater, Eloise is a fraud, and they are both monsters. I will expose them.

It's time to reclaim my power.

———◄◦►———

Beatrix opens the door and her eyes flit to my chest. For the first time, I notice a streak of crusted ice cream discoloring my silk blouse. *Shit.* As if people need more help to conjure images of me stuffing my mouth with sweets. Embarrassment heats my cheeks, and I picture her judging my snack habits. *You know you'd lose that extra weight if you weren't such a fat pig sitting around eating ice cream all the time, Suzanne.* I shift my purse strap to unsuccessfully cover the stain and ask to come in. Her eyes look everywhere but at mine. Does she know? Did Poppy tell her? Has Eloise confessed? Maybe they all know, and they've been laughing behind my back. Had Eloise and Poppy feigned surprise when I told them? I shake my head to bring myself back to the present. I am on a mission, and I can't let my self-doubt and insecurities deter me.

Beatrix doesn't make a move or even answer my request to join her inside. I try again, "Sorry. I just have a quick question. It won't take long." I internally chastise myself. Why am I always the one apologizing. I vow to remove the word 'sorry' from my vocabulary. It's everyone else's turn to apologize to me.

Her entire posture stiffens. She steps onto the front porch and closes the door behind her. Every muscle in my body contracts. *Is she really not going to let me in?*

Beatrix is the opposite of Eloise, whose lips are sealed shut with thick, tight stitches. Instead, Beatrix uses secrets as currency. She spends her secrets without care or remorse, the same way she spends her husband's money. A secret for a secret. Nothing is safe with her. I brush off this odd behavior. Perhaps she has guests and doesn't want them to overhear our gossip. There are no other cars in the driveway, though. I shake my head to escape my thoughts because I can't get out of my head lately.

I need my friend. I crave the solidarity and the comforting words. A coffee, a hug, anything. Instead, I'm being forced to discuss this private matter, standing on Beatrix's front porch like some uninvited solicitor trying to sell her my religion.

Left with no choice, I continue, "Tobin is cheating on me—"

She gasps. "Suze, I was just kidding the other day at lunch. Surely, you didn't take me seriously. I'm sure he bought your bracelet to be nice."

I narrow my eyes. I can't think of any reason why she'd be covering for Eloise. An image of them all sitting around laughing behind my back flashes through my mind.

"Now, darling, don't tell Suzanne, but you were absolutely correct the other day. Tobin is sleeping with someone: me."

"Eloise, you're so bad. Tell me more."

They'd clink glasses and laugh at their fat, dumb friend. My misery is nothing but a joke to them. Burning spots blossom on my chest.

I shake my head again. "It wasn't what you said. I found things."

She takes a step back and raises her hand back to the door handle. "I believe it's Eloise."

"Eloise!" she cries before laughing. "I'm sorry, but really? Eloise? I don't even think she sleeps with her own husband. Bryony was probably conceived in a test tube."

"I have my reasons." I cross my arms on my chest. But do I? I'm suddenly not so sure. No. I haven't got this wrong. My intuition is screaming. It's Eloise. It has to be. And this is my chance. I study Beatrix's face, and she looks relieved. Now, she doesn't have to worry about accidentally telling me. Beatrix isn't afraid to spill secrets, but Eloise's secrets are different. Beatrix has always feared Eloise. She's not the only one. Now that I've uncovered the truth on my own, Beatrix doesn't have to worry about being blamed. "Has Eloise mentioned it to you, or to Poppy, maybe? We've been friends a lot longer than you've known Eloise, so I would hope your loyalty would lie with me. If you know something, tell me."

Beatrix holds her hands up in defense. "I swear, Suzanne, I have no idea what's going on with Tobin. And I'm sorry, but I just can't picture it. I mean, Eloise? What makes you think it's her?"

My brain is tripping over itself. I can't explain it. It's impossible to put it into words. I just *know*. "Call it a gut instinct. Either way, I'm going to get evidence, and you better believe I'm going to do something about it."

Her eyes widen slightly. I must look like a crazy lady with my disheveled, stained blouse, and hair hastily thrown in a bun, on top of showing up on her doorstep accusing one of our friends of sleeping with my husband. I turn around and walk quickly back to my car so I don't burst into tears and embarrass myself further.

I hear the door close and turn around. Beatrix is staring out the floor-to-ceiling window to the right of the front door. Her hand holds the curtain back, and I can just barely make out her face. I freeze with my hand on my car door handle. A cool breeze lifts the hairs falling out of my bun, and they tickle my face, sending a shiver down my spine. The temperature outside is a pleasant seventy degrees, but suddenly I'm freezing. They all know. Every single one of them. They've known this whole time and instead of telling me, they've made me the butt of their jokes. I wrench my door open and throw my purse onto the passenger seat. After I heave myself into my SUV, I slam the door shut. I want to scream but I can still feel Beatrix watching me. Her stare crawls over my skin like ants. I hold my breath to hold in the emotions. The second I pull out of her driveway, I scream to the empty car, "fucking bitches!"

I drive around aimlessly for an hour, not sure what to think or what to do. I could confront Tobin. Just come right out and ask him. *Hello, dear. How was your day? Oh, mine was lovely. Say, question for you, are you fucking Eloise?* Another option, throw all his belongings on our front yard and welcome him with a bonfire of his shit. Then I remember who I'm dealing with. My anger is fueling these fantasies, but that's all they are. You don't confront Tobin. You don't throw his things anywhere. I know better. I find myself pulling into the parking lot. The large sign over the store says "Guns."

It's for the serial killer, I tell myself.

For protection.

Chapter 18

Eloise

I 've found her. Electricity hums beneath my skin. I'm floating. Bryony keeps side-eyeing me with her eyebrows knitted together. She can sense my happiness but doesn't dare ask what's causing the sudden shift in my mood. Robert is still traveling, which makes what I have to do next wonderfully simple. While Bryony is at school, and in between brunches and other obligations, I'll become a huntress, stalking my prey, choreographing our last dance.

Tara doesn't have any outdoor hobbies, such as running or hiking. Here's where I get creative. Thoughts of a new method are absolutely titillating. Everyone has a routine, days upon days of sameness. What people don't realize is that the very same routine that makes their life simple and comfortable actually puts them in the gravest danger. Simply going about their daily lives makes them an easy victim. Anyone looking hard enough can uncover when they are at their most vulnerable by learning this daily schedule. It never takes very long, either. A few weeks of stalking and I'll know what time you wake up, leave for work, where you stop for coffee every morning—I could place your order for you—whether you eat lunch at work or prefer restaurants, and the route you take home. On weekends, you sometimes vary your activities, but not by much. You have your favorite places, so the patterns eventually emerge, and people like me are committing those patterns to memory. We know where you'll be going and what you'll be doing before you do.

We met at Neiman's. Tara will remember me as the helpful patron who convinced her to buy the dress she was hemming and hawing over. That is, if she remembers me at all. Neiman's changing room hall leads to a viewing area with three floor-to-ceiling mirrors strategically angled to provide shoppers multiple reflections of themselves so they can admire their potential purchases in the most flattering light from any angle. Aggressive sales associates stand by doling out compliments, even when undeserved. Tara stood twisting her hips. The dress was entirely too short for a woman with her body type. From her screwed-up face, I assumed she was thinking the same.

"It's for a first date," she explained to the saleswoman. "Do you think it's too forward? We've only met online. I don't want him getting the wrong idea." She bit her lip and continued her twisting.

"It looks fabulous on you," I had said, standing in front of my own room, waiting for my selections to be hung inside. "If you feel good, who cares what he thinks?" I gave her a wink and stepped inside to try on the handful of dresses I'd selected.

However, with Tara standing at the end of the hallway and the thousands of Taras reflected in the mirrors behind her, my own dress had suddenly became much less important. I tried on a few, keeping the rustling of my clothes to a minimum so I could listen to Tara's progress.

When I heard her thank the saleswoman, I quickly changed back into the outfit I arrived in and grabbed five of the dresses randomly. We met again at the register, but she didn't mention our earlier encounter. This was good. Too wrapped up in her own date, life, and world, she'd already forgotten about me. Unfortunately for Tara, I had not forgotten her. Tara paid for her ghastly, too-short dress and thanked the yawning woman behind the register. She turned to leave. Our gazes connect. She offered me a pinched smile before walking toward the store's exit.

I stepped forward, placed my dresses on the counter, and as the woman began ringing them up, I pulled out my phone.

"Oh my God," I exclaimed. "My daughter. She's been in a car accident. Will you hold these for me? I'll be back; I have to run."

Concern washed over her face. "Of course, yes. I'll hang these right here with a note and let everyone know. I'm so sorry. I hope she's okay."

I thanked her profusely and jogged in the direction Tara retreated. The double doors swooshed open, and I spotted her immediately once I stepped through them. I always know I've selected the right one when the universe delivers them at my feet, like a dead mouse from a cat. If I hadn't seen her, or if she hadn't driven right in front of me, allowing me to memorize her license plate, then I'd have known she wasn't meant to be. But instead, as fate would have it, Tara chose that day and that time and that parking spot, and My Darling she will become.

A shiver travelled from my toes and out through my fingers, a prelude to the ecstasy to come.

Chapter 19

BRYONY

Annabelle and I lean on the counter in the mall's food court, waiting for our smoothies.

"I think I'm going to dump Chase." Annabelle hunches over and rests her chin in her hand.

I almost tell her to stand up straight and am horrified that my mother has so easily wormed her way into my thoughts. "Right before homecoming? Why not wait?" I ask.

"You don't have a date." She straightens, and my muscles unclench. "Why don't we go together? It will be way more fun. Besides, who cares about homecoming? It's just a stupid dance." The girl forced to wear an unfortunate matching yellow visor and apron, hands us our smoothies. Annabelle pauses, eyeing me over her drink with a raised brow. "Will your mom even let you go? I'm sure Queen Eloise can't be pleased after her precious Bryony came home hungover and half-dead." She laughs.

"She hasn't said. She's in one of her weird moods where she's super happy and not bitching about every stupid thing I do. It won't last long; it never does, so who knows?" I shrug. "Oh shit, don't look. It's Crystal and her loser friends. If they see us, they'll come over."

Annabelle ignores my warning and looks across the mall's food court to where Crystal and some girl whose name I can't remember are looking around for a place to sit.

"Aw, stop being mean. They aren't so bad."

My head jerks back. "Not so bad? They're annoying. I can't deal with them today. Let's get out of here. Any other stores you need to go to?"

"Nah, I'm bored with the mall. Check Snap and Insta and see if anything's going on."

We slowly make our way through the brightly lit concourse, weighed down with bags hanging on each wrist.

"Ooh look at the light," Annabelle says when we get outside. "Sit on the bench and turn your face to the right. I'm going to get a killer pic for you."

I take a seat and pose the shopping bags around me, moving my hands and chin slightly as she snaps away. The more options to pick from the better.

Annabelle lowers her phone. "Wait. I think I see your mom."

My gaze follows the direction she's pointing. "What the hell is she doing?"

We watch my mom standing in front of Nieman's, a dazed look on her face. *What is she looking at?* A black SUV drives past her, and she steps off the sidewalk, stopping in the middle of the road like an idiot. She stares in the direction of the SUV, then disappears into the rows of parked vehicles.

"She's such a bitch. How dare someone be driving by when Eloise wanted to walk on the road." I huff air through my nose.

Annabelle dramatically slaps her hand to her chest and sucks in a deep breath, putting on a hoity-toity falsetto. "Bryony, you wouldn't believe the injustice I experienced today."

I place the back of my hand on my forehead and pretend to faint. "Don't they know who I am? To drive on the road that I planned on gracing with my feet. The horror!" I lean over the bench, laughing, and Annabelle snaps a photo before bending down, hands on her knees, cracking up.

It's my favorite shot of our impromptu shoot. A natural laugh, the sun hitting my face just right.

Later that night at home, I'm in my bedroom looking at the photo. The guilt smacks me like Mother's hand across my cheek. I chew my bottom lip and delete it.

I hate her.

I love her.

Chapter 20

Eloise

The ladies, all distracted by their banal life problems, have been neglectful of our Gatsby-themed garden event. For this reason, I've been forced to take the lead on everything. None of this is a surprise. I'm used to doing things myself that I want done right. And while I would have preferred to tour the location and provide Mia, the establishment's event manager, with the final instructions myself, I also didn't want to get stuck in a group text of whining women.

"Alright, ladies, we are a few weeks away from the big event, so let's focus and get the final preparations wrapped up." I clap my hands to demonstrate that it's their attention I demand.

"We aren't your children, Eloise. We're perfectly capable of participating without the dramatics," Suzanne says. I don't let annoyance show on my face. It's not my fault her husband wasn't getting what he needed from her. There is no need for her to take her attitude out on me. I should let it slip that I saw Tobin at a restaurant the other night with an attractive redheaded woman. It would provide for an amusing reaction. Or I could accuse Poppy or Beatrix, maybe even both. I smile to myself, envisioning the confrontation. But I'm so busy with this event, needy parents from the school, managing Bryony's musical career—almost all of the recruiters reached out after the concert—and, of course, Tara. Suzanne's final mental breakdown will have to be put on hold for another day.

"Would you prefer to lead this discussion, Suzanne?" I ask.

Beatrix stifles a giggle behind her hand. Poppy has suddenly become very enthralled by something on her phone, and Mia, leading the tour, clears her throat and adjusts her cheap black blazer. I'm reminded of Melissa and her baggy jeans. Another woman whose mother didn't provide the tools necessary in her upbringing, educating her about the fact that an entire profession exists for the sole purpose of adjusting clothing so that your pieces fit properly. I decide I'll slip her my tailor's card before we leave.

When Suzanne chooses not to respond, I continue, "Now ladies, if you look back here, there's a lovely patio." I walk outside and turn to face them with my arms extended. "I believe this is the perfect area for a cocktail hour, weather permitting." The ladies follow me out and *ooh* and *ahh*. Lush greenery encloses the space, giving it a secret garden vibe. In the center, a stone fire pit juts from the ground. "Picture strings of market lights hanging across in rows. With the fire pit going and several cocktail tables strategically placed." I'm directing their attention to the locations to properly communicate my vision.

"Oh, I love market lights. We just hung them across the pool and they are so pretty," Poppy says, clasping her hands together and bouncing on her toes.

I step around the women and indicate they should follow me back inside through the glass doors into the empty room. "This," I say, sweeping my arms across the room, "will be where we'll serve dinner. I'm thinking lots of black and gold, feathers, glitter, fringe, very art deco. Clean lines, but glitz and glamor. The waiters in black tuxedos, the waitresses in tuxedo dresses with feather head pieces." I turn to Mia in her ill-fitting pantsuit. "Are you writing this down?"

"It can't be cheesy, though," Beatrix adds. "The line is so thin with these themed parties. No Party City decorations. It needs to be like we're stepping back in time into the roaring 20s. Understood?"

I stare at Beatrix. I don't need her help and wish she'd just stand there and look pretty. It's all she's good for.

"Yes, got it," Mia says, scribbling furiously in a notebook.

"We'll need a stage over there." I point at the far end of the room. "We have a live band, but there will also be speeches after dinner and before dessert."

"Speaking of dinner," she says. "I have the chef preparing a tasting menu for you ladies. Shall we?" We're led into a smaller dining area where a table is set for us. After taking our seats, we're each given a sheet of paper and pen.

"These are for notes. Chef Donavan will bring out samples, and we can finalize the menu," she says.

"I have a great idea," Poppy says. "We should have themed cocktails."

This is not a great idea. Certainly not a novel one. We have themed cocktails at every party.

"Yes, Poppy, wonderful idea," I reply. "Do you want to brainstorm some ideas and call the bartending company to ask them to come up with some drinks?"

Her shoulders slump slightly. I'm guessing she was hoping to throw the idea out and have someone else do the work. We nibble our way through various fish, beef, and pork courses. There will be a vegetarian option, but none of us are vegetarians, so we let the chef pick. After the menu is chosen, we're told design concepts should be completed in approximately two weeks.

"Afternoon cocktails to reward our hard work?" Beatrix asks as we walk to the parking lot.

"I'm busy, not today," Suzanne says.

"Busy." Beatrix laughs. "Doing what? Watching Netflix?"

Suzanne stops short, and her face takes on a deep shade of red. "None of your fucking business, Beatrix." She quickens her pace, gets in her car, and speeds out of the parking lot with the sound of squealing tires announcing her exit.

"What the hell is her problem?" Beatrix asks.

"Menopause, maybe," I say.

Beatrix and Poppy laugh.

"Eloise, don't be mean," Poppy says. But her face doesn't match her words.

Chapter 21

BEATRIX

I pace my hallway, chewing on my thumb's cuticle. I never in a million years thought Suzanne would figure out Tobin was cheating on her. She's usually absolutely clueless. I've underestimated my friend. If she figured that much out, how long will it take her to realize she's right about the affair but wrong about the mistress's identity? It's not Eloise she's looking for. It's me.

"Shit," I say to no one. Unlike Eloise, I don't have full-time staff. My home isn't custom. My life isn't perfect. And as terrible as Eloise may be, at least she isn't sleeping with her good friend's husband.

It's only ten in the morning, but I need a drink; stress does that to me. Some women eat, I drink. I walk to the kitchen and pour myself a vodka over ice. Normally, I'd go for the wine, or something less harsh this early, but with everything going on, I need the sharp sting of pure alcohol. I take a long gulp and enjoy the warm sensation coating my belly the second the vodka hits it. I remind myself to go slow, to pace myself.

Unlike the last time. David was not pleased to come home from work and find me passed out drunk on the couch. I didn't remember puking over the side of it either, so it wasn't a good look.

Maybe it was guilt turning me into this cliché. But when I think about Tobin, I don't feel guilty. Instead, I feel the tingling between my legs and the anticipation of our next meeting shooting warm bolts of lightning through my chest. God, just thinking about him now is turning me on. I take another long pull of my drink and laugh. What is wrong with me?

David is a perfectly fine husband. But perfectly boring. There's no excitement with him. It's all the same. The same conversations, the same sex, the same everything. Tobin is different. He's not nice, or kind. In fact, he's an egotistical asshole. That edge is what draws me to him again and again. I guess I am a cliché. The worst kind, really.

I need to tell Tobin that Suzanne knows. I refill my drink and try to remember where I left my phone. As I'm walking down the hall, I stumble. Left hand on the wall, I hold up the glass with my right hand. Have I had more than one of these today? I don't remember drinking that much, but the floor is shifting, and my head is floating. I'm drunk. How did this happen?

I shrug and continue the search for my phone.

"There you are." I giggle and snatch my phone from the couch, then dial Tobin's office. His assistant answers. He'll be mad I called him at work, but this is an emergency. He'll get over it. I concentrate on keeping the vodka from slurring my words.

"May I speak to Tobin, please?"

"He's in a meeting. Can I take a message?" she replies in a bored, monotonous voice. With her boss away, I've probably interrupted her Instagram scrolling. I picture her tiny form behind the large desk in front of Tobin's office. Striking black hair, brown eyes so dark the irises are hard to distinguish from the pupils, and a double D chest squeezed into a too-small top. Who's the cliché now? I'd expect nothing less of Tobin, though. He views women as objects, put on this earth for nothing other than to fulfill his needs. Jokes on him, though. I've been using him just the same.

I know all about his assistant because I've visited him at work. I pretended to be a client and showed up unannounced. He was upset at first, but his mood altered the second I closed the door and opened my trench coat to reveal my naked body beneath. I didn't lock the door behind me and had been disappointed when Tobin reached behind my back and locked it himself. I was really hoping to see the look on what's-her-name's face when she walked in and saw us fucking on his desk. I had even practiced what I could say to further the shock. I imagined her opening the door, her red lips rounding in an oh shape, the whites of those black eyes forming a perfect circle around them when they widened in surprise. I'd pull Tobin closer, make him keep going. 'Either join us or lock the door when you leave, sweetie.'

I start laughing.

"Uh, hello?" Her voice interrupts my fantasy. I've forgotten what I'm doing for a second. My mind is scattered, and then the pieces snap back in place. I'm calling Tobin. He needs to know his wife is on to us.

"Do you know when he'll be done?" I ask.

She huffs in annoyance. "No. Can I take a message or not?"

I'll also have to tell Tobin how his assistant treats people. She doesn't know I'm not a client. She could be treating all callers this rudely.

"No, I'll call back," I snap before hitting the end call button with more force than necessary. I go for my drink and realize it's in need of another refill.

Chapter 22

Eloise

Tara is thirty-four, 5' 3", medium build, with strawberry blonde hair and brown eyes. Not a person who you'd notice. An extra on the set of life. She moved to Virginia from Michigan when her mother died. Her father had died years earlier. She has a few work friends but no one she's particularly close to, and she has just started online dating on Tinder. This new online dating thing all the girls are doing is so dangerous. You never know who you're talking to or who you'll be meeting. But they all do it, so that takes the scary out of it. They can explain it away, make it seem okay and not have to think about how they are putting their life in danger every time they open the application on their phone or go to meet a complete stranger for a date. Not even the media scares them, the Tinder Date Gone Bad articles or women being raped and killed by men they met online. 'It would never happen to me,' they say to themselves, 'those girls are dumb; they must not have taken the proper precautions.'

She bites her nails when she's nervous, has the same thing for breakfast every morning—black coffee and a plain bagel with cream cheese, not toasted—she usually eats lunch alone and eats dinner—takeout or frozen meals—from her couch watching *Wheel of Fortune* and *Jeopardy*. Tara is lonely and insecure, and a psychiatrist would likely diagnose her as depressed with a dash of anxiety disorder. Her life is sad. Most people would feel sorry for her if they knew all this about her. However, I'm not most people.

Online dating has sparked a new zest for life within her. She bounces a bit when she walks, is chattier with the girls at work—a bank where she is a vice president—and she feels hopeful. She's always wanted to be married, to be a mother, and to have a fairytale ending. Now she may just get it all.

I've gone on a few dates. Not a ton and they were okay, but it's different with you. Is that weird to say? I mean we haven't even met! LOL

This is what she types to Mark, but Mark isn't Mark; it's me, Eloise. I've made her trust and fall in love with me all through typed messages. She's never even heard my voice. Mark is in technology sales. He's on the road a lot and very busy with work, but also very wealthy. Women will forgive almost anything for a bit of cash they may be able to sink their manicured claws into one day. He gives her everything she needs: compliments, attention, and someone to really listen to her, not just pretend to. We've been talking for two weeks, and I've cracked her open like an egg. I know her entire history and life story, but also the secret thoughts she 'never shares with anyone.'

She doesn't ask me the right questions, though. Why can't we talk on the phone? Why can't we video chat? Mark is rich and young; he should have a phone with all these capabilities.

This is how those catfish scammers stay in business. People will ignore every red flag when they are desperate and lonely enough. They'll ignore every instinct screaming at them that something isn't right. All for hope. For the idea of love and security and the life they are determined to have.

This is all very sad for Tara but incredibly convenient for me.

Chapter 23

THE WATCHER

P oor Tara. Eloise has her claws hooked into the jugular of another innocent victim. The most perplexing thing is that Eloise is *so* obvious. She thinks she's so clever, so incognito. Blending in among society, a true pillar of the community. It's something I always circle back to. *How does she do it?* She's like a clone, a Stepford wife. She looks the part and sometimes acts the part, but it's never quite right, always a bit off. The layers she hides behind are so thin, like the skin of an onion. A flick of a finger and they'd flake off, revealing the devil below.

The only logical conclusion is that these people who fawn over her and fight for her acceptance and attention are teetering on the edge of evil themselves. She's surrounded by narcissists, so it's the perfect cloak. They're too absorbed in themselves to see what's so clearly right in front of their faces. Does she do this on purpose, or does evil attract evil and her social circle has grown by complete happenstance? Or maybe she's just that good.

Tara seems like a nice woman. Lonely but kind. She dresses nicely but not flashy. She keeps her face clean and natural, maybe a bit of mascara for nights out. She works at a bank in some management position, probably a vice president. Isn't everyone at a bank a vice president? That's the thing they say, right? I wouldn't know; I've never had a real job. She doesn't go out much, just work, home, and occasionally happy hour with co-workers in Georgetown. She doesn't mind eating alone and can often be found at a bistro enjoying a Cobb Salad, either reading the Washington Post or a book. She prefers self-help. Most of them have bright covers with curse words in the titles, which are all the rage these days. She must be sick of coming home to an empty brownstone each night, as she recently posted an account on an online dating app. I wonder if Eloise has ever considered using a dating app to find out more information on her victims, or is that another way I've outsmarted her?

Through Brant, the fake profile I created, I learned Tara has never been married but has been in a few long-term relationships. She's very career-driven, something men—at least the ones she's attracted to—don't particularly care for, according to her. She likes to read, knit, and travel. Has a fondness for animals and often volunteers at a local shelter. She prefers a quiet night at home enjoying a home-cooked meal, a bottle of wine, and a movie. Romcoms are her favorite.

Brant is always too busy to meet for coffee, lunch, or dinner. His "job" keeps him on the road. I keep waiting for the day when she'll finally tire of the excuses, but I have a feeling that having someone to talk to at night, someone to compliment her and ask her about her day, is enough to fill the void and curb the loneliness. Tara is boring but sweet. My old friend's guilt twists and turns through my guts.

She doesn't deserve to die.

Chapter 24

Eloise

A documentarian or biographer may say the summer of Billy's death was my tipping point. His lifeless body in that creek being the inciting incident that awoke the sleeping monster. They'd be wrong.

With one last look over my shoulder at Billy's corpse, I stepped into the shade of the trees and followed the path back toward my house. When I came to the end of the path where the trees ended, and the field of golden grass began, I started running. It would be unusual to have watched your friend die and lazily stroll for help, I decided.

"Mother!" I screamed, my face red and sweating, tears streaming down my cheeks. I ran through the front door and found my mother in the kitchen.

"Eloise, what are you fussing about?" She turned, wiping her hands on a dish towel, her features tight with confusion. Her eyes widened with surprise when she met my gaze. I wasn't the type of child who got worked up over just any old thing, so she must have known that whatever was going on, it was serious.

"It's Billy, Momma, something's wrong!" I exclaimed.

"Wrong?" my mother asked.

"We were at the creek." I stop, out of breath. Finally, when I'm able to speak again, I continued, "We were catching frogs ... one of the frogs got away ... I was chasing it, not paying attention. When I turned back, he was laying, down not standing anymore, his head—" I burst into tears. So distraught, unable to finish.

"Eloise, what? What happened to Billy's head?" my mother asked, her voice more panicky and louder with each syllable.

"Momma it was all bloody. He wouldn't get up," I cried.

She was already moving, grabbing my arm, pulling me after her. My shoulder hurt from being yanked. I wanted to yell at her, to tell her to get off me. But I had to play the part now. I was young, but I knew every second of every minute on that day would be very important. We were running toward Billy's house. With a fist, my mom pounded on the front door, screaming his mother's name. "Betty Sue, Betty Sue!"

She came to the door, wearing the same look of confusion my mother had when I had burst into the kitchen.

"It's Billy; you have to come quick," my mother cried. Justin appeared behind his mother. "Justin, call an ambulance," my mother demanded of him.

The two mothers and I ran back in the direction of the creek. "Faster, Eloise," my mother kept saying. But I couldn't move any faster. My legs were shorter than theirs, didn't she know? When we got to the opening of the path, Billy's lifeless body came into view. Betty Sue elbowed her way past us and ran into the water, scooping him into her lap. The sound escaping her lips wasn't human. She rocked and screamed with her dead child cradled in her arms. Her face turned toward the heavens, and tears streamed down her cheeks. She begged for a lot of things that day, for him to be returned, for God to take her, not him.

I stepped behind my mother and buried my face in the folds of her skirts, hiding my smile, muffling the sound of my laughter. My quaking shoulders must have given her the impression I was crying. She crouched down and hugged me so hard I could barely breathe.

"Go back and meet the ambulance," she whispered. "Bring them back here. Can you do that?"

I could, and I knew I had to, but the summer sun was right in the center of the sky without a single cloud to blanket its scorching rays. I was so hot and bored with the entire affair. My book was seeming real nice right about then. I sighed, but made it seem like more of a whimper and turned around and walked back the way we'd come. I was done running for the day. My legs were tired.

Did I enjoy watching Billy die? Yes, of course I did. Did it awaken something in me? No. It simply happened. Then it was over.

My thirst for blood would come, but it was much more gradual. That doesn't make for good TV, though, does it?

Darling Billy was not my first Darling.

My Darling was out there, not far from the home I grew up in, living her life with her loving family. None of them realizing how short that life would be.

Chapter 25

BEATRIX

"You're late," I say when I open the door for Tobin. "I've been sitting in this shitty motel room for an hour."

He stops and looks at me with his jaw flexing. "I had work."

"I don't give a fuck about your work."

His head tilts to the side, and his lips spread into a smile. I shiver; his eyes look cold, mean. I suddenly don't feel safe. The motel is in a bad part of town; it's rundown, and the other occupants are drug dealers and sex workers. Yet, I didn't feel unsafe walking from my car into the lobby, then from the lobby to this god-awful room. Even knowing that a blacklight would probably reveal enough stains of human excrement to send me running and screaming hadn't been enough to scare me away. It wasn't until Tobin walked in that I felt truly in harm's way. Which is strange, as I've been alone with him more times than I can remember.

We've all noticed how Suzanne flinches whenever he approaches her. She tries so hard to control it, but those things are the work of our subconscious. I always assumed—I think we all did—that there were things happening behind their closed doors, things that would make us all question Tobin and the shiny boy-next-door persona he likes to play in public. I've never seen bruises or anything of the sort, so I'm sure he just yells at her. Suzanne is annoying, so I'd probably yell at her, too, if I had to live with her.

He's unbuttoning his shirt, then his pants. So presumptuous of him. I hate that it makes me forget my entire reason for calling him here last minute. I find myself reaching to undress myself. I shake my head.

"Wait," I say, holding out a hand. "We need to talk."

His smile turns into a smirk, and it finally reaches his eyes. "We can do plenty of talking. I love it when you talk to me."

"Not that kind of talking." I fail to keep the annoyance from my words.

He rolls his eyes and sits on the bed. The faded floral comforter doesn't match his style. He looks shiny and new, with his blonde hair carefully combed back and his tanned six-pack peeking out over his black boxer briefs. "I have a wife for that. What do we have to talk about that's more important than fucking?"

"Suzanne knows."

"Knows what?" he asks.

He's infuriating. What else could I possibly be implying? "Knows about us," I say, waving my hand back and forth between us.

He shrugs. "So?"

"So? I just told you your wife knows you are having an affair, and your answer is so."

"I could care less what Suzanne knows or doesn't know," he says, laughing.

My hip juts and jaw drops. I want to correct him and tell him, 'It's *couldn't* care less, you dumbass', but I contain myself. "I figured you'd, I don't know, be a bit more worried. She doesn't know who you're sleeping with. Just that you're having an affair."

"Interesting," he says, looking off to the side. He shrugs again. "Yeah, still don't care. Let's get this over with."

My eyes narrow. Tobin is using me, but I'm using him too. It's just sex, nothing more and nothing less. Still, I don't particularly care about being used. I turn to grab my purse and start walking to the door. "I'm not in the mood anymore," I say over my shoulder.

"Wait," he says, and the sharpness of his tone makes me quicken my pace. "Wait." He softens his words and stands. His arms wrap around me. "I'm sorry," he whispers into my ear. He traces my neck with his lips. "I've had a long day at work, and I just need you. Your body." He's turned me around, and as one hand is in my hair, pulling my face close to his, he speaks into my mouth while kissing my lips, my neck, nibbling my earlobe. "I'm taking my stress out on you. You don't deserve that. You look beautiful tonight." The other hand slides from my waist up to cup my breast. My annoyance melts away. Before I realize it, we're both naked on the ratty floral comforter.

When we're done, he rolls off me onto his back. His skin is slick with sweat, and his breathing is still rough. I roll on my side facing him with my head propped up by my hand.

"Find out what she knows, okay? Make her think she's got it all wrong. She thinks you're sleeping with Eloise—"

"Eloise," he says, propping himself up on his elbows. "Why the hell would she think I'm sleeping with Eloise?"

I shake my head and laugh because it is funny; it's hilarious, actually. Suzanne is such a fool. I should feel guilty, I know I should, but the entire situation is so ... comical. Or is it? "You aren't sleeping with her, are you? I mean, it's not like I could tell you not to, all things considered. But, I mean, I hope you would tell me."

Tobin pushes himself off the bed and starts pulling his clothes on. "You women are all the same." He shakes his head and laughs to himself.

My entire body heats with shame. I get up and start dressing quickly, suddenly not wanting to feel so exposed, either my body or my feelings.

"Forget I asked," I say, finishing first. I gather my purse and leave Tobin alone.

Chapter 26

Eloise

Mark has finally made arrangements with Tara. A dinner at Taberna del Alabardero, an upscale tapas restaurant in downtown DC. *Dress nice*, he tells her, *tonight will be special.*

Tara knows the exact dress she'll wear. She purchased it at Neiman's on a whim and never wore it. It was more expensive and revealing than her normal attire. But tonight is special. Mark makes her feel beautiful and confident. She puts the too-short dress on, curls her hair, and does her makeup with the help of a YouTube tutorial while smiling at herself in the mirror.

When she first started talking to Mark, she told him she had created a strict set of rules for herself after she downloaded the dating app. One of these was she would never meet a man for a date unless they had talked on the phone. He wore her down by saying he didn't want the first time hearing her voice to be over the phone or the first time seeing her face to be in pixels. He was so romantic. She'd agreed completely.

I'll be coming straight from a meeting in the city, he'd messaged. *I can't believe I won't be able to pick you up like a proper gentleman. You understand?*

Nothing would spoil her evening, certainly not the inconvenience of having to drive to the city. He was a busy man, even working on a Saturday. His work ethic was admirable. She was very career-driven herself. In fact, she'd dedicated much of her life to her career. A career, he told her, he fully supported. Even in these modern times, so many men still didn't think this way. A successful woman intimidated them. He was confident enough not to let things like that bother him, he explained, and she fell more in love.

She told him it was all fine, that the night would be perfect no matter what. They arranged to meet at the parking garage a block from the restaurant.

If I can't pick you up, I at least want to walk in with you. A beautiful woman on my arm. How did I get so lucky?

I could practically see her in front of me getting ready, distracted by thoughts of her and Mark strolling arm and arm through the front entryway. Turning the heads of the other patrons. Jealous women, wondering how she stole this handsome man's heart.

I park my car and wait behind it in the darkened parking garage. It's Saturday night, lots of people, lots of chances to get caught. But no cameras. Everywhere you go, there are cameras these days. Millions of eyes are always watching, recording every move. This concrete dungeon is the exception. It circles down below the city, a hidden cave spiraling its way to hell. My plan isn't without risk. At any moment, someone could come and interrupt us. I realize this makes it all the more thrilling and

I consider how I can incorporate this added twist into future Darlings while I wait for Tara's arrival.

As expected, Tara is early. She drives her old Jeep Cherokee slowly toward me at exactly 8:03, though she's not supposed to meet Mark until 8:30. Ready to sit in her car and overthink the evening, I'm sure. I roll my shoulders back and inhale a slow breath before stepping frantically into the path of her oncoming vehicle. I wave my arms above my head. I don't scream or cry out, as that could attract the attention of more than just my intended target, so I let my face do the talking. Eyes wild, mouth extended in a silent scream. She slams on her brakes and jumps out of the car.

"Are you okay? I almost hit you!" she cries. My eyes flick to her thighs—her dress has inched further up her legs, and I ignore my initial urge to grimace.

"A man," I say, wringing my hands. "He came out of nowhere."

"A man? Did he do something to you?" She's so worried, so willing to help. She's also scared. Her head swivels around, looking for this man I speak of like he'll jump from a shadow and attack us both.

"He stole my purse. I had just gotten out of my car." I point to my vehicle, which costs what she probably makes in a year. "I wasn't paying attention. So dumb. I'm always telling my daughter, 'Pay attention to your surroundings, never let your guard down.' Especially at night." I'm setting the tone, proving she can trust me, a mother, a wealthy mother at that. There is no one more trustworthy. She's now standing next to me, her arms partially raised, as if wanting to wrap me in them, to comfort me. "I didn't even hear him. He grabbed my purse and took off."

"Are you hurt?" She looks in my hand and sees what they clutch. "You still have your keys. That's good. Why don't you sit in your car? Let me park."

I take the few steps it requires to get back to my car, on visibly shaky legs and sit in the driver's seat. She'll get in the passenger's side after she's parked her car, and if she doesn't, I have an alternate plan. They always do what I want, though. Tara pulls into the spot next to me, and as if I'm controlling her every move, she opens the passenger door and slides into the seat.

"Is there someone I can call? Should we call the police?" she asks with a comforting hand on the top of mine.

I suck in several breaths, composing myself from the imaginary attack. "Yes, the police. We'll need to alert the police."

She begins to reach into her purse to retrieve her phone.

"Do you mind if we wait for them up on the street?" I ask. "This place is making me nervous."

She checks her watch, likely regretting her involvement for the first time. I know her conscience and desire are competing within her. She doesn't want to be late for her date. *Just my luck*, she's thinking, *of course, this would happen on tonight of all nights.* She's too nice to deny me, a woman in need.

"Yes, I can't blame you. You must be terrified. Let's go up to the entrance and let the attendant know what happened. We'll get you help." She offers me a sympathetic smile and shuts her door.

And now she's mine.

Chapter 27

Eloise

T ara and I are exiting the parking garage and merging into DC traffic before she realizes what's happening.

She opens her mouth to point out that I didn't stop at the parking garage entrance. Her eyes are narrowed but not wild with panic. Perhaps she thinks I'm confused, shaken from the incident. I cut off her attempt to speak before any sound could escape her lips.

"I'm sorry, darling, you picked the wrong evening to be altruistic," I say, already reaching down into the pocket on my door to retrieve the taser. Her eyebrows furrow, and her mouth opens and closes. Before she has a chance to realize the danger she's in, I've passed the stun gun from my left to right hand and dug it into her neck, holding it there, sending the electricity that will disrupt the nerves controlling her muscles, rendering her body useless. Her state is temporary and highly variable. Had her body been subject to the electricity for one to three seconds, she could recover immediately, but I can't have that now, can I? However, the magic number is between three and five seconds. I hold it on her neck for the full five, and an additional second for good measure, giving myself between five and sixty minutes before she regains consciousness. I need between twenty-five and forty to get to my destination, depending on traffic, which can be unpredictable in our bustling metropolis. I keep one hand on the steering wheel, and one placed on the stun gun. If Tara is one of those people who will inconveniently wake up too early, I'll just hit her again while she's too dazed to fight me. My thirty-five percent window tinting affords a nice shield between Tara and the other drivers. From their view, she's simply napping. Two women after a long day of womanly things, one tuckered out and resting while the other drives her friend home safely.

I risk a few moments to take my hand off my weapon to turn on the radio. Nine Inch Nails fills the interior, and I bob my head, singing along, picturing the fun Tara and I are about to enjoy. Murder isn't my only secret indulgence. I consider playing "Creep." As if I didn't know who Radiohead is and needed Robert to educate me. My eyes roll at the thought. I do love that song, but I'm not in the mood for it at the moment.

"Is this music to your liking?" I ask Tara. A bit of drool trails from the corner of her outstretched mouth, glistening from the glow of the headlights and streetlamps passing through the car's interior.

She's disgusting.

I will make her beautiful.

I turn into our driveway and punch in the code for our gate. She'll be the first murder committed in my house. This makes her special.

We've been afforded total privacy. Robert is out of town, and Bryony is out for the evening. The shock on her face, when I agreed to her plans without argument, was rather humorous, seeing as the last time I agreed to that type of freedom, she came home the next day incapacitated by a hangover.

It will be my drooling Darling and me. The possibilities are endless; I couldn't select just one. Tonight, Tara and I will just *be*. We'll step into the breeze and see where it takes us. We will be one: her pain, my euphoria. If this evening were a painting, it would be hung in the Louvre, and people would flock to lay their eyes on it. A work of art that ignites something in onlookers they never knew was there.

"Tara," I sing her name as I pull into the garage. "We're home, darling."

Her eyes flutter open for a brief moment. She attempts to speak, but her garbled words blend into nonsense.

"Up, up, up. I am really not in the mood to carry you in." I get out of the car, walk over to her side of the vehicle, open the door, and give a slap, slap, slap on her cheeks. I'm losing my patience, and my words are becoming less kind.

"Get up, Tara. We have things to do." A harder slap and her eyes snap open. I stare at her, my green eyes lit with anger, the rest of my face as smooth as marble. "Don't scream, don't try to run, don't try anything. I don't want to use this again." She wilts back from the stun gun I wave in her face. "But I will."

I help her from the car and guide her into the house. She's stumbling and leaning on me, too consumed with her attempts at gaining back her facilities to admire my beautiful home. I'll have to give her a tour later. No reason to deny her that pleasure in her final hours. I flip on the light and illuminate the staircase that leads down to the mostly unused portion of our house. During construction, half of it was walled off for storage, and the rest of the space was used for entertaining. It features a separate entrance to the inground pool, complete with jacuzzi and sauna, a speakeasy-inspired bar, a movie theater, and a small bowling alley.

I usher Tara into the storage room which I'd prepared for her. The shelves of boxes and files have been moved to the side, and the entire room has been draped in plastic. A built-in shelf lines one wall, filled with an array of metallic devices and tools. Her panicked eyes scan the room, and with renewed energy, she whips around and tries to push past me. I give her a quick two-second jolt of electricity to the belly, and she takes two steps backward into the room.

"Enough of that. Take a seat." I point to the single chair in the room's center.

She collapses to her knees, hands steepled in prayer, leaning toward me. "Please, I won't tell anyone; just let me go. I swear." She stutters through more useless begging.

I throw my head back and cackle. "That wouldn't be very much fun now, would it?"

Her hands plop down to her sides, and she slumps forward, finally appearing to accept her fate. Something incomprehensible stutters from her lips.

"Stop muttering, it's so unbecoming. What is that you just said?"

"I didn't even get to meet him."

It takes me a second. I'm so shocked her mind is still consumed by this fantasy. So shocked I'm at a loss for words. "Oh, have you really not—you haven't figured it out yet?"

Her head snaps up, and anger flashes across her face. Is she mad about her little missed chance at love, or does she finally get it?

"I'm Mark. It's a pleasure to finally meet you in person." I reach my hand out to shake hers. I've removed my jewelry, and I don't like how my fingers look when not adorned with platinum and diamonds. She glares at it like I've tried to hand her a dead animal. "Apologies, my sense of humor is an acquired taste, not for everyone."

"What is happening?" She whimpers.

"Get up, sit in that chair, and I'll give you answers as you earn them. The first one is free." I nod my head to the metal seat. It's bolted to the floor, and the spindles are thick beams fused together in a simple yet effective design. I need her in the chair. It's not like we have all the time in the world. I have Bryony to think of.

Still reeling from the effects of her earlier torture, she struggles to stand before her legs finally remember how to hold her weight. Two steps, and she's slumped forward in the chair. I walk to the shelf, grab two zip ties, and turn back to her.

"You just sit still and let me do this." I dole out orders to her like she's an unruly child.

When one wrist is securely attached to the chair's armrest, she surprises me with a sharp pain in my bicep. When I rip myself from her mouth's grip, I look down in shock. The little bitch has broken skin. How can she be so ignorant not to realize that filthy mouths are filled with billions of over five-hundred species of bacteria? She has the audacity to smile at me, her teeth stained red with my blood. I quickly mask my shock and return her look with a cool smile of my own.

Before she can react, I punch her in the nose. I've been taking boxing classes since my twenties, and while I may not look like I have it in me, you never want to be on the receiving end of my fist. Every bone in her nose breaks, and she screams and grabs at it with her free hand. Her once-straight nose is sagging to the right. It would take a very skilled surgeon to fix the damage I've inflicted with one hit. She won't be alive long enough for that to be of any concern, though.

"Shut up and put your other hand here. If you do, I'll give you a shot of morphine to ease the pain."

She looks at me through tear-filmed eyes, likely not sure whether to believe me. She must have decided the promise of relief was worth the risk because she places her last free hand down and I expertly secure it to the chair.

"You'll have to wait for your morphine. I need to deal with bacteria your mouth has now transferred to my body." I shake my head and walk out of the room, locking the door behind me. The bite wound will have to be properly cleaned and sterilized. The risk of infection is too great to put it off.

After cleaning and bandaging my arm, I change into leggings and an oversized cashmere sweater. I'm walking down the front steps when I hear noises in the kitchen. I freeze and hold my breath. How would Tara free her wrists from the zip ties and so quickly? Drawers open and close—she must be looking for a weapon, a knife, hammer, something to kill me with. I walk on my toes up the last few stairs and grab a vase from the marble table. I quite like this vase. I bought it on my last trip to Switzerland, and though I'll be disappointed to see it shattered over her head, desperate times call for desperate actions.

Sliding down the hallway with my back against the wall, I run into the kitchen with the vase poised to strike. Bryony turns and screams, collapsing to the floor with her arms wrapped above her head in protection. I'm able to correct my aim inches from her head, and the vase shatters upon impact with the floor.

Bryony jumps up. "What the fuck, Mother!"

I place a shaking hand on my heart. "Bryony! You frightened me. I thought you were an intruder. You know I've been on edge ever since I was attacked." Calm now, I'm able to continue with far less unnecessary emotions. "First, do not use that word, you're entirely too educated to curse. Second, what are you doing here?" I want to look at the door that leads to a tied-up Tara, but I hold my gaze steady on Bryony. The anger at Bryony's unexpected entrance and not having the chance to gag Tara makes my entire body shake. My tongue finds my teeth and I count in my head.

"I texted you. I got sick of staring at Annabelle on her phone fighting with Chase." She shrugs. "Decided to come home. If I'd known that it was a death sentence, I probably would have chosen death by boredom instead."

"Don't be so dramatic. Have you eaten? Why don't we go out and have a nice dinner, the two of us?"

"It's ten at night. I was going to grab a snack and watch TV."

"Ten already. Where has the time gone?" I gasp.

"I was wondering what you were still doing up."

"I've been trying to organize the storage area, and I guess time flew away from me."

"Like you are actually doing the work?"

"I hired someone, and they didn't complete the task to my standards. So yes. Me."

She grabs a soda from the fridge and shuts the door with her foot. I bite my tongue until I taste blood. Without a word, she takes her provisions and retreats to her room. When enough time has passed for me to be sure she won't be coming back to collect some forgotten item, I head back to Tara.

"Slight change of plans, Darling." I fill a syringe with enough morphine to numb the pain from her broken nose and hopefully put her to sleep. "We'll have to continue this conversation at another time."

"What do you mean? What is happening?" Tara whimpers. The blood still flows from her nose over the dark, crusted dried blood covering her face and the front of her chest.

I grin, find a vein, and plunge the needle into her neck, depressing the syringe and injecting the clear liquid. "Hush now, answers are earned. I'll tell you how later. Now you enjoy your sleep, and we'll continue tomorrow." I secure her mouth with a gag. She struggles to breathe around her broken nose. Stepping back, I shake my head. What a shame it will be if she dies tonight with me not here. I check my watch and note the time. I have four hours before her next morphine dose is due.

Her head slumps to her chest, blubbering, tears streaming, perhaps hoping whatever I've injected her with will kill her, ending this torture. I go upstairs to prepare for bed. As I remove my makeup and apply night serum, I ponder how I shall proceed. Tara was supposed to be dead tonight and buried early in the morning. I've got a situation on my hands. Bryony could be gone all day tomorrow, sleep half the day, or hang around the house; there really is no telling. If my responsibilities weren't so all-encompassing, I'd have the control over her schedule that I'd prefer. I have exactly three days until Robert gets home, which will greatly hinder my chances of getting Tara's body removed from the house unseen. A dead body rotting in our basement just won't do. The smell alone could create a dilemma.

I'll have to keep Tara quiet, Bryony unaware, and get through tomorrow. Then Monday, while Bryony is at school, I'll torture Tara, kill Tara, and dispose of her body. I really am brilliant.

Chapter 28

Suzanne

Tobin is late getting home again. The number of times Tobin has come home at a reasonable hour lately is significantly less than the times he's out until who knows when at night. It's been...amazing. A relief. I can almost trick myself into believing my life is perfect. In those moments, I can hear the old me screaming from within. Begging me to remember who we are. Reminding me not to forget. Whispering to love myself, my body, my face, my heart, my everything. This old me knows we are better than this life; she's so confident and proud. She'd never have let it get this far. But she didn't help me. Her words weren't enough. And now, it's time for me to take things into my own hands and right so many wrongs.

I grab my keys and break a rule. It won't be the last one broken.

When I pull up to Eloise's house, I park by the gate on the side of the road. Her home is almost impossible to see from where I stand. Her stupid driveway is as long as a road. Thankfully, the trees are bare, so I can tell there are no lights on, at least not in the front. I stand, straining my eyes, for almost an hour. Several cars drive by. If any of them are her, or Robert, or even Bryony, I decide I'll tell them I popped by, just got here, and no one was answering the call from the gate. It will be suspicious, but I'm starting to not care what people think of me. Exposing the truth has taken over any rational thought or fear of embarrassment—or worse.

If Robert does come home and finds Eloise out, I can explain that Tobin is also out. Maybe he'll believe me then. I just need proof. If Robert is working with me, I have a chance of walking away alive. And if not, it's a risk I'm willing to take.

Right now, I'm just crazy, stupid Suzanne. The one everyone thinks is a joke. Robert is an intelligent man and a fair one. With him as my partner, we will take Tobin and Eloise down.

The ladies will regret ever ignoring me.

And maybe I'll punish them next.

My limbs are stiff with cold, and I'm shivering. I've texted Eloise, but she hasn't responded. As I'm walking back to my car, I see her pull up to her gate. My stomach drops; I'm sure she'll see me. Excuses for why I'm here fly through my brain, but they're unnecessary. She doesn't even look at me. The ever-observant Eloise has somehow completely missed my presence. I let out a long sigh of relief when the gate opens and her tires begin rolling forward. I want to see if she's alone, but despite my newfound bravery, I'm still nervous she'll catch me. In a last-minute decision, I scurry back to my spot at the fence and look through the metal railings. It's impossible to see through her tinted windows, not with how dark it is outside. My shoulders slump and I grip the metal tighter. I want to run after her, scream in her face, shake her, and force a confession.

A vibration from my jacket pocket startles me. It's a text from Tobin.

I'll be home in an hour. I haven't eaten and expect dinner when I get there.

Tobin isn't with Eloise now, but the timing of her arrival and this text doesn't rule out the possibility that they were together earlier tonight. With one text, my reality roars in, a wild, whipping wind smashing my fantasies and devouring my newfound power. I'm blown back, reduced to a shivering child. I need to be home before he gets there with dinner prepared and my clothes, makeup, and hair pulled together.

I hate him.

I hate Eloise.

It's enough to keep the fire within kindling.

I'll make them pay.

Chapter 29

Eloise

If Bryony senses something is amiss, she doesn't let on. I suggest shopping at Tysons and lunch at Urbanspace to get her out of the house and away from Tara. She says she isn't in the mood, but after being told it wasn't a request, we are in the car and on our way.

Playing doting mother is usually easy for me, but today the thrill of what awaits me tomorrow is almost too much to bear. My heart pounds with anticipation, and my skin tingles with excitement. I find myself forgetting to listen to Bryony when she speaks. I'm deep in my own thoughts, imagining the things I'll do with Tara before I kill her. Burns? Carve drawings into her skin? Or is it a more intense pain I'm after? My murders to date have been very quick. My Darlings dead before they could register what was happening to them. But lately, there's been a voice whispering in my ear, a hungry ache in my stomach. The evil seed planted in my heart, the one I've grown up watering, its vines twist longer and thicker each day, wrapping themselves around my organs. This should worry me. I can smell the sweetness in the air. A shift coming. The walls are closing in. My secrets are too big to be contained, ready to crack those walls.

I'm not sure I care.

I'm not sure I'm ready.

I'm not sure I wouldn't enjoy the world knowing.

I am sure I'm more intelligent than the police, my friends, my family...and if I were to be caught, it would just extend to the players who've joined my game.

The more, the merrier.

I pull an olive-colored sweater from the rack and hold it in front of Bryony. A shiver makes me visibly shudder. I'm changing, I'm not sure into what, but I'm excited to find out.

After shopping, we eat a lovely meal. Both Bryony and I are in pleasant moods. After lunch, we decide we're tired and head home. When Bryony goes to her room, I call Melanie, feigning a few coughs, and give her the day off, with full pay, of course. I wouldn't want her to catch this terrible cold. No, no, don't be silly, I'll be fine, you don't need to bring by meals. I can hear the relief in her voice, a four-day weekend, lucky her.

Later that evening, I make myself and Bryony a light dinner of salmon salad with a special seasoning of crushed sleeping pills added to her dressing. I haven't checked on Tara all day and am becoming impatient.

We sit in a quiet living room after dinner, Bryony on her phone and me reading a book. When she yawns for the twentieth time, she exclaims she can't believe how tired she is for only eight thirty. I encourage her to go to bed. It must be the shopping; it's worn you out, dear. She mutters in agreement with drooping eyes and trudges up to bed.

The metallic smell of blood and the stench of urine hits me as soon as I open the door to Tara's den. She's slumped over to the side, and at first, I can't tell if she's died on me. I take a few steps toward her, and she moans. Her head lolls up, she opens her eyes, and she jerks back in the chair.

"Ah, you aren't dead yet, I see. Good, that is excellent. Slight change of plans." I walk over to the shelf and refill the syringe. "It seems you will live to see another day."

She tries to mutter something, but she sounds as if she has a mouthful of rocks.

"Good night, My Darling," I whisper in her ear as I plunge the needle into her neck.

Bryony is at school, and she has violin practice after, which gives me six hours. I won't get to do all the things I'd imagined, but that's okay; Tara and I will still have fun today. I place a hand buzzing with excitement on the basement door handle. A piercing ring echoes through the house: the doorbell. I squeeze the door handle and grit my teeth as I storm toward the front of the house. At the front door, I pat my hair down, brush the front of my shirt, and stitch a smile on my face before opening it to find Suzanne. My smile drops slightly.

"Suzanne, hello. I wasn't expecting you today."

"Eloise, may I come in?" She doesn't return my smile, so I let my lips fall back into a flat line.

"Of course." I usher her in with a sweep of my arm. "Can I get you something? A coffee? Tea?"

"I won't be long." She takes two steps into my entryway, but instead of greeting me with our usual air kisses, she holds her purse at her chest like a shield. "I have a question for you, and then I'll be out of your way. I'm sure you're very busy." She spits out the last statement like it tastes foul. "Where were you Saturday night?"

Her bluntness hits me in the chest so hard I'm physically drawn back. "Excuse me?"

"Saturday, where were you?" Splotches of red begin molting her chest and neck.

This witch-hunt for her husband's mistress may have inadvertently taken her down the wrong path. The mercy killing is back on the table. "Well, let me think. I believe Bryony and I—"

"No," she cuts me off. "Bryony was at Grace's house. Where were you?"

My eyes narrow, and my fingernails dig half-moons into my palm. How does she know where Bryony was? "What is this about Suzanne?" I match her tone with my own curt reply.

"It's not a difficult question. I just want to know where you were."

"No, it's not, but it is a rude and imposing one, and quite frankly Suzanne, where I or my daughter were is none of your business. Now, I'm willing to forget this little display of emotions and chalk it up to a bad day. If you will kindly leave, we can pretend you didn't show up at my home, unannounced and uninvited, demanding I give you a play-by-play of my comings and goings. Leave now, and I will not tell people about this indiscretion of yours. If I do, I can assure you, your social circle is going to be much smaller by the time I'm finished."

Her mouth flops open. The blotches on her chest connect. She's a red tomato. It reminds me of Tara, and dizziness overtakes me for a moment.

Suzanne turns around in a huff and stomps back to her car. I follow her and stand in the open doorway.

"Suzanne."

She stops and turns around.

My tone is now high and cheery. Breezy even. "We must get the girls together and wrap up the rest of the Gatsby dinner details. I'll schedule brunch. Bye now, have a lovely day."

She returns my wave with a pinched smile, and I shut the door, sick of looking at her ugly face. I don't have time to figure out what Suzanne was on about, though it's clear Tobin's affair is really making her unravel. She's become a liability.

With one hand on my hip, I pinch the bridge of my nose with the other. Time has run out. So many distractions. Images of killing Suzanne flash through my mind. I shake my head.

Back in the basement, I place two fingers on the side of Tara's neck. Her pulse is weak, and her breathing is slow and ragged. This shouldn't take long, and it curdles my blood that I can't stretch out the experience. I pump her full of enough morphine to kill an elephant, take a plastic bag, and cover her face with it. For a split second, her body comes to life. The instinct to stay alive lives within us all I suppose. Her wrists fight against the restraints as her body convulses. Her outstretched mouth strains to suck in the life-saving air her lungs desperately seek, but all she accomplishes is moving the plastic, creating a satisfying sucking sound. After a few minutes, her body gives up, her muscles unclench, and she is gone. I step back and rub my fatigued arms. The planning, manual labor, fake Mark relationship ... all of it for nothing. It's enough to make me want to do something destructive, like drive a vehicle into a crowd of people or blow up a building, any release for the rage molding itself to my mind.

Time check: three and a half hours until Bryony is home if she skips practice, four and a half if she doesn't. An unusual sensation is increasing my pulse, and my throat aches as if invisible hands are squeezing my neck. It's a feeling I have no words for, and one I don't like. I will not be bringing My Darlings home with me in the future. I'm not used to dealing with feelings, frustration, and things not going my way. It's making me spiral out of control. I'll have to reflect on this later. Right now, I need to get Tara's body upstairs, outside, and to the area on our property I've selected as her final resting place. The stairs will be the most difficult.

Once she's cut loose from the chair, I shove her body onto the plastic tarp I've laid on the floor. I remove her clothes and clean her cold skin until it's red from my scrubbing rather than blood. Two hours and fifteen minutes left. The grip on my neck has now turned cold and has extended to my entire chest.

The stairs loom over me after I open the door. They seem to have doubled in number. With my hands gripping Tara's wrists, I drag her to the bottom of them. I pull her body up far enough so she doesn't slide back down, and I sit, catching my breath and wiping the sweat from my face. Sweating this heavily is for pigs, and I'm disgusted by myself. Rested, I continue the arduous task of heaving her body up a few stairs, sitting for a moment, then repeating the process until she is laying in my kitchen with her hands above her head, face frozen in a warped, soundless scream.

Two hours left.

I'm hot, and my arm muscles burn from the buildup of lactic acid. This was a terrible mistake. I should have killed her in the parking garage and left her there for some innocent passerby to find. I gulp down two glasses of water and continue dragging her out the back door, over the porch, and through the backyard. The thought of being done and running a bath is the motivation to keep pushing on.

I find Tara's grave a few feet into the woods that line our perfectly manicured lawn. When her body thuds into the pre-dug hole—grave digging a task I had replaced my morning run with for the last few weeks—I could cry with relief. If I were the crying type. I'm almost done with her. I leave her to retrieve the hydrofluoric acid that I paid a silent partner of mine to purchase and pour it over her body. This will expedite the decomposition process. The whole ordeal is sloppy and so unlike me, but occasionally, we need to learn our lessons the hard way. Her flesh begins to bubble and melt, and I take pleasure in watching. I then shovel dirt over her mangled body, cover the disturbed dirt with fallen leaves, return the shovel to our shed, and walk back to the house.

The hard part is over, but my work isn't done. After I collect everything from the basement and wrap it up in the tarps I used to cover Tara's temporary holding chamber with, I stand in the room and for a split-second, reconsidering dismantling it. Perhaps I made the earlier decision too hastily. This house could become a house of horrors. It just requires better planning. I could keep this room for future Darlings. I'm positive I'd be able to keep Bryony and Robert ignorant of its use.

I'm not ready to commit to that notion, so I continue cleaning and drive to the dump to dispose of the evidence. Five dollars and some friendly banter later, I'm on my way back to my house. Bryony is watching TV when I arrive. I tell her to order takeout so I can go upstairs to take a long bath.

I lay in the hot water with my head leaned against the tub and eyes closed. My body aches. I enjoy the pain.

Bryony's face materializes behind my eyes. I've imagined hurting her, emotionally and physically, but never killing her. I've put too much time and effort into creating her. However, I envision my hands wrapping around her neck then standing over her grave. I feel no sadness, no happiness either.

If Bryony and Robert were to fall victim to a tragic accident, so be it. Rules were made to be broken.

Chapter 30

THE WATCHER

Guilt, anger, sadness. My emotions continue to intertwine. I stood watching Eloise drag Tara's lifeless body through her yard and shove it into a shallow grave and I almost ran from my hiding spot behind a mature oak. I didn't. My feet wouldn't move.

I hate myself.

I can't go on like this.

I should end things.

I don't deserve to live.

A perpetual bystander I've become. So comfortable watching and waiting. But for what?

I don't even know what I want anymore. I could have stopped all of this, but my own fear, my own anger, my own selfish desires froze me into inaction and complacency.

Eloise has done worse things than murder people. I'm living proof. I wish she had killed me. I wouldn't be here contemplating whether I should do it myself instead. The pain would have been temporary. What she put me through, it's not something you get over. Time does not heal all wounds. Not mine, at least. Eloise ripped a gash in my heart so deep it's been pumping poisonous blood into my body for decades, rotting my insides. Decaying my body. And now I'm nothing but a walking sack of meat and bones and hatred.

The night of Tara's murder, I stood shivering, hidden among the oaks. Was I shivering from the cold or from the scene playing out before me? Probably a bit of both. Eloise didn't look regal and untouchable like she normally does. She looked old and tired. Tara's body was left in a hole. No place for her friends to stand and grieve over.

I ran over and crouched beside her shallow grave and wept silent tears over her mangled body, a shoddy replacement for her loved ones. The terror she must have felt in her final moments now permanently expanding her features. Her face bloated and bruised beyond recognition.

Footsteps.

So close.

I'd left my back exposed. Flight or fight instincts kicked in, but a flicker of numb relief flashed. This was it. The end.

I turned. She hadn't seen me. The choices spread in front of me.

I could kill her and dump her in the grave with Tara. She'd be forced to spend eternity cradling her victim. Their bones eventually mixing under the dirt.

I am a coward.

I ran.

I scrambled away from Tara, despite my heart pulling me toward her, and disappeared back into the trees. I couldn't watch anymore. The tear in my heart widened more, as it always does around Eloise.

Tonight, I'm numbing myself with tequila. I couldn't stand the quiet of my apartment. The ghosts of Eloise's victims visit me there. I see their faces in the corners of the dusty rooms, and in my mind when I close my eyes. The bar is loud and full of young people. The crowd keeps the hauntings at bay. I scan the room and take in the faces of the women surrounding me. So young, so vibrant, so alive. Any one of them could fall prey to Eloise.

They could be next.

Chapter 31

Eloise

My mom bought me a new black dress for Billy's funeral. A stiff and itchy dress. But she also got me a new pair of patent leather Mary Janes, which I liked very much. I was sitting on my front porch rocking in the white wooden rocking chair with my feet held straight in front of me, enjoying how the sun reflected off the shiny material, when Cricket strutted up my front porch steps, uninvited.

"Eloise, bless your heart, you poor thing. You must be so traumatized." Her dress looked much less itchy than mine. I lowered my legs and stared at her. She rushed over and placed a hand on my shoulder. "Just look at your face. You're pale as a ghost. I just don't know how anyone gets over something like that." She clucked her tongue and shook her head, her blonde curls bouncing, swinging around her face. I stared at them, mesmerized, while Elton John's "Tiny Dancer" rang through my head. It was one of my mom's favorites. She'd turn up the old cassette player she kept in the kitchen and sing along with it, playing the song on repeat. I do enjoy that tune. It has a lovely melody.

She helped herself to the rocking chair next to me, looked around and leaned closer, lowering her voice. "What'd he look like?"

"What'd who look like?" I asked.

The concern returned with an exaggerated frown. "Are you in shock? Is it too hard to talk about Billy?"

"No, why would it be hard?" I was genuinely confused by her questions.

"Well then, what'd he look like when he, you know—died?" The last word came out as a whisper. As if "died" was a bad, dirty word. Billy was dead, it wasn't a secret; anyone who heard her would have already known as much.

I stopped rocking. "He looked dead. How else would he look?"

She rolled her eyes. "I know that dummy. But was he all—" She made an exaggerated face, tongue hanging out to the side, eyes rolled back into her head.

"No," I said, annoyed by her ignorance and bored with the conversation. "You know when that deer got hit by the car over there." I pointed at the road.

She nodded.

"And its guts and insides were all over the pavement, blood everywhere."

More head bobbing.

"It was like that, but only here." I put my hand on the back of my head. "The back of his head cracked open, whap." I smacked my hand on the arm of the rocking chair, and the noise made her jump out of her seat. I covered my mouth with my hand to hide my giggling. "He was rolled over, face in the water, so I could see through all the blood and bone, right to his brain."

"I don't believe you; you're exaggerating," she said, placing one hand on her hip.

I shrugged. "You asked."

Momma came out and told me it was time to go, sending Cricket on her way. Billy's funeral was a big hoopla, standing room only in the church, and southern churches are big, as we southerners take our churches very seriously. It was a lot of boohooing and talking. I kept turning around in my seat to get a good look at all the crying, but my mom kept pinching my arm and hissing at me to stop fidgeting. I liked seeing everyone all upset, and it wasn't fair that my mom was making it more difficult to enjoy the funeral. It's not like anyone was paying attention to me anyways; they were all too busy with their crying and sniffling.

After the funeral, we all went to the cemetery and stood around, watching them lower Billy into the ground. I'd seen plenty of cemeteries but had never seen what it looked like under all that green grass and rows of stones. The hole they dug for Billy went down a whole lot farther than I expected. I wanted to get closer, but when I went to take a step forward, my dad grabbed the back of my itchy dress and pulled me tight in between him and my mom. When I leaned forward to see past them, I met Cricket's eyes. She was staring at me with her typical smug expression. I grinned and wiggled my fingers at her, hoping my description of dead Billy would haunt her dreams, keeping her tossing and turning at night for a long time. Her smile fell, and she looked down at her shoes. Plain ole matte black ones too.

After the burial, everyone shuffled to their cars, and we all drove to Billy's house. There was lots of food set out, like a party, but it was the saddest party I'd ever been to. Everyone standing around talking in whispers. I filled a plate with a bunch of sweets, went out to their front yard, and huffed in annoyance when I saw Justin swinging on the tree swing, where I planned to sit and enjoy my treats.

He looked up from his lap when I got closer. "Can I have a turn when you're done?" I asked.

"What?"

"When you're done swinging?"

He dug his toes into the dirt to stop the movement. His momma would probably scold him later for scuffing up his nice shoes. I thought he was going to get up, but he just stared at me. This would make most people uncomfortable, but not me. I could sit and stare at someone for hours, and it didn't make me feel any way whatsoever.

Finally, he stood and threw the wooden seat at me. "I don't give a damn about the stupid swing, Eloise." He stomped off in the opposite direction from the house. I jumped out of the way and only lost one macaroon to the ordeal. I put my plate on the ground and calmed the swing, then I grabbed my plate of sweets and enjoyed them while lazily swinging in the shade.

It wasn't long after the day of the funeral that Justin found his momma hanging from that very same tree.

Chapter 32

Suzanne

Beatrix is an absolute bitch, but she's an honest bitch, which is exactly why I've invited her to lunch. I have barely eaten since I learned of his affair since I started planning. I let my mind slip away from me a bit. There were so many feelings. It's not the time for that. I need to hold it together. This may be my only chance.

I put on a pair of black slacks I haven't been able to button in years and a fitted sweater I haven't felt comfortable wearing in ages. My morning was filled with hair, nails, and face. I feel younger and more confident, with anger and the desire for revenge growing. Not just the desire, the hope for revenge. Something I'd all but given up on.

"Suzanne, you're looking absolutely stunning. Have you done something new with your hair?" I stand and exchange air kisses with Beatrix. Before we've fully settled into our chairs, a server is hovering over us requesting drink orders.

"Just water, please," I reply.

Beatrix's lower lip juts out in a half pout, as drinking alone would go against an unspoken social rule. "Me as well, with two lemons." She turns her attention back to me. "Now, what was so important that we had to meet right away, and without the other girls?"

"It's Tobin—"

"Are you still on about Tobin and Eloise? I really don't think—"

"I know it's Eloise," I insist.

Her finger begins spinning her wedding band, round and round. Her eyes dart around the room, falling everywhere but on my face, and two perfect circles of red bloom on her cheeks. *Not so funny when your cruel jokes turn out to be true, is it?* I let her squirm in her seat. Punishment for planting the seed of suspicion in the first place.

"Maybe you're right," she says. "A woman's intuition usually is." She retreats into her thoughts.

"Are you ready to order?" The friendly server asks, placing our water on the table.

"We need a few minutes," I reply, sharper than I mean to.

"It's always the ones you don't suspect now, isn't it?" Beatrix says, leaning forward.

"Mmhmm." I take a sip of water. "Doesn't she seem—secretive to you? Like she's never quite being herself. I don't think any of us even know the real Eloise, if I'm being honest."

"Always saying the perfect thing, wearing the perfect outfit, volunteering first. Nobody is *that* perfect," she agrees. "What are you going to do about it?"

"I don't know yet. I think I'll confront Tobin first, let him know I found out about the affair and see if I can get him to admit he's sleeping with Eloise. Then I'll call Robert, of course. He has a right to know."

"You could always call Robert first." She shrugs.

If Robert and I could work together as a team, neither Tobin nor Eloise could find a way to talk their way out of it. Tobin wouldn't have a chance to forewarn her either. There'd be no time to align their lies. And more importantly, I'd have protection.

"Isn't he back in town?" I ask. "I thought I remember Eloise saying he'd be getting back this week."

"He is," Beatrix says, her red lips turning up. She is sitting in the audience, waiting for the curtains to fold back, and we're all jesters taking the stage for her entertainment. Sweat prickles under my arms and I sit on my hands to stop myself from smacking the scheming look off her face.

"Or I could investigate more, find evidence of him and Eloise on my own," I say, letting my voice trail off. I revel in her face, attempting a shocked expression. Her jaw hinges open, and eyes bulge, but the rest of her skin is too full of Botox and fillers to move with them. It gives her a cartoonish appearance. The din of the room—forks scraping on plates, hushed conversation and laughter—fills the silence.

"Do what you want; I'm just offering a suggestion," Beatrix snips.

She's so used to getting what she wants that she can't even handle me choosing how to manage my fucked-up life the way I want to. I'm so sick of everyone controlling me. I need a new life, new friends, and a fresh start. Maybe I'll move back to Ohio when this is all done. I need to get away from all these awful people.

Ohio may not work, though. I need somewhere Tobin can't find me.

Chapter 33

SuzANNE

B ack home, I'm pacing my bedroom. I've already done more searching through Tobin's office, closet, dresser, and nightstand, extremely careful to put everything back exactly where I found it.

My phone is clutched in my hand with Robert's contact already pulled up. I'm about to hit call when I hear Tobin come in. My pulse quickens, and sweat beads down my back. The house already feels smaller. That's his way. Always taking up too much air, too much space, too much everything. He's like a black hole, just sucking the life from any space he occupies. Most people would consider him charming and charismatic. I used to be one of those people. They don't know the real Tobin. I wish I could take a pin and pop his inflated ego.

My phone slips from my hand and clatters on the pinewood floor. "Shit," I mutter to myself, bending to check if the screen shattered. Tobin would be angry if I needed another replacement. I hush myself. I don't need to worry over what angers Tobin anymore.

"Suze," he calls. I glare in the direction of the familiar sound of his footsteps.

"Coming," I reply.

I'm expected to be waiting for him. Greeting him when he walks through the door.

I find him standing in the hallway, waiting, looking at his watch.

"Where were you?" he asks, not with anger, not with love. It's a trick he plays, hiding his emotions. This is one of his less devious games, yet anxiety twists my heart and shallows my breathing.

"Bathroom," I reply, then suck in a breath.

"And how was my girl's day?" His smile is back, muscular arms extended.

I walk into his arms and allow him to shower me with fake love and fake affection, bracing for the shift I know is coming.

"It was fine."

"Ah, great to hear," he replies. The phone is out now that he's done his duty. "What's for dinner?" he asks with fingers flying over the phone's keyboard.

"Nothing planned, but I'm sure you'll manage."

The phone is suddenly not so interesting. If looks could kill, I'd be dead, but I'd have keeled over long before tonight if that were the case. For years, I'd done everything in my power to avoid this look, and to avoid what comes after the look.

"You know the rules, Suzanne. I asked what's for dinner. Is that the answer you want to go with, or would you like to try again?"

I walk over to the side console where my purse is, throw my phone in it and sling the strap over my shoulder, then with my hands clutching the strap to hide their shaking, I walk out the front door without another word.

Chapter 34

Eloise

I consider myself to be at the pinnacle of good health, not just for my age but for any age. However, too much manual labor has caused me to be bedridden. Any slight movement and my back seizes, sending painful spasms shooting down my legs. After a restless sleep, I call Melanie first thing in the morning and tell her to come immediately. The first thing she did, at my insistence, was call my doctor. He's come and gone, leaving a prescription of both pain relievers and muscle relaxers. Robert is due home late this evening. I can't stand to be immobile, but I do like the idea of being waited on.

"I have your dinner here, Mrs. Williams." Melanie balances a crystal tray which holds my meal. She places it on my nightstand and fluffs a pillow to support my back while she gently helps me into a sitting position. "I also found this earring in the kitchen; I almost stepped right on it." She holds out a cheap stud, cubic zirconium from the looks of it.

"It doesn't look like yours or even something Ms. Bryony would wear. Should I show her? Maybe it's one of her friends."

"No," I snap. "It's cheap, and whoever lost it won't miss it."

She tries to cover her surprise or confusion by turning her back and tucking the earring into her pocket.

I realize I've overreacted and don't want her thinking something as silly as an earring has bothered me. "I'm sorry. These medications and the pain are making me grumpy. I don't know what I'm saying. Thank you for finding it. Place it on the nightstand, and I'll be sure to ask Bryony myself."

Her face softens, and she visibly relaxes. "Yes, of course. It will be right here." She pulls it back out and places it down. "Give me a shout if you need anything else." Melanie brought a set of walkie-talkies so I could beckon her without having to move. Her ingenuity, as usual, is impressive. It's a shame I can't leverage that kind of thinking outside of the management of our household.

I finish my meal and take my medicine, and within almost exactly thirty minutes, they take their hold. My eyelids become heavy, and I'm slipping away into a dark world of nothingness.

"Eloise. Eloise." Someone is calling my name, but from where? It sounds as if I'm standing at the end of a hallway, and my name is bouncing off the walls toward me from far away.

"Eloise, wake up." A large hand shakes me. I open my eyes to a dark shadow standing over me, holding something in their hand. I want to scream, but I can't break free from the fog of sleep engulfing me. Another shake and my eyes begin to adjust to the darkened room. Robert turns on the light next to the bed, and the brightness sears my eyes.

"What are you doing?" I demand.

"This was thrown through our front window. How did you not hear it?"

I sit up and rub my eyes.

"What is wrong with you? Have you been drinking?" he asks.

"I threw out my back, and the doctor put me on painkillers. What was thrown through the window?"

He passes me a brick, and I turn it over in my hands. My fingers trace its cool, rough surface. I still don't fully understand what's happening.

"This was wrapped around it." The piece of paper he holds looks like a standard notebook paper, white, college-lined. Then I see the writing:

I know what you did.

I narrow my eyes. "It must be a prank. Maybe some child in Bryony's class."

"Quite the prank." He makes a choking sound, almost a laugh, but not quite.

"What time is it?" I ask. I look at the clock on the nightstand and see it's just past two in the morning. "There is no sense waking her up. We can ask if she's having any trouble with one of her friends in the morning."

"Hmm," Robert says more to himself. He's studying the page as if it will suddenly speak to him and reveal its author. I'm observing him, wishing I could crack his skull open and read his thoughts. "It's just...it doesn't look like a kid's handwriting, does it?"

"They are almost adults, Robert. It's not as if their handwriting would be any different from yours or mine. Really."

"I guess you're right. I'm going to see if I can find something to put over the window tonight. I'll call someone to come fix it in the morning.

Sorry to disturb you. Go back to sleep. I'll get this handled." He leans down and kisses me on the forehead.

"I'm so glad you're home. We missed you." I smile, but the second the door closes behind him my lips plummet into a frown. I don't know what this person thinks they know, but the next item shattered with a brick will be their face.

Chapter 35

Eloise

With my back finally healed, I'm out of bed and downstairs. Robert was able to get our window replaced, and I'm standing in my kitchen with the crumpled note laid on the counter. *I know what you did.* Between the attack in the woods and now this, it's getting harder to brush everything off as coincidence. I can't imagine anyone would know about My Darlings. The police would have already been called, and I'd have been hauled to some filthy interrogation room, dealing with questions I had no desire to answer.

I drum my nails on the marble. I understand that a position such as mine comes with its fair share of jealousy. I want for nothing; everyone loves me. I'm rich, beautiful, and I'm not just part of the inner circles ... I run the inner circles. Many people live under the false assumption that cliques end when adolescence does. This is highly incorrect; they only get worse, especially for the upper class. At school, there is the mommy clique, where you earn your place by being the best, most involved mom of all the moms. You throw the best birthday parties, volunteer for every school function and field trip, bake the most delicious cupcakes for the bake sale, and, of course, earn a coveted position on the PTO board.

Then there are the society cliques. Country clubs are the hives where the swarms of women socialize. Most women are born into these groups. Their parents were wealthy, as were their grandparents, and so on. They're given a free pass; no work required. Simply having the proper lineage is all that's needed. Within these country club groups, there are several layers. No one talks about them, but they exist; everyone knows they do. There are two types of women considered at the bottom of this unspoken totem pole: new money and trophy wives. You see it all the time, these women trying so hard to break in, yet making the same faux pas. They believe if they talk about how much they spent on their house, how many nannies they have, their newest designer handbag, and the trip they are planning to Fiji, then they will be accepted and respected. Instead, the other women laugh and talk behind their backs. The coveted invites to brunches and dinner parties never come. No matter how many tennis lessons or how much volunteering they do, they're always stuck on the outside looking in, crying to their husbands at night, not understanding what they could possibly be doing wrong.

There is one way in, though. A husband of an outsider has what is seemingly a simple game of golf with the husband of an insider. A business transaction occurs. The new husband earns the established husband a significant amount of money. Suddenly, the wife is in. It was never about her; there was never anything she could have done. It's always about money. You can't talk about money. You can't flaunt money. But if you somehow manage to make someone else a lot of it, you're in. The world is a shallow place. The rich always want to get richer, and everyone is looking out for themselves. Once again proving I'm not so different from everyone else, am I?

I fold up the note and stuff it into the back of one of the drawers. Poppy, Beatrix, and I have plans to go dress shopping today. The note's mystery can wait for another day.

I pull into the parking lot of the boutique Poppy suggested. The goal is to find 1920s-inspired gowns, so our normal shops wouldn't do. Air kisses exchanged, we walk in and begin exploring the racks of sparkles.

"Did anyone invite Suzanne?" Poppy asks.

I catch Beatrix's eyes sliding toward me, waiting to see if I'll respond first. I pretend to be very interested in a floor-length mermaid-style dress I'd never be caught dead in.

"She's been...off lately," Beatrix says. "Have you ladies noticed?"

Poppy's eyebrows attempt to meet in the center, a fresh Botox appointment preventing their full descent. "I haven't spoken to her much. Poor thing must be a wreck over Tobin. Anyone know if she's told him what she knows?"

"No, I had lunch with her the other day," Beatrix says. "I suggested she find out who it is and tell the husband, whoever that husband may be. The two of them could do it together. What a sight. Can you imagine?" She laughs and pulls out a black minidress, holding it up against herself and admiring her reflection in the mirror.

"You're assuming this mistress has a husband then?" I ask.

Beatrix narrows her eyes. "I—well, I guess we don't know."

Poppy clucks her tongue and shakes her head. "Shame. I don't understand why people cheat. Divorce is so much easier. It's not like we don't all have prenups. Let the attorneys sort out all the fuss and move on."

"I would assume," I interject, "they do it for the thrill. It's new, something devious. There is also the thrill of being caught. It's all entertainment, especially for a bored housewife. And men, well, we all know they have no self-control when it comes to these things."

Beatrix's jaw flexes, and her grip tightens, twisting the dress she holds. I suddenly get it. I've been so distracted by my own life; I can't believe I missed it. I want to laugh out loud. It's Beatrix. She's the one sleeping with Tobin.

"Beatrix!" Poppy exclaims. "You'll ruin that dress. I'm sure David would never cheat on you. Eloise, stop being so gloomy. We're supposed to be having a fun shopping day."

"Oh! You didn't think I was implying..." My lips curve down in an exaggerated frown, and I place a hand on my chest. "I wasn't trying to upset you. David would never. We all know that. Nothing for you to worry about. I think I'll try this one on." I hold out a white, floor-length gown with a plunging back. Swarovski crystals are sewn into the fabric covering the entire dress.

Poppy gasps and claps her hands. "It's gorgeous! Yes, you must try it on right this minute."

When I come back out with the dress on to show the ladies how perfectly it hugs my toned body, Beatrix is gone. Some sort of emergency. I shrug. This love triangle Beatrix has gotten herself entangled in isn't my problem. After a slow circle for Poppy, we both agree it's the one and I hand over my black Amex to pay the five thousand dollars for it.

With the dress carefully arranged in a garment bag hung over my arm, we walk out to the parking lot. I look at my car and drop the bag. My fists tighten into small balls at my side. Poppy notices I've stopped walking and turns around with a confused look on her face. She follows my glare, and her palm rises to the side of her face while she sucks in a horrified breath.

A gash in the black paint of my Rolls Royce runs from the front of the car to the back.

I turn around and march back into the store, demanding to see the footage from the last hour. The shopgirl, flustered, stutters when she explains they don't have any cameras in the parking lot. There's nothing to see.

I want to wrap my hands around her neck and cut the flow of oxygen from her mouth to her lungs. Scratch my nails down her elfin features until lines of blood drip down her face. Instead, I smile a teeth gritting smile and thank her for her assistance.

"This was Beatrix," I say to Poppy, who has picked up my dress from the ground and is staring at me with her mouth in the shape of an O.

"Beatrix? No, she would never—"

"You're right, it's my anger speaking. Forgive me." I take the dress and shake my head at my car. "As if I didn't have enough to deal with, and now this."

"Don't stress yourself out, honey. Let Melanie take care of the car. You can focus on the event. That's what we pay the help for now, isn't it?"

"Mhm," I say more to myself.

I drive home, planning all the ways I could kill Beatrix while inflicting the most amount of pain. Tiny little slices with a knife, letting her body drain blood for weeks. Cutting her into pieces, one small body part at a time. I'd start with the tongue in that big mouth of hers.

Chapter 36

Eloise

M elanie is in the formal dining room cleaning the china. When I get close, I note the faint scent of lemon drifting from the bowl of warm water she's dipping the rag in and wiping down each piece with. I tell her the vehicle has been vandalized and ask that she please schedule it to be picked up. I let her know the entire thing would need to be repainted.

She drops the rag in the water and places her hands on her hips, biting her lower lip.

"Do you have something to say?"

She continues to annoyingly gnaw on her lip, avoiding eye contact, Spit it out," I huff.

"I mean, first the attack on your run, then the window, now your vehicle. Do you think these are related? Could someone be targeting you? Maybe I should call the police officer who was here when you were assaulted? I put his card somewhere..."

I force a smile. "I appreciate the concern, but that won't be necessary. When you're a woman of my position, you always have enemies, and usually they are the people closest to you. A few minor incidents are of no concern to me."

"Bryony was upset about the brick. Maybe you could talk to her?"

"Maybe you could mind your business and not tell me how to raise my child. Further, this validates my suspicion that the culprits are kids. I'm sure Bryony has gotten herself in a tiff with one of her schoolmates and now we all are left to suffer. Keep your ears open, and please tell me if you learn anything. I'd much prefer to avoid any further expensive replacements or repairs."

Seemingly unfazed by my outburst, she replies, "Yes, of course. Should I finish the china?"

I pause, an idea forming. "Actually, finish what you're doing. When you've gotten the car sorted, I'd like you to formally invite Suzanne and her husband Tobin over for a dinner. Check Robert's schedule and select a night both he and they are available. That chef you hired, the woman, what was her name? Doesn't matter. Hire her. I want the best food, a full tablescape, the works. Let me know when the details are arranged."

"Would you like this before or after the Gatsby event?"

"Before. As soon as possible if schedules allow. I'm going to take a bath now. I need to relieve some stress before my back begins hurting again."

While the water runs, I send a group text to Beatrix and Poppy. *Beatrix, so sorry you had to run off so quickly, hope it was nothing too serious. I have Melanie putting together a dinner for Suzanne, Tobin, myself, and Robert. I'll let you ladies know if I learn anything new. XOXO*

Poppy replies that it's a wonderful idea, and she thinks Suzanne will be so pleased. With the moving dots appearing and disappearing, I can only assume Beatrix, for once in her life, is at a loss for words.

Chapter 37

BRYONY

After spreading the pink gloss over my lips, pleased with the shiny pucker in the visor's mirror, I flip the mirror closed and look at Annabelle. "New color, you like?"

"Yeah, put some on me." She leans over with an exaggerated pucker, keeping her eyes on the road. I swipe the wand across her lips, most of the gloss landing on its intended destination.

I turn up the radio, and we shout along, laughing at our off-key performance. The gravel parking lot is already full by the time we arrive. The thudding bass reverberates from the field where a bonfire casts orange flickering light on crowds of half-drunk teens. Annabelle grabs hold of my hand. "Try not to go all vampire on us tonight, 'kay?" She laughs. I stop walking. She tugs on my hand. "I was just kidding." Her head thrown back, another laugh. I force a smile on my face and try to forget about the last bonfire.

The night becomes a blur of stale beer and faces that look like jack-o'-lanterns from the fire's light. At some point, those smiles turn from friendly to menacing. The entire world spins too fast. My vision blurs, and I hold out the red Solo cup and look at the fizzing gold liquid sloshing inside. I don't remember having more than one or two beers. As if in slow motion, the cup is out of my hand and falling to the ground. Everyone and everything moves faster than my mind can keep up with, but also slow; it's too confusing. All the lights are extinguished. The world goes black.

My heartbeat pounds in my head. Each pulse sends a throbbing pain reverberating through the interior of my skull. My mouth tastes sour and foul, and my throat burns from what must have been vomit. I can't remember puking, or how I got home, or anything really.

"Wake up, Bryony." My mother's voice sends a chill down my spine. I open my eyes to her standing over my bed. She looks eerily calm. It's when she looks like this that I fear her the most.

I try to sit up and wince at the increased pain each small movement brings. "I'm sorry. I didn't drink that much." My voice sounds hoarse and strained.

"You don't remember, do you?" She starts laughing, the sound like glass shattering. My entire body shakes. I'm less afraid of what I've done than I am of what she's about to do to me. She stands, throws my phone in my lap and leaves. Bile creeps up my esophagus. I swallow it down. My entire body quakes after I unlock my phone and see hundreds of notifications of texts, calls, and every social media app.

When I open my texts, I see why.

I crawl out of bed and take out my violin. I play Bach's Partita No. 2 until the notes lose meaning; it's just chaos and noise. A chainsaw. My fingers bleed. My muscles ache. I don't stop. The music chases away the shame and the ache. Minutes or maybe hours later, there's no telling, I open the door to go to the bathroom.

Mother is standing in the hallway outside my door. "You're a good girl, my darling."

Pride swells in my chest, replacing the shame.

Chapter 38

Eloise

Billy's remaining family members left town soon after his mother's funeral. Maybe the adults knew where they ran off too, but no one ever shared that information with me, and I didn't care enough to ask. There was a whole bunch of flowers and stuffed animals left at the creek, but no one wants to think of a dead kid every time they go to play, so one day Billy's memorial was gone too. Life carried on.

By middle school, I had adapted my approach to others, having learned quickly how to get people to fall in love with me and want to be my friend. As a matter of fact, I was the most popular girl in school. This meant I could be mean to whoever I wanted, and everyone else would go along with it. Most bullies will pick the easiest target, the poor kid, the one who studies too much. Those kids already felt bad about themselves, which took all the fun out of torturing them. I preferred the ones who got a bit too big for their britches. I'd let them into my inner circle and bam, turn on them for no reason other than my own amusement. Their social standing plummeted. I'd let them swim in the mud for a bit, before picking them back up, washing them off, and letting them back in. Little girls are willing to give up almost anything to be included, and women are no different really. Would the other girls in my group try to stop me the next time I targeted one of our friends? Of course not.

One evening, I overheard my parents talking about me. My mom suspected something was off. Not quite right. My dad suggested therapy or long-term care. The idea intrigued me almost enough to play up my strangeness. I wanted to see what a mental institution was like, more to see what the patients were like than anything. After thinking about this option for a few days, I decided against it and quickly learned how to act so as not to arouse my mother's suspicions. I began telling her I loved her, and gave her kisses, hugs, things of that nature. She looked much less worried all the time and talk of therapists and mental institutions ceased.

What happened to Heidy, well, that can't be blamed on me, although some people certainly did try to.

We were in my least favorite class: art. I much preferred literature and history. I enjoyed learning, and I still do. Especially history. The study of the fall and rise of entire empires over the silliest things. Entire wars are fought over religion; it's so preposterous. I am not against the mass killing of citizens and military men. Lives lost are of no consequence to me. But these gods they claim to worship, these all loving, all forgiving gods. They don't seem to be the types of beings who would support murder in their names. I'd sit in church every Sunday and look around at that room full of sinners. Wife beaters, adulterers, petty thieves, and worse, sitting in their pews, walking out of the church believing their sins were atoned and they earned their right to damn others to hell. Hypocrites, all of them. If there is one thing I am not, it's a hypocrite.

Immoral and evil, yes. If there is a hell, I probably have a one-way ticket there, but at least I have the good sense to know my place, and I don't twist the version of my moral beliefs to decide another's fate.

Heidy wasn't the type of girl I'd usually pick on. She was a bit slow. Already an outcast. Already fallen. But I was more spontaneous back then. Less thoughtful. It was seventh grade, and I was sitting behind the paint-splattered desk, mindlessly cutting pieces of colorful construction paper for whatever project we were working on. Heidy was making her way up the center aisle. I rolled my eyes when I saw the scissors clutched to her chest. We'd been taught how to hold scissors in kindergarten, yet there she was, pointy side facing up, hands wrapped around the finger holes. It wasn't *so* awful what I did. She's not entirely without fault.

My backpack was on the floor next to the aisle; I simply nudged it with my toe and slid it in her path. How was I to know Heidy wouldn't let go of those scissors when she tripped and fell?

But she didn't, and down she went. Those sharp blades pierced right through her neck. A slight shift in either direction and Heidy's fall would have been a nick to the skin, a trip to the nurse, and a stern lecture in the proper handling of scissors and other sharp objects.

Unfortunately for Heidy, luck was not on her side that day in art class. Somehow Heidy managed to stab those scissors right through her neck and into her carotid artery. It was a bloodbath. She convulsed on the floor, blood squirting from her neck like a water fountain. Kids screamed and ran out of the classroom. I sat and watched.

Later, when my mom came to pick me up, and I was covered in Heidy's dried blood, the principal told my mom I was in shock. To witness such a gruesome thing at such a young age. How tragic. They recommended therapy. All that work to avoid therapy, poof, wasted. My mom nodded and agreed while she dabbed her eyes with a hankie.

If you haven't guessed already, Heidy died that day. No one saw me push my backpack out in front of her path. One girl made the mistake of asking me about it. "Wasn't your backpack under your desk?" she'd asked.

She later regretted that.

Chapter 39

BEATRIX

M y husband and I are eating dinner. He's home, and I'm sober—ish, it's an unusual evening.

"You seem somewhere else tonight. Is everything okay?" he asks. Always so kind, my husband. I'm such an asshole.

He's right—I'm inside my head, my thoughts tumbling. I look into his concerned eyes and my breath catches. His brown eyes are so caring, so thoughtful. The lines around them, on his whole face really, are deeper than when we first met. His dark hair is now almost fully gray. These details tell the story of him and of us. We've been together since college, grown old together, him more gracefully than me. I'm an awful person. Why am I like this? I take a long gulp of my wine.

"Yes. Fine," I say. I can't even muster up the energy to sound convincing.

He sighs and puts down his silverware. It's the first dinner we've had that is just the two of us in so long. The guilt sinks my stomach further.

"You're barely eating, barely paying attention to me. What's going on, Beatrix?" Even when he's annoyed, he looks concerned. He's never even raised his voice at me, not once in our entire marriage. Even though I've deserved it plenty of times.

My mind races to think of an excuse. I can't tell him the real reason I'm having trouble concentrating. He can never find out about Tobin. Tobin was a mistake. I need to end things immediately. I know this, but every time I start to work up the courage, my body takes control of my mind, my clothes are off, and I'm once again acting like the person I am and not the person I want to be.

"There's a lot going on." I sigh. "That Melissa girl's murder has really gotten to me for some reason."

"Did you know her?" He reaches out his hand and rubs the soft skin between my thumb and pointer finger. It's so familiar. So comforting. I could cry.

"No, it's nothing like that. It's just—this is going to sound crazy. I'm actually slightly embarrassed. Have you seen the photos of her?"

He nods.

"She looks so much like me. I don't know... I am having all these *thoughts,* and my anxiety is through the roof. It's silly, I know."

He doesn't say anything; simply looks into my eyes so deeply as if he's looking inside my head. I try not to squirm or look away or to do anything that would send him digging further for my secrets.

"I'm worried about your drinking, B."

I jerk my hand from his and knock over my wine. We both stand and grab for napkins, patting at the mess. Thankfully, I drank half the glass already, so the liquid doesn't get far. I'm sure this action helped confirm his suspicions. I thought I had been hiding my drinking and doing a good job of it. Apparently not. Better he thinks I have a drinking problem than a fidelity problem. I use the time we take to clean the table and sit back down to decide.

My hands folded in my lap, my chin tucked down, I peer at him through my lashes. "I'm so sorry, David. I've been drinking a lot more than I should lately. I'll do better. I promise." A single tear trickles from my eye. It's all I can muster. He reaches forward and wipes it away with his thumb.

"You don't have to apologize to me, babe. You're under a lot of stress. I've been gone so much. And with me always at the hospital ... I just want you to be happy and healthy, okay? I love you."

I excuse myself to go to the bathroom, where I burst into tears. These ones aren't forced by good acting. I have never hated myself more than I do right this very second.

I pick up my phone before I change my mind. "We need to talk Tobin. Your wife is on the hunt for your mistress, and she can't figure out it's me. We need to end this. I can't do it anymore. Tell her it was just some random woman, tell her whatever. She'll stay with you and everything will be fine. Besides, she already knows. Don't fuck up my life, or I swear to God. Don't call me back, just fix this. Now."

I hang up the phone, wipe the mascara from beneath my eyes, force a smile on my face, and rejoin my husband. I'll be better. I'll do better. I can fix this.

Chapter 40

Eloise

G race has asked for a few moments of my time to discuss Bryony. She's heard what happened to her at the bonfire and is very concerned. There are some things she'd like to tell me.

There are things I'd like to tell her, like to mind her own fucking business. But ever the lady, I oblige and have Melanie prepare tea in the sunroom for the two of us.

"I think Bryony was drugged," Grace says, cutting immediately to the chase. We both turn our heads at Melanie's gasp. After placing the tray with the tea set on the wicker table, she pours us each a cup. Her shaky hands causing the tea to spill.

"Thank you, Melanie; we can manage our own sugar and cream," I say. She looks relieved and scurries back into the house to busy herself with her duties. I pour a splash of cream in my cup, while Grace drops two sugar cubes in hers.

The video of Bryony from the bonfire creeps into my mind. When Annabelle brought her in looking half dead, I thought she may have overdosed, that her partying finally warranted a trip to the hospital. I was already thinking of the excuses I'd give for her sudden departure after I shipped her off to a rehab facility, preferably out of state or country. Between moments holding her hair while she was sick in the toilet, I went through her phone. The videos made their rounds before the party had even broken up. Bryony stripping off her clothes and dancing, Annabelle desperately running after her and trying to cover her. The glassy, faraway look in Bryony's eyes while she laughed and continued to dance, fall, run, dance. Finally, Annabelle was able to grab hold of her. Annabelle dragged a laughing Bryony away while screaming at the crowd to stop filming.

It was mortifying. And it was everywhere online.

She hasn't left her room since. She may be hanging from her ceiling fan for all I know. Too ashamed to live with herself. I haven't bothered checking.

"I don't believe a word that comes out of either of those girls' mouths right now," I say, casually sipping my tea. "Bryony has made her bed, and now she's going to have to deal with the humiliation that comes with lying in it."

Grace winces and places her cup on the saucer. "I understand how upset you must be; I'm furious myself. Annabelle is grounded, possibly until she's thirty. But when I sat down with her and got the full story, she swore Bryony only had one beer, two at most. Now, that's still unacceptable but I just don't think she would act that way after two beers. Unless something was put in one of those beers, like that date rape drug, what's it called, G something."

"GHB." I sip my tea and think. "You don't think Annabelle is covering for her friend? These teen girls are quite adept at lying, as I'm sure you know."

Grace shakes her head. "I don't. Annabelle seemed very scared that someone there had been trying to rape Bryony or worse. The kids say they aren't worried about the serial killer. I'm sure that is just them putting on a bravado to compensate for how terrified they truly are."

"The serial killer? Surely they don't think?" I'm the only one laughing, so I fix my face to match Grace's concerned look. "Yes, you're right. It's just too awful to even think of. If it was the serial killer, that means ..." I turn my head and pretend to stifle a sob.

When I look back, Grace's eyes shine with tears. "Should we go to the police? They could look through the footage, see if anyone in the background stands out, that isn't a student." She places a hand on her heart and looks at me in earnest.

I choose my next words very carefully. My brain begins systematically reviewing its options, and branches of possible outcomes grow from the problem tree. I could insist that no, Bryony wasn't drugged; we have it wrong. She simply drank too much. Or, I could go along with this, and continue to feign terror. Together, we put a call into the police. If brought to the police, they would consider all the unusual recent events, the attack, the brick through the window, and now this. That could lead to an even deeper investigation into me, something to be avoided.

"I think I should speak with Bryony first before I do anything. This is quite humiliating for her, and I would hate to put her through any more than she's already endured. If she was in fact drugged, that is extremely concerning. I think a trip to the doctor would be a good first step. I'm not sure how long these drugs stay in one's system, but it is worth trying nonetheless." There are several ways to test for the presence of GHB in one's system, hair being the most reliable, which can be detected for up to a month. Blood and urine are the least reliable means, only lasting hours, at max a few days. It's a risk. I could drop a few hints about her drinking problem. The hospital would most likely do a blood test and send us on our way with some pamphlets. Whatever drug she was given most likely is now gone without a trace. Whoever this person is who administered the drug, well, that's Bryony's problem. She's becoming quite irritating lately. Maybe their next attempt will be more successful.

"What an absolute nightmare. I don't understand what has happened to our safe little town. You always think these things happen in other places, but not here," Grace says.

I nod in agreement. "Yes, you would think. But is anywhere really, truly safe? The world is an ugly place, especially for young women."

We finish our tea and I thank Grace for being such a great friend and bringing me this information. She wishes me well and sends Bryony her love.

When the door closes, my phone alerts me to a text.

Thanks for the dinner invite, we aren't able to fit it in right now. Maybe another time.

Who does Suzanne think she is rejecting my very generous offer? It's not as if I wanted to spend an evening entertaining her when she's been in such a state lately.

I grab a vase from the side table next to the front door and smash it to the ground. The second one destroyed in a month. Melanie hears the commotion and comes running in.

"I'm so clumsy. It's all the stress. Get this cleaned up for me, please?"

I collect my purse and keys and leave Melanie and the broken vase in my wake. Someone or several someones are making a fool of me, and I need to release some frustration.

Chapter 41

THE WATCHER

I shouldn't have done that. Using Bryony. I wanted to make Eloise feel *something*, anything. She's so absolutely obsessed with Bryony; I thought it would work. But I've known Eloise for long enough to know she doesn't feel. She is an emotionless hollow bag of meat and bones. Not even her own daughter in peril stirs emotions within her. She wasn't programmed that way; she was born evil, born without morals, born without feelings. Bryony could have died, and for what? Nothing. Not even that could breathe life into Eloise's black soul.

I haven't been able to leave my apartment since that night. Watching that poor girl strip off her clothes and run around naked and exposed while her so-called friends stood around laughing and filming her. Those videos will follow her for the rest of her life. Nothing dies these days, not with the internet, the world's time capsule. How will she ever recover? Girls are so fragile at that age. I should know.

I should know better.

I should *be* better.

Yet I keep proving I'm no better than Eloise. And that's the problem, isn't it? What we hate the most in other people is what we hate in ourselves. Maybe this is why I'm like this, why I've never been able to lead a normal life. Because deep down inside, I've always known that I'm just as bad as she is.

I haven't left my apartment in days, the slum of a box I call home. I've barely left the floor, where I sit curled in a fetal position, staring at the stains on the carpet, wondering how I got here and how things could have been so different. If it weren't for that night, I could have gone off to college, had a career, had a family. Instead, I spent the rest of my childhood and twenties locked in a prison branded a hospital for the insane and locked in the prison of my own mind.

Up until this point, it was the rage and insatiable desire for revenge that ravaged me. It consumed my every thought and drove my every action. But now it's guilt—at least, I think it is. I'm not sure I'll ever recover from this, just like I'll never recover from the night that turned me into this monster.

I pull myself off the floor and stand in front of the wall. Hundreds of photos and newspaper clippings. Bryony, Eloise, Poppy, Suzanne, Beatrix, Grace, Annabelle, Melissa, and every other woman and child who died at Eloise's hands. I pull down a photo of Eloise, then another. I'm clawing at the faces, ripping them, screaming. The neighbors will hear, I'm sure of it. I don't care.

The remains are a pile in the middle of the room. I walk to the bedroom and pack a bag.

I feel nothing.

A child laughs outside. This should be enough to stop me. It's almost six, the building will be full.

In the kitchen, I grab the lighter fluid I use for the grill.

My bag is at the front door. I walk to the pile of Eloise's ruined kingdom and squeeze all the contents on the shredded paper.

The first match doesn't light. I have time to stop this, time to reconsider. The flame comes to life on the first swipe of the second one.

I toss it on the pile, and the papers ignite.

I grip the handles of the duffle bag, open the door, and walk to my car without looking back.

Chapter 42

Eloise

B illy and Heidy, too much death for a child to bear. Surely, I must
be traumatized. Professional help is needed.

Momma had an appointment scheduled with a psychiatrist before
Heidy's body could be lowered into the ground. She gripped my hand
and led me into the office.

She knew better than to touch me like that, but I let her lead me.
Played the part.

Dr. Andrews looked over his glasses as he asked me about how this
made me feel, and that made me feel.

I sat in the center of a green couch with my feet crossed at the ankles
and hands clasped in my lap, answering his questions how I knew he'd
want them answered.

"Scared and sad." Is how I felt when I watched Billy die.

"Scared and sad." Is how I felt when I watched Heidy die.

A tear. A sniffle. A nod of his head. A scratch of his pen.

A 'that will be all,' and I'm ushered out of his office, and Momma is ushered in.

I stood at the door with my ear pressed to the wood.

"Antisocial personality disorder," Dr. Andrews explained. A hair checklist (which I later learned was actually "Hare") determined I possessed enough psychopathy traits to tack that onto the end as well.

Momma cried. I smiled.

It all made sense. And now, I would become who I was meant to be. Who nature intended.

Chapter 43

Eloise

I don't realize how hard I'm gripping the steering wheel until my hands start aching. I'm driving with no destination. The office buildings and neighborhoods fall away as I drive farther out of the suburbs and toward the rolling mountains. On the highway, signs start appearing for Shenandoah National Park.

My tires crunch over the gravel of a small parking lot at one of the trailheads. The sounds of my heavy breathing fill the car. I stare beyond my windshield; a low fog cradles the endless miles of the mountains like layers of sheer silk, muting the greens of the pines and blurring the edges of the peaks and valleys. I am still staring, thinking, analyzing. The scene before me turns monochrome, just shades of red. It's the rage taking over, skewing my vision. I know this, and I do nothing to stop it. I am a volcano that's been lying dormant for thousands of years, ready to unleash my fiery lava and wreak havoc.

An old pickup pulls into the small lot. Its rust and dents tell the story of a long, pathetic life. A man steps out and offers a friendly wave in my direction. I fix my face and return his innocent graciousness with a wave of my own. He continues to prepare for his hike, filling a large backpack with water and other items. After changing into a pair of boots and retrieving hiking poles from the bed of the truck, he walks over to my car and leans down so his bearded face fills my window. The creases of his weathered face deepen, and his blue eyes shine. He's a trusting man, and his friends and family would probably describe him as funny, caring. All the standard platitudes given to the dead, even though they are no longer around to hear them.

I roll down my window.

"Everything okay?" he asks.

"I think I'm a bit lost," I reply, half shrugging and giving him a sheepish smile.

"Well, let's get you on the right path. Where you headed?"

My purse is in the backseat. I lean back to retrieve it. Most women would be afraid to turn their back on a stranger they've met in an isolated parking lot on the side of the road. Especially when one is only steps away from endless miles of perfect body-hiding locations.

I twist forward with my bag now in my lap. "Now, let me see here. I've written the address down on a piece of paper. I thought I had the directions memorized, but silly me, this memory just doesn't work like it used to." We both chuckle in solidarity.

He steps back so I can open the door and join him. It will be easier to search through my large purse with it on the hood of my car. "It's in here somewhere, let me just..." I continue rummaging through my bag. I've already found what I'm looking for, but he doesn't know this. He begins to whistle a happy tune. I command my back not to hunch and show any signs of annoyance.

"Ah, here it is," I proclaim.

I run my finger down the cool metal of my Glock 19's slide, sending a shudder of excitement through my entire body. I turn around, the friendliness gone from my face. "I'm going to need you to put your hands up and walk toward the trail," I demand.

He throws his arms above his head in defense and the walking poles clatter to the ground beside him. He's still smiling, thinking this is all just a misunderstanding. "Whoa there. Nothing to worry about. I'm not gonna hurt you, ma'am; I'm just here to help."

"If you could kindly do what I asked, this will be much easier on both of us," I say coolly.

"Okay, no problem. I have a wife; I know how scary it is out there for women right now. My Helen started carrying herself these days. So, whatever you need to feel like you can safely leave is a-okay with me."

He stops at the trailhead and looks back over his shoulder, hands still in the air. "This good? Need me to keep going?"

"You said your wife thinks it's scary out there. Why is that?"

"That serial killer the news keeps talking about. I get it, a big bloke like me comes knocking on your window, middle of nowhere. You don't know me from Adam—"

"Keep walking. I have a story to tell you." I stay a few steps behind, both of us carefully stepping over roots and rocks. This isn't one of the main trails, and it's not as well-kept. "Have you ever met anyone famous... I'm sorry, I didn't get your name."

"Name's Rusty."

"Wonderful. Rusty, have you ever met anyone famous?"

His face twists as if he can't decide if this is a joke or if he should be scared. "Nope, can't say I ever have." His voice is starting to quaver. Thoughts of this all being a silly misunderstanding are likely being replaced by fear, but he's trying to remain calm, hopeful.

"Well, Rusty, today is your lucky day. You've met someone famous. I am Eloise, and I am the one they are looking for. Soon, you'll be famous too. But you aren't my usual victim, and this isn't my usual method. So you may just end up as a few-sentence blurb buried in the middle of a newspaper. Forgotten."

Rusty has now stopped walking, his entire body shaking. It's starting to click. He's starting to see. I can only imagine the thoughts running through his terrified brain. If he hadn't decided to hike today, or if he had picked a different location, or if he hadn't stopped to talk to me. Or is he thinking of his Helen and the grief she'll experience. Imagining her opening the door to the police officer, there to let her know her husband has died.

"It's unfortunate, but the police and media will most certainly bumble this one. Never connect your death to the rest. Perhaps I'll tell them, anonymously, of course. I do hate to not get credit for my work. We shall see. Well, you won't, but the rest of us will, including your dear Helen. And now it's time for us to say goodbye."

He starts to run.

The gun recoils in my hands as the bullets leave the barrel and fill Rusty's back. He falls forward, face in the dirt, and circles of blood grow bigger until his entire shirt is dark red. I take a quick look around and listen. Nothing but the sounds of the forest answer, the rustling of the leaves, a few birds.

Feeling much better about my day, I follow the path back to my car, get in, and drive home.

Chapter 44

Eloise

"**I** received an email from the school today; they're requesting a meeting with us," Robert says over dinner on the evening of Rusty's untimely demise. "Any idea what's going on?"

Bryony hasn't left her room since the incident. Melanie brings her meals to her and keeps fussing about how she's barely eating them. I place my fork and knife next to my plate, careful to leave them perfectly spaced and vertically aligned.

"There was an incident," I explain the party, the videos, and Grace's hypothesis that Bryony was drugged.

"Christ, Eloise. And you're just telling me this now?"

"I've been trying to decide how to handle it."

"She's my daughter too, and I should have a say in how *we* handle it."

I pause. Look down at my lap. "You're right. I should have told you immediately. I'm just so overwhelmed with all that's happening. You must understand?"

His face softens. "Of course. I shouldn't have been so sharp with you. I'll kill whoever did this to her." His face turns a shade of red I've never seen. There is a tingling between my legs. It's very rare that I'm turned on by Robert, but I suddenly have the urge to throw him on the table and ride him until we both scream in ecstasy. It must be the red; I do love that color. I shake my head to expel those dirty thoughts.

He checks his calendar and confirms that he can spare a few hours to visit the school with me tomorrow. We finish our meal in an amiable silence. I retire to our bedroom to read, and he locks himself in his office. I'm already asleep by the time he joins me. Or maybe he never does, because when I wake in the morning, he's already gone. I received a text letting me know he'll meet me at the school at ten. It's eight, which gives me two hours to get ready.

Principal Michaels has just told Robert and me that he believes it's best that Bryony does not return to school and that she should finish the semester via the district's online option. "For her own protection," he adds.

"This is the most egregious display of victim blaming I've ever witnessed. The amount of money we have paid this school for tuition and through donations, and this is how you treat my daughter?" Robert pounds his fist on the principal's desk making Michaels jump. My back remains stiff, my eyes unblinking. I'm not as easily frightened.

"Mr. Williams, I understand you're upset—"

"Upset? I'm more than upset! I'm ready to sue this entire damn school."

I place a hand on Robert's arm. I'm not sure what he's angry about. It's me who will be publicly humiliated when I'm removed from the PTO. "It seems they've made their decision. Let's not cause more of a scene. I'm not sure I want my Bryony in a school that protects a potential rapist anyway. Who knows what else is happening within these walls."

Principal Michaels' Adam's apple bobs up and down. He takes a hanky from his pocket and wipes the sweat beading on his brow.

"You know very well this is a safe place for students. We don't condone violence, but we also don't condone underage drinking. I'm devastated this happened to Bryony. You have to understand this isn't a punishment. I—the entire staff is worried about her. Those videos..." At the mention of the videos, his face turns red. "We are all worried the content of those videos will get her bullied and could increase the psychological damage of having to relive it. You know how cruel kids can be."

"Yes," I say. "I do. I also know how cruel adults can be." I stand and look down at Robert. "Robert, let's go; there's nothing more to discuss. They've made their decision."

Principal Michaels clears his throat. "Eloise, I want to make sure we're all on the same page. This also means you'll be stepping down from your role as PTO president. I don't want to make a big thing of it all, no announcement no—"

I place my hands on his desk and lean toward him, our faces inches apart. "If you think I would even want to be associated with your shitty school from this point forward, you're a bigger idiot than I've always thought."

I start walking to the door and realize Robert hasn't moved from his chair. "Let's go, Robert. Now," I demand.

When we reach the parking lot, Robert is shaking his head. "You aren't worried that online school will hurt her chances of getting into a good college?"

"She's not doing online. We'll find a nice boarding school, more prestigious than this dump, maybe even in Europe."

I don't give him the chance to answer. Bryony is my job; I'm the CEO of her life. I'll figure out what we'll do with her, and he will go along with it. That's all there is to it.

Chapter 45

THE WATCHER

I found a cash-only motel to crash at. I didn't use my real information to sign the apartment lease, but the fire was a rash decision. According to the one mention of it online, no one was hurt. However, the building's occupants have all been displaced. Because of me.

I've tried reaching out to Bryony with no luck. My DMs continue to go unread and unanswered. I'm so worried about her. What she'll do to herself, what Eloise will do. I shouldn't have put those drugs in her beer. It was so stupid. So foolish. What was I even trying to accomplish? I don't even know at this point.

My mind is slipping away from me, farther than it's ever gone. I bang my head with my fists. I don't know what Eloise has been up to, and maybe that is part of my problem. So much of my headspace has been consumed by Eloise, where she is, what she's doing, what she's eating, who she's with, who she's killing. Without her, I'm reminded of how empty I am. The black nothingness inside, or is it white? Black is all the colors and white is the absence of any. My insides are an unending cavern of white. I am not a person. I am nothing.

But Bryony is a person, and I've taken that from her. My nihility is contagious, and it spreads within her, taking over her organs, mutating her plasma. I want to fix this. Tell her that nothing matters when you are a teenager. Everything feels so much bigger than it is.

Someone should have said these words to me. And I should have listened.

This is the beginning of the end. I can smell it, feel it, taste it.

Bryony still has a chance. She can get away from Eloise, run as far and fast as she can. Her story doesn't have to end like mine.

Eloise birthed Bryony, but Bryony can rise above her. Do what I never did. Eloise birthed me, too, in a way. I didn't get away. I wasn't brave enough.

But you are, sweet Bryony.

I want to tell her these things, but how can I convince her when I lived unconvinced my entire life.

Chapter 46

Eloise

Doctor Andrews, the savior, the expert, gave me permission. Armed with the knowledge of who I was, the possibilities extended before me. I'd learned and adapted so much in my short thirteen years, and now I knew what I had to.

I sat in my bedroom after the appointment and laughed and laughed. Why change? I saw no point in working on fixing that which wasn't broken.

It was time to be who I was born to be.

I entered the kitchen. Momma was seated at the table, staring at nothing with a coffee mug clutched in her hands.

"I'm going to go hang out with my friends," I said.

She moved slower than normal. Her face was pale, her eyes red and puffy; she'd been crying. Of course she had.

"Maybe not today, Eloise."

I grinned. "Yes, today."

Before she had a chance to protest, I practically skipped out of the house, running down the front porch stairs and making my way to the row of shops and restaurants kids hung out at during that time.

I'd walked that walk a thousand times, but on that day, the sky was bluer, and the sidewalk seemed to glow, showing me the way.

I found Layla with her worshippers sitting on a bench in front of a diner where the kids often gathered. Layla was a year younger than me, but despite my feeble attempts, I could neither lure her into my inner circle nor destroy her pristine reputation. She didn't need me. She'd mastered the same art I had. But there can only be one leader.

I'd been working for months to sever the ties she'd worked so hard to form. Not overtly, I knew how to bide my time and wait for the right opportunity.

On that day, everyone was on edge. A second child had died. The air hung thick with foreboding, full of whispers that worse was coming. We were cursed, all of us. The old women even felt it, blaming a tornado they were sure would turn the sky green and send us running to our shelters at any moment.

Layla stood and approached me, arms outstretched. "Eloise, my gosh, are you okay?"

I studied her face and the inflection of her words.

Her arms encircled me, and I hugged her back. "I'm fine." With a heavy sigh, I sat on the bench in the now unoccupied space. The girls crowded around, too close, fawning over me with unwanted attention and words of sympathy.

The entire school knew what I'd witnessed. I'm sure some of their sympathy was authentic. The rest were just happy to have a connection to the tragedy.

"We're gonna go to The Greasy Woman's, wanna come?" one of the girls asked. The Greasy Woman was a story that had been passed on for generations. In true local lore fashion, The Greasy Woman's story had morphed over the years, slightly changing as each group of older kids passed it onto the younger ones.

Our version had The Greasy Woman being brought to Mississippi by her husband, the details lost over time. A politician's son killed her husband, receiving no more than a slap on the wrist. She responded by standing outside the politician's home every evening, watching. Somehow, she broke in and sprinkled arsenic on their dinner. The family became sicker and sicker, and finally, one by one, they died.

With no proof, there would be no justice for them either. However, everyone suspected it was her. She was shunned and forced from town, making her home deep in the woods in an old, abandoned shack. Depending on who you ask, she still occupied the crumbling building, and others claimed it was her ghost. Either way, the kids in our area grew up terrified and mesmerized. The old shack became a place to get away from the prying eyes and ears of adults.

The four of us made our way to the woods, the same woods Billy's creek flows through, and follow the path to The Greasy Woman's shack. We sat on the old stumps in front of the shack, that kids use for chairs. I sensed the girls getting bored.

"Want to play truth or dare?" I asked. So innocent. So nonchalant.

The dares and truths start out innocent enough: Run into the shack and call out for The Greasy Woman. Who do you have a crush on? Do your funniest impression of each other.

I turned to Layla, and she picked truth. "Tell us one thing about each of us that annoys you."

She squirmed, and I reminded her of the rules. She *had* to tell the truth.

The mood shifted slightly.

My turn again. It was time to put the secrets I'd been collecting to good use. I asked Layla who the last boy she kissed was. Layla didn't know that her friend was obsessed with that very same boy. But I did.

More poking. More prodding.

The girls were glaring at each other.

"Dare," spat the girl whose heart had been broken.

"I dare you to punch Layla," I said.

Layla stood. "Enough. This isn't fun; I'm going home."

The girl stood, marched over to Layla and punched her in the nose. Layla bent over, hands covering her face, and when she stood, three jaws dropped at the blood covering her face.

"I'm ..." the girl backed up, shaking her head. "Layla, I'm sorry—"

"Don't be sorry," I said. "It's just a game. And it's not like she didn't deserve it."

Their jealousy was my instrument. And I was about to play them a beautiful song.

A few more prodding words, then I stepped back and let the music take over. Layla was on the ground with the two girls standing over her kicking and punching her. I expected a fight or some mean words thrown at each other. Never could I have imagined this scene.

I reveled in it. Smiling, I spun with my arms spread and my head thrown back.

When I looked back, one of the girls had a rock held between two hands hovering over Layla's head. In the split second before her arms swung down and she smashed her skull open, I saw regret flash across her face.

The fighting stopped, and the girls stepped back.

"What have you done?" her friend asked.

Billy's death had marked us. Death had imprinted on us. He was only the beginning.

"Stop," I demanded.

"We have to get help. We—"

I held up my hand. "We will not. This will be our secret. Do you want to go to jail? Do you know what happens to little girls in jail?"

Two heads shook.

I expected it would take more convincing, but they surprised me.

We dragged Layla's body to an old well and, with much effort, lifted her over the stone lip and waited a surprisingly long time for the muted thump of her body to reach the bottom. Pinkies were hooked, sealing the promise to never ever talk about that day. We swore our loyalty to each other. We'd protect each other forever.

And with Layla out of the way, all of the girls were mine. My Darlings.

Chapter 47

BEATRIX

I expect Suzanne to look like a deteriorated version of herself, but her resilience has surprised me. It's a risk, coming here, knowing she's on the hunt for her husband's mistress and me being that mistress. She may look better than she has in years, but I know her mind is in a much different state. I've had a real shit morning, though, so my mind isn't doing much better.

"Beatrix, let's open a bottle of wine. It's five o'clock somewhere," she sings while she reaches up to grab two glasses and continues rummaging through drawers in search of her opener.

"Not today; I have an awful headache. Water is fine."

She pours herself a glass of merlot and takes a long sip. The ball of guilt sitting in my stomach grows claws that reach up my throat and squeeze. Suzanne was one of the few women I was somewhat fond of. Eloise is a self-absorbed witch, and Poppy is an idiot. Suzanne has her issues, but she's nice. I didn't feel bad about screwing her husband at first. Not for her or for my husband. I didn't think at all, I suppose. I just acted for my own selfish self. I didn't even like Tobin very much. He was good-looking, and I was bored. I justified the first time with alcohol. Everyone drank too much one night at the club's annual holiday party. I ran into him in the long hallway leading to the bathrooms. We didn't say a word, but he grabbed me and pulled me into one of the offices. After bending me over the desk, he hoisted up my skirt and took me from behind. One hand around my waist, one hand rubbing my clit until I screamed. Even with every nerve dulled by vodka, he brought me to orgasm within minutes. It was like the lines of coke we'd do in college; you can never have just one. It was only sex, though. There were no feelings. And that's how I continued to justify it.

"Have you called Robert?"

She turns her head to the side, staring out the window. I hope she doesn't cry. I don't have the energy to comfort her today.

"No, not yet. You heard what happened to Bryony? I didn't want to bother him with this when he has all that to deal with."

My muscles unclench. I had encouraged her to involve Robert, but I'm starting to doubt that feeding into this Eloise theory is a good idea. Poppy would have made a better scapegoat. Now that I've had some time to think about it, I'm scared about what Eloise will do if Robert is pulled into this twisted imaginary relationship Suzanne has fabricated.

"If you ask me, that child is out of control. I heard they are claiming she was drugged. Which she probably was, but not by anyone else but her dealer and her own hand. She loves attention as much as her mother. I'm sure the videos of her going viral are the best thing that's happened to her this year. She's probably loving every second of it," I say.

Suzanne puts her glass down and frowns. "Surely, you don't think that. That poor girl must be humiliated."

I shrug.

"Will you still be going to the Gatsby dinner?" I ask.

"Yes, of course. Is there a reason you think I shouldn't be there?" Her words are starting to slur, and I'm wondering if this is her first glass of the day. Probably not. My hands twitch. I need a drink.

Suzanne's eyes narrow into slits. Tiny pin pricks of panic crawl over my skin. *Too far, Beatrix. Just shut up.*

I shift in my seat and sit up straighter. "Of course not! We all want you there. I'd be devastated if you weren't."

I decide the shorter of the two gowns I was debating between would be my dress for the evening. Nothing underneath. Easier access for when I borrow Tobin for a few minutes that night. One more taste before I cut him off for good. Watching how fast Suzanne is going through the bottle of wine, it shouldn't be too difficult to sneak away. There is a small matter to take care of before I end things. A slight bump in the road. Nothing we can't figure out. If he would just return my fucking calls.

Chapter 48

Eloise

As expected, I finished all the planning and preparations for the Gatsby event alone. Suzanne is too preoccupied with her destroyed marriage, Beatrix is hiding like a coward, probably afraid she'll finally get caught, and Poppy is disorganized and can never be trusted to follow through on her commitments anyway. Regardless of the lack of help, and everything I currently have going on in my own life, I have put together what is guaranteed to be the most talked-about event this year. Which I'm sure the other ladies will gladly take credit for when the admiration comes pouring in.

I'm hanging my dress on the back of the bathroom door when Melanie knocks to let me know my hair and makeup team has arrived. I have her bring them upstairs. My black hair is pulled back into a faux bob, with finger waves on each side. My makeup isn't done to my standards the first time. I lecture the girl and make her start over. Her hands shake as she applies it the second time, and I'm worried I'll have to fire her on the spot and find a replacement. At this hour, all the best makeup artists will be at other women's houses. It will be a complete inconvenience, but everything must be perfect tonight, especially me. To my surprise, she gets it right. My lips are a deep shade of maroon, and my green eyes pop from the razor-sharp winged eyeliner and gold eyeshadow with just a hint of glimmer. I'm positive all heads will turn my way, especially the men's.

Robert comes into the room as one of the girls is zipping up the back of my dress up.

"You look absolutely beautiful, love."

"I do, don't I?" I say while admiring myself in the full-length mirror. Remembering myself, I quickly add. "These girls did a wonderful job; they are truly magicians."

They, of course, deny it, tell me how beautiful I am, all the things the help is expected to say before taking their generous tips and leaving. Robert puts on his tuxedo, and we descend the spiral staircase to Melanie's ooh's and aah's.

"Do you want me to see if Bryony would like to come down and see how lovely her parents look tonight?" Melanie asks. I am grateful for Melanie's caring for Bryony. Without her, I'd probably forget she was locked away in her room, forget to feed her, and forget to make her bathe, until one day I'd walk in and find her dead in her bed. It would be yet another inconvenience I'd have to figure out. These inconveniences were starting to become cumbersome, adding up too quickly and getting in the way of My Darlings.

"Let's let Bryony sleep. She's still very distraught over everything, and I don't want to push her too hard. You're so wonderful for thinking of her, though, Melanie. I'm not sure what we'd do without you." I place a hand on her arm and give it a comforting pat. The doorbell rings, and Melanie straightens.

"Oh, that will be your ride. Let me get the door."

Robert wraps my arm within his and escorts me to the limo. We pull in front of the venue thirty minutes after the start of the party—late enough that there should be an acceptable amount of people to witness my arrival but not too late to be considered rude.

We walk in and make a circle of the room, saying our hellos, which provides me the opportunity to inspect every detail. I mentally note the things that were not executed as per my instructions. Each of these items will be discussed later in detail with Mia. There is an hour left before dinner. Most guests are mingling outside, as the weather is pleasant and the back patio has been transformed into a beautiful oasis. The market lights reflect off the ladies' glittering gowns, adding to the effect.

I spot Poppy, Beatrix, and Grace and join them at the bar while Robert goes to find the husbands. I kiss the air next to each lady's cheek and we exchange our greetings.

"You all have truly outdone yourselves this time," Grace gushes. Poppy has the good sense to look slightly ashamed when she accepts the praise.

"Are Suzanne and Tobin here yet?" I inquire.

Both women shake their heads. "I haven't spoken to Suzanne. I'm not even sure if she's coming," Poppy says.

"Oh, I doubt she would miss the opportunity to be seen in public with Tobin," I say. "Can't blame her. Wanting to claim her territory."

"What do you mean?" Grace asks.

Poppy's face turns as red as her dress.

"You haven't heard? Tobin's been having an affair. Suzanne hasn't figured out with who, but I wouldn't be surprised if it's someone we all know."

Grace uses her drink to hide her shock. "How unfortunate."

"Indeed," I agree.

The bartender approaches and takes my drink order.

"A black martini, extra vermouth, please."

Poppy scrunches her face. "I don't know how you drink those things; they are way too bitter."

Beatrix, who has been looking everywhere but at us, meets my eye and smiles. "I read an interesting article the other day; apparently, they've found a link between those who have a preference for bitter food and psychopathy."

The bartender places my drink on a cocktail napkin in front of me. I take a sip and smile. "And you know what they say about people who recite useless facts?" I enjoy Beatrix's smug smile melting into a pout. "They do so to overcompensate for their less-than-average intelligence."

Robert's hand grazes my lower back, and he kisses the side of my forehead. I turn with him to go check on dinner and look over my shoulder back at Beatrix. "Have a nice evening, darling."

On the way to the area where dinner will be served, a woman standing off to the side catches my eye. She is very tall and very striking. Her auburn hair falls in glossy waves down her back, and the front of her royal blue dress plunges low enough to expose entirely too much of her cleavage. She's not the type of woman one forgets. She's standing alone, separated from the clumps of couples laughing over martini glasses and champagne flutes. When we make eye contact, she lifts her glass my way and smiles. It takes a lot to unnerve me. In fact, I can't remember it ever happening before this very moment, but the look she's giving me, her presence, everything about her feels wrong. I shiver. Robert asks if I'm chilly and offers his jacket.

"No, let's go inside. I have things to do." I step over the threshold and try to busy myself with fixing each table setting, checking that the silverware is placed perfectly and adjusting the crystals and flowers in each centerpiece. But I can't get those eyes, so dark the pupils blended in with the irises, out of my mind.

Chapter 49

Eloise

T he mysterious woman was nowhere to be seen during dinner. I searched every table. If she were sitting at one, I would have seen her. This only increased my desire to uncover her identity. After dinner, the dance floor opened, and the band began to play. The silent auction is set up next to the bar where people can bid for things like luxury vacations, spa days, jewelry, and other things of the sort.

Grace cornered me, clearly excited to finally get me alone. "How is Bryony doing? Annabelle says she's not returning any of her calls, and her phone's been turned off. We're so worried."

"Bryony will be fine."

"I heard she was told she couldn't return to school. Where will you be sending her?"

Her questions are bothersome. I don't want to talk about Bryony tonight or think about her, and it certainly is none of Grace's business.

I glance around the room, hoping she'll get the hint. "What's wrong?" She gasps. "You look like you've seen a ghost."

As if her name has summoned her, Bryony stands by the main entrance wearing a dress that makes her look like a trophy wife marrying a rich man thirty years older than she is.

"Bryony is here," I say, forcing a smile. "I'm so glad you felt well enough to join us. It is a special evening. Excuse me, she must be looking for me."

As I'm crossing the room, I freeze. The woman from earlier is standing in a corner with Robert, her head thrown back and hand on his arm, laughing at something he's said. She leans in and whispers something in his ear, her lips grazing his bottom earlobe.

I swallow my scream. Are the two of them conspiring against me? I am certain when outlining the rules of tonight that I didn't need to mention that Robert shouldn't be seen flirting with another woman, and I most certainly didn't need to tell Bryony she was not invited. I look at the now empty spot Bryony had occupied seconds ago.

A hand grabs my bicep, and I whip around to find Poppy looking nervous and fidgety.

"Not now, Poppy, I'm in the middle—"

"Have you seen Tobin? Suzanne is here, and she's running around asking everyone if they've seen him." She looks around and leans in closer. "Or you."

"It's not my job to help Suzanne keep her husband's dick in his pants. She can figure out where he is all on her own. She'd be better off asking Beatrix."

"Beatrix?" Poppy looks at her feet and then shakes her head. "Suzanne's a bit drunk and making a scene. Should I—"

"Do what you want, Poppy. If Suzanne wants to make a fool of herself, that's not your problem or mine." I turn away from her and halt. The corner where Robert and the woman had been just seconds ago is empty. I spin in a circle. Everyone is getting drunker, talking louder, and the dance floor is full.

"You are never going to believe what I just saw." Robert is standing next to me. Where did he come from?

"Who was that woman you were talking to?"

"What woman? Anyway, I just saw Tobin and Beatrix coming out of a room, and they looked like they were definitely up to no good. Hair all messy, adjusting clothes like they had just fucked. Holy shit, can you believe it?"

I sigh. "Yes, I can believe it. Answer me," I hiss. "Who is that woman, the one you were with over there." I point to the exact spot the two of them were just standing in.

He shrugs and takes a sip of his cocktail. "She said her name is Alyssa McDaniels. Just moved here. Nice lady. Her husband is out of town, but they joined the club, and she heard about this event and wanted to meet some folks. They seem like a nice couple."

"The only person she seems to be meeting is you. I've never heard of this Alyssa."

Robert smirks. "Eloise, I don't think I've ever seen you jealous."

My head jerks back. "Jealous? I think not. Also, Bryony is here."

His stupid smirk disappears. "What is she doing here? Where is—"

A commotion from the bar cuts him off. All heads in the room swivel in the same direction. It takes me a moment to understand what has drawn all our attention. But then I see a very drunk Suzanne being dragged toward the exit by Tobin. She's screaming something unintelligible at him. Finally, she rips her arm away and falls to the floor in a heap of green silk. The drink she was holding flies from her hand and covers several people in a clear liquid. The room collectively gasps. Beatrix, a few feet away, stifles a laugh. Suzanne picks herself up, her face red, hair now in disarray, and yells something to no one in particular. I can't hear her, but her lips seemed to say, 'Fuck all of you.'

"My goodness, what a scene." I say and take a sip of my drink.

"Looks like my man Tobin got caught with his pants down." Robert laughs.

Several people are helping the drenched guests with napkins, others have gone back to their conversations, and several others simply stare into Suzanne's wake, shaking their heads. The party returns to normal, but Suzanne has given everyone something to talk about; how embarrassing for her.

I slip away from Robert to follow Suzanne out and observe from a distance. It takes my eyes a second to adjust, but finally, I spot her standing alone in a shadow in the parking lot where Tobin must have ditched her. A figure approaches her. I squint and clench my fists. Bryony taps her on her shoulder. I quietly get closer so I can hear what they're talking about.

"Don't listen to any of them." She nods her head toward the building. The absolute betrayal makes my blood turn to fire. "You're beautiful and nice, and you don't deserve friends or a husband like that."

"Excuse me? You don't know anything about me, my husband, or my life. You're a child." Her words are still soft, blending together, and she sways on her feet.

Bryony says, "I know more than you think. And more than *she* realizes."

I'm tracing. I'm counting. I'm calming down. I will not kill them here. Tobin saves them both. His car skids to a stop and he jumps out, grabbing Suzanne's arm and dragging her to the other side.

"Don't pull her like that!" Bryony says.

Tobin stops and looks at Bryony with such hate that I'm sure he's about to attack her. He shakes his head and shoves Suzanne into the car.

"Mind your fucking business." He gets in the car, spinning gravel and driving away like a maniac. Bryony's back is to me. She watches them leave.

I slink from the shadows.

Bryony doesn't turn. "How long have you been standing there?" she asks, hugging herself, staring in the direction Tobin drove off in.

"Just now. I've been looking everywhere for you."

She turns and huffs a laugh. Her bravery is a weed I must prune from my perfectly manicured garden. "You found me."

"So I did." I step closer. "Care to tell me what the fuck you're doing here?"

She looks genuinely surprised. Her arms uncross from her chest, and she studies the pavement beneath her feet. She looks up. "You invited me here. I got a note—"

"Show it to me immediately." My hand extends toward her.

Her hand rummages through her clutch, then she looks up and shakes her head. "I didn't bring it. It was your handwriting on your stationary. It said something like you are expected to dress presentably and behave."

My stationary is bespoke, designed and imported from Europe. Either Bryony is lying, or my little anonymous nuisance has played a trick on us.

"I left no such thing. Go home. Now."

She turns and is already calling for a car service. I've done us both a favor. With her out of the way, there is only one unwanted guest left to deal with.

As I walk back into the party, I roll the name around my mouth. Alyssa McDaniels. Either she is lying about who she is, or Robert is. Either way, I do believe Alyssa, whoever she is, would make a perfect Darling. Her and I will be getting to know each other very soon.

Chapter 50

Eloise

High school was much the same as middle school. My circle of admirers grew with my breasts. Boys chased, I teased, and girls were jealous but were too afraid of being left out to do anything about it. And two were too afraid of rotting in jail or at the bottom of a well. I controlled our school. They were my puppets, and I was the master.

One winter evening in junior year, a few of my closest friends and I were on our way to The Greasy Woman's shack. What used to be a spot all the local kids would go to, also became mine. An unspoken rule everyone knew was to keep off my territory. I call them friends because that's how they considered me: a friend. They weren't my friends. They were my pawns, little figurines I moved around for enjoyment. Friendship was never something I valued or desired unless it suited my needs, of course. There were seven of us. Myself, five girls who had passed what I was calling The Rituals, and Becca, a new girl who had recently moved to Mississippi from Texas. Becca was used to being popular, used to being accepted, and she'd clearly analyzed the school and knew immediately that I was her way in. After allowing her to sit at our lunch table and in our section at the Friday football games, she believed she'd completed her mission. What she didn't realize was it hadn't even begun.

We walked through the woods in a single file, our breath creating little clouds of white. The crisp air had the faint smell of campfire, but everyone knew better than to complain. The only sound echoing through the forest was our boots crunching on the dead leaves. The path opened into a clearing. The six of us had been there many times before, but this was Becca's first time.

I put my backpack down and handed around the bottles of Boone's Strawberry Hill. The girls passed them around, taking swigs. There were a few fallen logs that most of the girls plopped down on, chatting and giggling. I remained silent, standing in front of them. I preferred a clear mind for these evenings. The girls were very good actresses. They gossiped, laughed, and made Becca feel welcome and relaxed, doing exactly what I needed them to do.

"Alright, girls." At the sound of my voice, all chatter halted. They turned their attention to me, some of them stone-faced, some of them with fear flashing in their eyes. Becca, quite drunk now, was smiling, excited to see what came next. "Becca, we explained tonight was a special night for you. Each one of us has gone through this. It's your turn to prove your loyalty to us, and we will in turn, be loyal to you. Think of it as a pact. We're more than friends. We're sisters. And tonight, you will officially become one of us."

She laughed, then turned her lips down in an exaggerated frown. "Sounds serious." She was being sarcastic, thinking this was all a silly joke. A harmless prank. Her gaze fell on each of the girls, searching their faces for the punchline. They all avoided eye contact. A few shuffled in their seats.

"Oh yes, very serious, darling."

Her eyes widened.

I could sense the fear starting to vine its way into her. It was so visceral; it was as if I experienced it vicariously. The tingling ran from the tips of my toes and up through my body. "Stand up," I demanded with my hand outstretched and my fingers pulsing up and down to emphasize my instructions. She put her bottle down and slowly stood, still looking around at the other girls, waiting for one of them to offer comfort or let her know this was all a silly game, a joke even. The few girls who were still standing took their seats on the fallen logs. They sat in a semicircle behind her, and I stood in front of them. Becca shivered from cold or fear, perhaps both. I let the moment drag on, and the sounds of the forest seemed to come alive around us, filling in the pause. Wind blew through the leaves, and an owl hooted somewhere off in the distance.

"Now, strip," I said.

"W-what? What do you mean, strip?"

"Your clothes, all of them, off."

"But it's freezing. I can't take my clothes off. No way." She crossed her arms and jutted her hip out. No longer scared, she wasn't going down without a fight.

I smiled; I knew she was going to be a fun one. "You can refuse. We all have free will, after all. Don't we, ladies?" I directed my question at the girls, not expecting anyone to answer. "I can assure you, you won't like what happens if you don't go along, though."

"Screw you and screw this. I don't want to be part of your stupid group anyway." Becca started to walk away, but two girls stood and blocked her way.

"At this point," I said. "It's not about being part of the group or not. You're already in the group, Becca. Now you must follow the rules or the night won't end well for you."

"This is insane; I'm going to tell my parents about this."

"Oh, I don't think you will." I sprinkled my voice in powdered sugar, softened my face, and walked toward her, putting a comforting hand on her shoulder.

She jerked back.

"I'm just being dramatic." I laughed. "We've all gone through this, including me. Don't take my theatrics too seriously. This is all a bit of fun. Mississippi is so *boring,* as I'm sure you've discovered." I rolled my eyes. "And just think, once you're done, you'll have a whole group of sisters who will love you forever. We'd never want to hurt one of our sisters, would we, girls?" Heads shake around me in unison. Becca shrunk into herself, a cornered animal, then slowly removed her jacket, then jeans, then T-shirt. Her legs crossed, her arms attempted to cover her body. She stood in front of us in her underwear, head hung in shame.

"Fully undressed, darling. I know it's cold, but the quicker you move, the quicker it will be over. Chop, chop, chop. Let's go."

Her head whipped up. With her lips curled back in a snarl, she didn't break eye contact while she reached back and unclipped her bra, letting it fall forward over her arms and to the ground. Then she stepped out of her underwear. Naked, white skin glowed in the moonlight, and she stood up straight, arms stiff by her sides, hands clenched in fists, chin jutted up.

"Good girl." I clapped my hands, and the girls sprang into action behind her. A hand reached out, passing me the metal pole with the heated brand fixed to the end. I walked toward her, face inches from hers and whispered, "This will only hurt for a minute." I placed the iron against her hip while two other girls held her in place, each one gripping an arm. Once again transformed from a girl into an animal, a noise filled the night air that if I hadn't witnessed it coming from her mouth, I would have never believed a human girl produced it. I felt a pulsing between my legs and moaned while the perfect circle seared into her skin, a permanent reminder of me. Leaning in, I kissed her on the cheek; she was mine now.

The girls holding her up released her arms, and she crumbled to the ground into a fetal position. I kneeled beside her and smoothed the hair from her face that had matted to her forehead from sweat. "The hard part is over, my darling," I whispered into her ear while lovingly caressing her cheek. I stood, brushing the dirt from my jeans.

I instructed one of the girls to bring her a Boone's. They helped Becca sit and held the bottle to her lips, encouraging her to drink. It would take the edge off the pain, a girl cooed in her ear. Becca's eyes rolled into the back of her head, but she obeyed.

"A few more parts of the ritual, then we can all get back to enjoying our evening. It's so beautiful out. Look around you at the stars and the trees. Listen to the animals." I held my hands above my head and tipped my face to the sky. "Do you feel it? We're so close to it all; that's the universe humming within you, girls. Not many people get to experience this, but we are special."

While the girls helped Becca over to the log and sat her on the ground with her back propped up by the fallen tree, I retrieved a wooden box carved with intricate details and sealed shut with an ornate brass lock. I turned the key to open it, then walked toward Becca to show her what was inside.

Sitting in front of her with my legs folded and crossed and the box in my lap, I explained how one of the most important parts of our sisterhood is trust and loyalty. This next part of the ritual ensures that no matter what, your sisters will always remain loyal to you, and you will remain loyal to them. I opened the box and showed her the contents. Her face showed no emotion despite the shock she must have been feeling.

Chapter 51

SUZANNE

"What the fuck is wrong with you, Suzanne? You made a total ass of yourself tonight." I'm on the couch, and Tobin paces in front of me, his fingers pinching the bridge of his nose. "You're a sloppy drunk, an idiot, and I don't know why I ever married you. You disgust me. You are a fat, disgusting waste of a person."

These insults used to make me cry.

I have no more tears for Tobin.

I am a desert. Dry. Nothing but sand and searing heat.

"You're just trying to create a diversion for yourself." I hate how fuzzy my words sound, blending together. I shouldn't have drunk so much. I should have stayed sober, alert. "So, where were you, Tobin?"

The slap shouldn't have been a surprise, but alcohol has dulled my reflexes. I don't realize it's coming until his hand connects with my face, sending my head flying to the side. I can already taste the blood filling my mouth.

I will not cry. I. Will. Not. Cry.

"Look what you made me do!" he screams. He's so close, his spit speckles my face. It makes me want to vomit. "You and your big fucking mouth. Your fat ass stumbled around the party with that mouth running, and now you can't stop running it. Those people aren't just a bunch of no ones. There were colleagues and business partners there. You could ruin my career. Then how will you pay for every stupid diet you want to try so you won't be such a pig."

I've been listening to these insults for so many years; they don't even sting anymore. I'm not sure if I've become a sponge, and they just seep into me; they are who I am now, who I see myself as. Or if my skin has hardened to titanium, too strong for them to penetrate. I'd like to think of myself as strong and impenetrable, but I know that's not the case, no matter how hard I wish it to be true.

"Just tell me who she is?" I say, refusing to back down.

"What are you on about, you stupid cow?"

"I know you're having an affair. Just tell me so I don't make a fool of myself by continuing a friendship with the woman sleeping with my husband." The tears finally come. My husband can hit me, call me vile names, but what breaks me is the humiliation of him sleeping with one of my friends. It's *her* betrayal, even if it is Eloise.

Tobin sneers. "Do you really think I would sleep with one of your stupid friends? You are all the same, shallow idiots. I have higher standards. I'm not even sure how I got stuck with you. I could have had anyone I wanted. And now look at my life. A worthless wife who can't even bother to keep her mouth shut from words or food."

"Then divorce me!" I can't remember the last time I raised my voice with him. It feels good. It's the fuel I need to continue.

"And give you half my money?" He starts laughing. His laugh is one of the worst sounds. Metal scraping together. I want to cover my ears. Even when he's not acting like an evil bastard, it sounds like a wild banshee. I want to tell him that I'll leave, I don't need his money, to just let me go. But where would I go? How would I survive? I've never worked, and I have no family. I'd be homeless. Or dead, because I'm positive, despite the fantasies I've created of freedom, he'd never let me get away alive. I'd be trading one impossible life for another.

"I'm sorry," I say, slumping forward.

"You're God damn right you're sorry, and this isn't the end of it either. Get upstairs. Go sit on the bed and wait for me."

I push myself off the couch and stumble up the stairs. He may be up within seconds, or he may make me wait for hours. This was part of the game. He reveled in the fact that I would be upstairs wondering what and when my punishment was coming.

I perch on the edge of our bed and wring my hands. Our bedroom looks like any other middle-aged couple's room. King sized, four-poster bed, floral comforter, nightstands, and a dresser. A few paintings of seascapes hang around the room. I've always loved the ocean, and I like sleeping surrounded by paintings of it. I find it calming. Especially with how much time I spend in this room being tortured. It helps.

It's also spotless. Not a speck of dust can be found. That's one of Tobin's rules, one that he checks often. He'll put on a pair of white gloves and walk around wiping a hand over surfaces and checking the glove. Every missed spot is a punishment.

"Take your clothes off." I didn't hear him come in. He's very good at entering a room without making a sound. I obey. There's no sense in arguing; it will only make things worse. "Hands against the wall, legs spread." I hear him walk to the closet and open the safe. My mind screams at me to run. There's no escape, and I tell it to shut up.

I hear the crack of the whip and try not to tense. It's worse when you contract your muscles.

After twenty-five whips across my back, he leans in and whispers in my ear, "Clean yourself up, you filthy pig." I lean my face against the wall, unable to move. I can feel the blood seeping from the gashes on my back and running down my legs. I'll have to treat the cream carpet tonight. Blood is much easier to deal with when fresh. I've cleaned enough blood from this carpet to know.

I think of Eloise's high cheekbones, her piercing eyes, and wonder if Tobin calls her a pig. I can't imagine her putting up with it like I do. Maybe that's what has drawn him to her: she is strong where I am weak, and she is jagged where I am soft. I limp to the bathroom and turn on the shower. Stepping in, the cold water stings when it hits my back, but the wounds can't be left untreated. That's how infections start; these aren't the kind of injuries easily explained away to an ER doctor. I stare through the glass wall and look at the medicine cabinet, mentally cataloging the bottles of pills in there and which ones could end it. There's a whole bottle of sleeping pills, a freshly filled prescription. That would work. A set of Tobin's razor blades. Up and down, a bottle swallowed, no more pain, physical or mental.

Or—

I could get rid of the source of my problems: Tobin and Eloise.

Chapter 52

Eloise

Suzanne, despite her ignorance, does have one thing right: I did sleep with her husband. I've slept with almost all of my friends' husbands. At least the ones I know who are capable of being discreet. I don't have continued affairs with them. Not like Beatrix and Tobin. I seek them out when they are at their weakest, use them for sex, and never speak of it again. I do this for several reasons, the first being I enjoy sex, as it feels good, and I never deprive myself of things that bring me joy. It's also in my best interest to always have a secret with people closest to me. Something I can hold over their heads, a protection of sorts. Just in case. You never know.

Robert likely also has women he sleeps with. If he does, it's really of no concern to me. What *is* a concern is him flaunting it publicly with such a lack of tact. That just won't do. Making me look foolish and weak, these are things I won't put up with. There has been an increasing number of undesirable things disrupting my carefully controlled life lately. It's time to start breaking some rules.

Alyssa McDaniels works in public relations. She is not new to the DC area, and she does not have a husband. She is very single and has lived here since birth. What ridiculous things to lie about. Did Robert not think I would find out? We've been married long enough for him to know my I.Q. is well above average. He's never been a liar, and I'm wondering why he's chosen now to give it a go.

If I'm correct, and she is in fact, sleeping with my husband, she knows who I am. This makes stalking her more difficult. My victims usually don't know me, making it easy to blend in with the crowd. I can stand in line behind them at Starbucks or push a grocery cart past them at Wegmans, and they don't look twice. Alyssa would be looking for me, especially now that she's so brazenly revealed herself.

There is a café across from her office building, a nondescript high rise, a tower of glass. After searching the area on Google maps, I've decided this is the best place for me to start casually tracking her unobserved. After requesting a table outside, I'm sipping my cappuccino and pretending to read a book. My eyes are hidden behind large sunglasses, so I'm able to scan each window, imagining which one is hers. I can picture her seated behind her large desk, long legs crossed, laughing while on the phone. My fingers tighten on the book, and I quickly loosen them before anyone can notice my knuckles turning white. Her schedule is what I'm after. Patterns of her life. Where she eats lunch, who she eats it with, how often she's in the office, with clients, and when she is with my husband.

At five past twelve, she steps out from the revolving door and puts on sunglasses. She's wearing an emerald green fitted dress. How appropriate, the color of poison and death. In the 1800s, green dye was infused with arsenic. It was highly popular, and the affluent couldn't get enough of it. Women dressed themselves head to toe in green, and rooms were wallpapered in it. The upper class ignorant to the fact that they were slowly poisoning themselves. Skin ulcers, open sores, hair loss ... these are just a few of the regrettable effects of arsenic. I imagine Alyssa's skin breaking out in painful, oozing sores and smile.

"Are you ready to order?" a cheerful server arrives, blocking my view of Alyssa. I snap my book shut, annoyed, and lean to peer around her. Alyssa looks across the street and halts. She pushes her sunglasses on her head and stares at me. The server tentatively turns in the direction I'm looking, bringing even more attention our way.

"Nothing right now, thank you," I say, not keeping the impatience from shortening my words. By the time the now-flustered server has left, Alyssa is gone. I place a fifty-dollar bill under my mug and gather my things. There is no reason to be caught here when she returns. It seems Alyssa is more intelligent than I anticipated. That begs the question: what is she doing with Robert? As a smart, beautiful woman, surely she could have any man. Robert is rich, yes, but he isn't much more than that.

Chapter 53

SUZANNE

Tobin used to apologize after the beatings. He used to cry, tell me it wouldn't happen again, and beg for forgiveness. He used to do a lot of things he doesn't do anymore. That was before. When they weren't punishments. There were a slap here or holding me against the wall by my neck there. It shouldn't have been, but it was much easier to explain those types of incidents away. Believe his lies. Still love him. Then it progressed and morphed from typical into sadistic. Almost overnight, in fact. I often wonder if he's always been this evil person hidden behind a handsome face and charming personality. Or if something in him snapped and his personality fractured. The monster took over because the monster was stronger.

As I said, there aren't any more apologies. I guess it's nice in some ways. It's honest. Because he's not sorry, he never was. He'd be sorry if he was caught, that I'm sure of. I'm not so sure he'd be sorry if I died. It would be an inconvenience with all the police questions, investigations, and potential gossip amongst co-workers and the club. That may be worth it, though, in his mind. I don't know. I stopped trying to figure out how his head works a long time ago.

Robert's saying hello on the phone. He sounds distracted, and I can hear the distant clicking of typing on a keyboard. "Suzanne who?" he asks.

After getting through the awkwardness of being so forgettable, I dive right into the reason for my call. "I have some uncomfortable news I'd like to share with you, pertaining to Eloise," I say.

"Eloise?" He sounds generally confused.

"I'd prefer to do it in person if you have time." The longer the conversation drags on, the more unsure I grow. This was a bad idea. I shouldn't have called him. Additionally, my back hurts. I glance at the bottle of Vicodin sitting on the kitchen counter. I'd much prefer to take one or three and go back to bed, forget. I'm not even sure what I'm hoping to accomplish. Somehow, expose Tobin without another beating? Maybe Robert will beat him up instead. I forget I'm on the phone and laugh, picturing round Robert trying to take on six-day-a-week-in-the-gym Tobin. I'm sure if the four of us, Eloise, Robert, myself, and Tobin were all lined up together and a stranger was asked to identify the couples, they'd, without hesitation, pair me with Robert and Eloise with Tobin. Robert and I are plain, softer, and we look our age. Whereas Eloise and Tobin are striking, beautiful, fit.

"I'm sorry, is something funny?" Robert's gruff voice interrupts my thoughts.

"Oh, no, sorry. It shouldn't take long. I know you're busy. Maybe I could come meet you by your office, tomorrow morning even. We could grab coffee. On me."

"I don't need you to buy me coffee, and I'm sure Eloise is capable of figuring out how to resolve her own drama."

"Please, Robert. It's not something Eloise knows about. Just five minutes. I promise." I hate how whiney and desperate I sound. He doesn't answer right away and sweat prickles my armpits. What if he refuses? Will he tell Eloise about the strange phone call he received from me? Will she tell Tobin? Before my mind can formulate a thousand more what if's, I hear a whoosh of air blow into the phone.

"Fine, we can meet tomorrow morning, and you can tell me whatever it is you think is so important." He gives me the address of a coffee shop near his office and starts to say goodbye.

"Oh, and Robert, one more thing if you don't mind."

"What is it, Suzanne? I'm at work."

"Yes, I'm so sorry. If you just—If you wouldn't mind, not telling Eloise about this call. Or about the meeting." I hold my breath and wait for his response.

He agrees. I only hope he's telling the truth.

The adrenaline is soon replaced by pain. My heartbeat pulses in the gashes on my back. I take two painkillers and send a text to Beatrix: *I called Robert, meeting tomorrow to tell him exactly what his wife has been up to.*

Beatrix doesn't reply, but I don't care because the pills are finally working. I limp upstairs and gently lower myself into my bed. I'm asleep the second my head hits the pillow. I'll be in trouble for not cleaning the house or preparing dinner, but I just can't find the energy to care anymore. It will all be over soon.

Chapter 54

BRYONY

My room has become both my cell and my sanctuary. My home, my prison. The humiliation of what I did at the bonfire makes the air so heavy it's hard to breathe, hard to move. The video—me dancing naked, stumbling around in front of everyone—plays on repeat behind my eyes every time I close them. The idea of not being in control of my body is terrifying. Like a zombie, dead inside, but something still moving my limbs, keeping me alive. No one is worried about who drugged me. It's much easier to point and laugh at the victim than place blame on a faceless perpetrator. It could have been much worse. Whoever it was could have gotten me alone, raped me, killed me. That may have been better. People don't laugh at dead girls.

They'd be crying over my grave instead of dancing on it.

My mother hasn't yelled at me or punished me yet. Not for the incident and not for my one excursion to her precious party. I wish she would. The fear of what's to come is as bad as whatever she has in store for me. Something *is* coming, and I want it over with. I tried to tease a reaction out of her but lost my nerve and left.

The fact that it has taken her this long means it's going to be bad, very bad. Maybe she'll do what the guy who drugged me failed to do: kill me, put me out of my misery. Or I could do it. I've thought about it. I'm too chicken. Every time I come up with a plan, I start crying and crawl into bed. I'm such a loser I can't even manage to kill myself right.

"Bryony, stop picking at your dinner and eat. Manners," my mom tuts.

I lift a bite of chicken to my mouth and slowly chew it without looking at her.

"You must eat, sweetheart. It will make you feel better." I look up at my dad, and his kind smile almost makes me cry. I want to run over and jump into his lap like I did when I was a kid. My dad travels a lot for work, but he always makes time for me when he's home. Not lately, though. They have both been weird lately. Or maybe it's just because I'm home so much I'm finally seeing what's always been there.

I've gotten used to the cold that's left behind when he leaves. The temperature of the house drops at least twenty degrees, the kind of cold you can't get away from no matter how many layers of socks and sweaters you pile on. It took me a long time to figure out the cause of that frigid shift. I look over at my mom's stony face. *It's you. You're the cold.* Even when she smiles, it's wrong. She's not a mom; she's not a person at all, really, just a badly drawn version of one. I catch my reflection in the mirror on the wall. Who am I to judge?

"I got the strangest call today," my dad says, turning his attention back to my mom.

Was that panic that flashed in her eyes? "Strange, in what way?" she asks, putting her fork and knife down next to her plate. If I had a ruler, I could measure the space between each utensil and the dish, and it would be exactly the same. Perfect Eloise, never a thing out of place.

My dad chuckles. "Suzanne wants to meet tomorrow morning. Says she has something important to tell me." He shakes his head and continues eating. My head swivels between the two of them. He doesn't feel the shift. He never does. But I do. My mom is now on the hunt. She didn't know about this phone call, and she doesn't like when things happen outside of her control. She especially doesn't like people knowing when she's not in control.

"That is interesting." She extends the last word for much longer than necessary. My dad, still unaware, continues eating. She, a as usual, makes the conversation about her. "I would have expected a call apologizing for her behavior at the event. But things continue to be quite unexpected lately, don't they?"

My eyes fall to my lap, and her stare crawls over me like cockroaches.

"It has been an eventful few weeks. Do the police have any updates on the man who attacked you on your run?"

"No. I fear many questions will remain unanswered regarding the attack, vandalism, and of course, darling Bryony's poisoning."

I hate the heat of embarrassment that overtakes my face and take a long drink of water to cover my shame.

She continues, "But Suzanne, now that *is* a surprise. You are going to go and see what she has to say, of course."

"She didn't really give me a choice if I'm being honest. She caught me at work when I was busy, and it was the only way I could get her off the phone."

"Mhm." Her eyes glow with that odd look they get before really bad things happen. I stare intently at my dad, begging him with my eyes to notice Eloise's shifted mood. I love him, but I don't understand why he's so blind to her. Is it easier for him to only see the good in her? If he knew what she was really like, he'd take me far away from her, and he'd save me. I like to think he would, at least.

The thought sends an invisible fist into my stomach. Her hold on me is so strong I can't even imagine leaving her without experiencing physical pain.

"Well," she says. "Do let us know what Suzanne has to say. This mystery has me intrigued, I must say." She grins over her wine glass before taking a sip.

"May I be excused?" I ask, moving my napkin from my lap to my plate.

She glares at me, and then her eyes dart to my dad. The speed at which her face morphs into a warm, sympathetic smile is enough to give me whiplash. "Of course, darling. If you're done, you may be excused."

"Thank you, Mother," I reply. My chair scrapes back, and I shuffle from the room. I don't look back. I don't want to know if she's following me with her gaze. I don't want to see the look on her face. My stomach is already in freefall, and I'm afraid if I do look, I'll vomit the few bites of dinner I managed to eat onto the dining room floor.

Back in my room, I turn on my phone for the first time in days. I'm still being tagged in videos. Different angles have surfaced. I should delete all my social media accounts. Go into virtual hiding. I'm not sure why I don't. There are hundreds of missed texts and calls from Annabelle. She's so worried about me.

Call me

I love you

Just come meet me

It will be ok

I scroll through each one and don't reply. The thought of typing even just a single word makes me incredibly tired. The only other person whose messages aren't vile or hateful is CaliViolinGrl. She's sent me several 'checking on you' DMs. My heart contracts. How can kids I've grown up with, my *friends,* be so quick to turn on me, yet this stranger continues to show me kindness? I think back on all the times I joined in on someone else's demise. Following the crowd like a lemming, too afraid of being left behind.

When Kayla Meyers confided in me that she lost her virginity to Annabelle's ex, I screen shotted the text and sent it to everyone I knew. The bullying started immediately. We all called her a slut, people threw food at her in the cafeteria, and her locker was graffitied with words like whore, STD Queen and the like. A small part of me knew it was wrong, and instead of helping, all I did was thank God it wasn't happening to me. I thought my selfish thoughts and joined in. Until enough was enough and Kayla drove her car into a tree.

This is probably my penance.

Or is it.

Because Kayla was the one who got herself into that mess. It's not my fault she couldn't handle the consequences.

I'm so stuffed full of secrets that my skin is stretched too thin. There's no more room for anyone else's secrets. I've spent my entire life being trained to be a good little girl and to follow the rules, including the most important rule: we don't talk about the rules.

It's not my fault.

I've behaved.

I've been a good girl, I haven't—

I shush Eloise's voice that is overtaking my thoughts and reply to CaliViolinGrl. Knowing she's across the country and has no connections to any of the assholes in my school makes it easier. *Yeah, I'm not ok, things are pretty fucking terrible actually.* Then I turn my phone off and get in bed to go to sleep. The sleeping pill I stole from my mom will be kicking in soon. Goodbye world, at least for now.

Chapter 55

Suzanne

Robert arrives late, but he arrives. I'm on my third cup of coffee, and the caffeine only adds to what my frayed nerves have already done to my insides. My knee bounces beneath the table as he slides into the seat across from me.

"Your wife and my husband are sleeping together." I wait for Robert's reaction, but none comes. No fist pounding on the table, no eyebrows raised, nothing.

He clears his throat. "That's a big accusation you are dropping on me there."

"Yes, I know." I giggle nervously and spin my wedding ring to give my hands something to do. The flight or fight response takes over. I suddenly want to be anywhere but sitting in this coffee shop with Robert. I shouldn't have come. And now the chain of events I've unleashed are barreling forward. It's too late to stop them.

"I have to be honest, this all sounds," he pauses, searching for the right words, I'm sure, "ridiculous. What evidence do you have?"

I blush and can't meet his eyes. What evidence *do* I have? None really. Just a feeling. I can't say that out loud. He'll dismiss me immediately. I shuffle uncomfortably in my seat, because I'm regretting coming here, but also because my back hasn't fully healed, and I can feel each wound throbbing.

"Umm, well, nothing concrete yet. I was hoping you could help me with that."

He sighs. I've lost him. "I'm going to leave now. I'm also going to pretend this conversation never happened, and we can all move on with our lives. My advice: if you and Tobin are having difficulties with your marriage, I'm very sorry for that, but that is something you will have to deal with together. You shouldn't be dragging other people into your personal affairs."

Without another word he stands, picks up his briefcase, and leaves me alone at the table with my regret and shame. The bile burns like lava in my throat. *What have I done?*

My gaze skitters across the crowd. Most are grabbing their steaming to-go cups from the counter and leaving. But a woman makes me freeze. She's sitting in the corner, hands wrapped around her own to-go cup, staring directly at me. A shudder quivers through my body. Her eyes bore into my soul, uncovering every thought and feeling. Even when I lock eyes with her, she doesn't turn away. She's not embarrassed she's been caught. She then does something completely unexpected: she winks. Yes, she's across the room, and yes, my anxiety is coursing through my veins, potentially distorting my perception. But I saw it. It was a wink like she's in on it. Whatever *it* is. I squint, trying to place this woman, trying to figure out if we know each other. Before I can figure it out, she's standing and walking my way.

"Hello, Suzanne," she says, sitting down in the seat Robert abandoned.

"I'm sorry, do we know each other?"

She tilts her chin up slightly, looking off to the side. "Hmm, you could say that."

"Pardon my rudeness, but I don't remember your name." A voice screams in my head, telling me to get up, run, get away from this woman as fast as possible, whoever she is.

"I noticed Robert was here. Left in a hurry, though, didn't he? Did you say something he didn't particularly care for?"

My eyes narrow, and I'm no longer sorry for not knowing who she is. This is not a friendly social calling. "Who are you?"

"I could tell you." She smirks and lowers her voice to a whisper. "But then I'd have to kill you."

I stand, and my chair clatters to the ground behind me, causing everyone in the room to look at us. I can feel tears pricking the corner of my eyes.

"Stay the fuck away from me," I say.

I start to walk out, clutching my purse to my chest.

"You're right, you know." I stop and turn. She's grinning. "It's so much worse, though. You don't even know the half of it."

I've heard enough. I run for the door. I can hear her laughing behind me. I don't turn around or look at anyone else. I don't care what anyone thinks. Robert must have told Eloise we were meeting. Eloise sent this woman to scare me. It's so like her to send someone else to do her bidding.

I slam the car door behind me and jam the lock button harder than necessary. My chest heaves from the sharp gulps of air I'm trying to feed my lungs with. I want to drive, but I'm shaking too hard. My head whips around for any signs the woman has followed me. All I see are women and men in business suits, typical workday foot traffic. I calm my ragged breathing and manage to start my car. The drive home is spent wiping the tears that stream down my face and blur the road ahead. I can't live like this anymore. Not knowing who to trust or what's happening around me is making me feel like I'm losing my mind. I've been living a nightmare with Tobin for years; with him, I know exactly who the monster is. That's almost comforting in a disturbing way. It's the not knowing that is terrifying.

But my courage is growing. I'm starting to think I'm no longer afraid to die.

Chapter 56

Eloise

Normally, when I'm sitting in my room in the dark, it's because of some ailment, but no, there is nothing wrong with me, at least not physically.

"Oh," Melanie exclaims, dropping the basket of laundry she's carrying in. "You scared me, Mrs. Williams." She takes two tentative steps into our room, her eyebrows creased. "Everything okay? Do you have a migraine? Should I get your pills?"

I'm seated in the sitting area in my quiet, dark room, trying to put the pieces of a very complicated puzzle together. Either I'm being targeted, which is very possible, or these things, these unfortunate incidents, are purely coincidence and completely unrelated.

"I'm fine." I flick my wrist to emphasize my point. "There's just a lot going on now, isn't there?"

She begins picking up the laundry and nods. "Yes, a lot going on. I wish there was more I could do..." She walks into the closet to finish putting away the clothes. I retrieve my phone and send an email to Suzanne, Beatrix, and Poppy, suggesting we get together for dinner to celebrate our successful event. Poppy replies almost immediately that she can't wait. I tap the chair's arm, thinking, contemplating which problem I should deal with first, when my phone rings. Private number. A call I'd usually ignore, but something tells me I should take this one.

"This is Eloise."

"Mrs. Williams, hello. This is Officer Donaley." My fingers tighten on the phone.

"How can I help you, Officer?"

"I was following up on the attack." The sound of papers shuffling in the background. "The one where you were running and thrown into a tree."

My shoulders relax. "Have you found the perpetrator?"

"No, unfortunately, I'm not calling with any news. I wanted to check-in. See how you were healing and if there has been anything else that could potentially help us find the person who did this to you?"

I consider telling him about the brick, but then I remember the note the brick was wrapped in. "I've healed fine, thankfully. I'm afraid I don't have any more information for you—actually, now that you mention it. There is one thing. No, I'm sure it's nothing—"

"Oftentimes, the nothings are the thread that leads to solving a case."

"Well, there is this woman. I recently hosted a charity dinner with a very exclusive guest list, one that I put together myself. This woman showed up uninvited."

"And you're sure this woman wasn't a guest of one of the folks invited to this party?"

"Absolutely positive. I finalized that list myself. Her name, which I found out after some investigation, is Alyssa McDaniels. The only reason I was able to figure even that much out is because she had a conversation with my husband, Robert. She told him she was new to the area and just joined our club with her husband. Well, after some further investigation, I discovered none of that is true. And now that I think back on it, the person who attacked me in the woods very well could have been a woman. Their build was small, and I never actually saw their face. I would never dream of accusing someone for no reason. I know how busy you and the rest of your colleagues are. But pieced together, it is all highly unusual, wouldn't you agree?"

"Could be nothing, could be something. I'll run a background check on Ms. McDaniels and see if anything pops up. In the meantime, if anything else unusual happens, feel free to call me directly. You still have my card?"

"I do, thank you so much."

"No problem at all, just doing my job, ma'am."

After I hang up, I feel lighter, as if the invisible hands that had been pushing down on my shoulders have gone. As if the fog dissipates within my head, it's suddenly very clear what needs to be done. And oh, the fun I'm about to have.

A distant rumble is followed by the crack of lightning. By the time I walk downstairs, the rain is drumming against the house. I push the curtain to the side of the front window. The sky has darkened, giving everything a forest green overcast. The rain intensifies quickly, but a movement at the head of our driveway catches my attention. I open the front door and wrap my arms around myself, wishing I had grabbed a jacket. Then I see them; the rain blurs the edges, but there is a figure standing at the end of our driveway. They're dressed in black, hood pulled up, legs spread wide, arms at their side, and they are looking right at me. Standing still as a statue. I can't see their face, but I can feel their gaze boring into me.

I will kill them, whoever it is, with my bare hands if I have to. I start running. Within seconds I'm soaked, and the water blurs my vision. My feet pound on the pavement, but the fallen leaves make the surface slick, and my legs fly out from under me. By the time I scramble up, they are gone. Ignoring the pain in my skinned palms and knees, I continue running to the spot where the person stood moments ago. Turning around in the circle, I search the darkened area for any sign of movement. They've gotten away. It has to be the same person who attacked me, the one who threw a brick through my window, and possibly the person who drugged Bryony.

With my fists at my sides, I scream into the darkness, "I will find you, and I will kill you!"

The only answer I receive is the wailing of the wind and a large crack of thunder. I rake my nails down my face and shriek.

I turn to walk back to the house. My foot hits something. A plastic box sits in the center of my driveway. I bend, pick it up, and march back to my house. Melanie is standing at the door, mouth hanging open.

"It's pouring out there. You'll catch a cold! Get in here, Mrs. Williams."

"I thought I saw a person."

She gasps, and her hand flies to her mouth.

"It's fine; I think it's just stress and the storm. My eyes are playing tricks on me. I'm going to go take a bath and get out of these wet clothes."

Melanie closes the door behind me, her eyes still wide. Her gaze flicks to the box in my hand, but she knows better than to ask too many questions. In my bathroom, I place the dripping box on my vanity and quickly undress and dry off before changing into fresh clothes. The box opens easily. Another piece of notebook paper is folded inside. I take it out and read the loopy, feminine handwriting.

Secrets, secrets are no fun, wait until I tell everyone.

I rip the paper up into microscopic pieces and flush them down the toilet, then slam the box into the mirror, over and over again, until the glass shatters and my reflection is lined with jagged cracks, making my manic face look even more deranged.

With my hands on the sink, I lean over it, out of breath. After composing myself, I straighten. I pull a brush through my hair and twist it into a low bun at the nape of my neck. I splash water on my face and smile at myself until my face looks natural, calm, pleasant. I retrieve the skeleton key and twist it to lock the bathroom door. No need for anyone to see the mess I've made of the mirror. I'll have to find a handyman to come repair it. When I had this house built, I insisted that all door handles be fitted so that they could be locked from the outside. When you are rich you can make eccentric requests like this without being questioned. It has come in handy on several occasions, for example, when I need an occupant to be locked in her room and unable to leave. Or, here, when I don't need Melanie prying any deeper. Foregoing my bath, I descend the stairs and find Melanie in the kitchen.

"It smells delicious, dear. What's for dinner?"

Chapter 57

BEATRIX

The last thing I wanted to do today was meet Suzanne, Poppy, and Eloise for breakfast, but Eloise, always so persistent, insisted. Tobin and I have an appointment this afternoon, one I can't miss.

I rolled my eyes when I read the email from Eloise inviting us 'To celebrate our successful event.' I mean, it was beautiful, and the food was great, but Suzanne made an asshole of herself, and that's really all people are talking about. Not the delicious filet mignon or the over-the-top table spreads. As much as Eloise would like to think that the details were the things that left an impression in the attendees' minds.

Despite wanting to be anywhere else, here I am, sitting in the French-inspired restaurant, sipping an orange juice, and waiting on the three people I have zero desire to see.

Eloise is the first to arrive. She walks to the table with her chin lifted. I almost expect her to wave to her subjects as she passes them, perhaps holding out her hand so they can kiss her ring. The urge to vomit suddenly overtakes me. "Beatrix, you're early. What a surprise," she says while kissing the air next to my cheek. I ignore the dig.

"I have an appointment today, which is what I said in the email. I can't be late."

"Yes, your appointment." She's not looking at me and is gesturing for a server, who isn't even ours, to come over. "Suzanne couldn't even be bothered to reply, so who knows if she'll show up. We don't have to wait for her to order. If she can't have the good manners to RSVP, we are under no obligation to wait for her."

I snort. "She's probably too humiliated to leave her house after how she acted."

"Mhm, yes. It was quite unbecoming, wasn't it? You know, she did the most peculiar thing." With her elbow on the table, she perches her head on the top of her fingers. The look she's giving me ices my blood. "She requested a meeting with Robert, which in and of itself is strange. But it's what she said that really has us both flabbergasted."

She's dragging this out. Does she know? With her hands on the table, she leans forward. "Suzanne accused me of having an affair with Tobin. It would be ludicrous, but you and I both know why it's truly so outrageous, don't we?"

"I have no idea what you're talking about, Eloise," I say through gritted teeth.

"It's outrageous because of you, darling. Suzanne isn't as foolish as we all thought, though, is she? She did figure out Tobin's mistress was one of her inner circle; she simply picked the wrong friend. She's been so focused on me that she's missed what's right in front of her face."

"And what is that?" I ask, knowing she knows. She'll use this. I'm now under her control.

"That you are the one who's been fucking her Tobin, not me—oh Poppy, hello sweetie, how are you?"

Eloise stands. I can't move. She and Poppy exchange hellos next to me. My hands grip the sides of the chair; I'm sure if I let go or try to stand, I'll collapse. The room spins.

Poppy's voice snaps me from my daze. "Beatrix, are you feeling okay? You look as white as the tablecloth."

"Ladies." I dart up from my seat and throw my purse strap over my shoulder. "I really need to go. As I explained, I have an appointment, a doctor's appointment. I'm not feeling well, and I shouldn't have come. I don't want to get either of you sick."

"Oh no, text me later and let me know what they say," Poppy says, face nothing but concern.

"Goodbye, Beatrix," Eloise says, a smile playing on her lips.

I refuse to meet her eyes and walk quickly out of the restaurant. How the hell does Eloise know? And what will she do about it? It doesn't matter. Not now.

My appointment is at two, in fifteen minutes. I was supposed to be there fifteen minutes early to fill out paperwork. I'm already late, but I can't bring myself to get out of my car.

With a huff, I pick up the phone and try calling Tobin. Voicemail. I try his office, pretending to be the assistant of an investor trying to get a meeting scheduled. They tell me he isn't in today but should be back tomorrow. I hang up when she asks if I'd like to leave a message. My cuticles have been chewed to a bloody mess, an old habit that returns when I'm stressed. I could reschedule the appointment, but I'm already here. I can't let Tobin's sudden disappearance disrupt my life.

I try Tobin's phone three more times, switching off the Show Caller ID in my phone's settings before calling to make my phone number show as private, but surely, he knows it's me. It's not like this wasn't a pretty fucking important day. On the fourth call, a woman picks up.

"Who the fuck is this? Stop calling." The phone call ends.

I'm staring at my phone, and it takes me a second to realize who the woman is, Suzanne. Her voice was rough, and her breathing was so hard and quick it made it impossible to hear anything that may have been in the background.

The sound of roaring wind fills my ears, a tornado barreling closer. Panic injects itself in every one of my cells.

I open my door, slam it shut, and march into the doctor's office, thinking of all the ways I'll make him regret ignoring me.

Chapter 58

Suzanne

It takes me much longer to get ready in the morning these days. It takes much longer to do most things. The whip sliced deep gashes in my back. He didn't hold back this time. I didn't think he had held back before, and I've learned how wrong I was.

In my bathroom, I hold a mirror in front of me with my back to the large mirror above the sink; it's hard to see from this angle, but some look infected. A yellow pus seeps out. For some reason, Tobin is still home, when normally by this time he'd have left for work. I should ask him to rub an antibiotic ointment on my wounds. But there's no telling what he'd do, so I suffer alone. I haven't seen him yet, so I don't know who's banging around downstairs, friendly, charming Tobin or sadistic Tobin. It's not worth the risk. I squeeze a large handful of the milky gel into my hand and twist and turn, trying to reach and slather the ointment on as many of the worst spots as possible.

I put on a loose tunic, a soft fabric that won't sting too bad when it rubs against my back and leggings, steadying myself to go downstairs. I have to face him eventually. No sense in putting it off much longer.

"Good morning," he mutters, not looking up from the newspaper, a mug of hot coffee steaming in front of him. He's dressed in jeans and a T-shirt. Definitely not going to work. I wonder if he's lost his job. Has that temper of his finally reared its head outside of our home? I can't believe it's taken this long.

"Day off?" I ask. I've been feeling much braver lately. Once you've resigned yourself to the idea that your death at someone's hands is inevitable, they become much less scary to be around. Tobin will most certainly kill me, and it's only a matter of when. Most mornings, I wake up hoping it will finally be the day. I'm tired. I'm ready for it to be over, and I see no other way out.

He looks up. Maybe it's the way the shadow is falling over his eyes, or maybe it's the devil inside him, but his irises blend into his pupils, and black eyes stare back at me. "You think it's your business? Worried there won't be enough of my money for you to spend and you'll have no reason to stay? If you think the money is the only thing keeping you here, I haven't made my position clear enough. So, let me spell it out for the fat piggy. If you try to leave, I will kill you. If you tell anyone what happens within this house, I will kill you."

"It's hilarious that you think I still care," I say while pouring myself a coffee. I no longer have to hide the shake in my voice, as it's no longer there.

He folds his paper and puts it on the table, intertwining his fingers on top of it. His head is bowed, and he's very still, very quiet. My stomach clenches. I may not be afraid of dying, but I am afraid of pain. To prove to him I'm no longer the quivering woman he believes me to be, I go about fixing my coffee as if we are having a casual conversation about the weather and not dancing this demented waltz of words.

"Why don't you have a seat? You clearly have things on your mind you'd like to discuss. We're both adults here, so let's have a conversation." There is only one adult here, one human. He is a demon with a pretty face. Regardless, I take my coffee and sit at the table. Before I can regret the seat I've chosen—the one right next to him—his hand is reaching for my fresh, hot coffee and throwing it in my face. The liquid burns, and I scream. He's out of his seat, smashing the mug into my eye socket, then covering my mouth with his hand. "Shut the fuck up, you stupid cow. No one can hear you."

You can't hide facial injuries. He's never told me, but I know that's why his beatings have always been on the rest of my body, places a pair of pants or long-sleeved shirt hide. I trace my burning face with the tips of my fingers, and the skin is already bubbling. His own cup has been knocked down in the scuffle, and he picks it up and holds it out to me. I don't have to ask what he's requesting. I stand and make him a fresh cup, the entire time wondering whether this one will also be thrown in my face. I force my hand to steady and place the mug in front of him. He will not feed on my fear, not today, and not ever again.

Tobin once told me why he was so great at negotiating. "It's the silence that you have to work," he said. "Silence makes people freak the fuck out. They can't handle it. You can get anything you want out of people if you just sit and say nothing. They'll fill that silence with everything you need to get them to do exactly what you want them to do."

This was back when we were first dating, before I knew the real Tobin. Another red flag I ignored. If I had been paying closer attention, maybe

I would have questioned the intentions behind the anecdote. What kind of person takes such pride in manipulating people? Now I know, it's not an innocent influence to close a business deal. No, with Tobin, it's much darker than that. The exploitation of people is his favorite game. I've never been a good judge of character, so it's really no surprise I fell for it, and then fell right in love with the devil.

He's employing this tactic now, staring at me, stoic, unmoving, waiting for my discomfort to bubble over so I'll fill the spaces, vomit words into his hands for him to use against me. I am no longer playing his games. I inhale a deep breath, letting it out slowly. If today is the day I die, I'm okay with that.

He's the first to break. "Your fat mouth suddenly has nothing to say, I see."

I return his aloof expression. "I asked a simple question, Tobin. A question someone who had nothing to hide would have no trouble answering." I laugh. "Well, nothing to hide beyond the fact that he is a weak man. So weak he has to beat his wife. Do you know what they do to women beaters in prison, Tobin? The same thing they do to child killers. Have you ever been raped by a man? I would imagine it to be pretty painful. Almost as painful as being whipped repeatedly across the back." This is the line I never dared to cross. It feels so good; I can feel the wind rushing past my face as if I've physically taken a giant bound over some invisible rope. Tobin has rarely spoken of his father. But the few pieces of information I've been given over the years has brought me to the conclusion that he is this way because of him. My guess is that he was not only beaten by his father but also sexually abused.

Tobin jumps out of his seat and grabs my head, slamming it into the table. Towering above me, he steps back to admire the damage. I lift my head, spit out a tooth, and wipe the blood from my jaw. There is no pain. Is adrenaline numbing me? Am I in shock? I'm not sure, but I smile a bloody smile and say, "Is that all you have?"

Hours or minutes later, I wake up on the floor. I feel the cool tile on my face first, then the pain. Hot, searing, unbearable pain. It feels as if every inch of my body has been beaten, and it probably has. My eyes flutter open. I'm lying next to the table. Squinting, I try to make sense of what I'm seeing. My vision focuses, and his shoes are inches from my face. They don't move when I struggle to a sitting position. The change makes my head spin, and I grip the chair, commanding myself not to pass out. I heave myself into it and brace myself with the table. It feels as if the floor has turned into liquid. I shake my head, refusing to slip out of consciousness again.

"Look who's awake. Anything else to say?"

"Fuck you," I hiss.

His smug face contorts into anger, then back to arrogance. "I'm not sure what's gotten into you today. I'm also trying to decide if I like it or if it's really pissing me off. I have to be somewhere, though. I'll have to decide tonight when we continue this lovely conversation we've been having."

"Going to see your slut?" I grab my head, as every word is a struggle to get past my swollen lips. "Tell Eloise I say hi."

Tobin's eyebrows furrow, "What the fu—you know what, I don't care. You're insane, a deranged idiot. And I'm going to be late." His chair scrapes as he stands. With one more disgusted look at me, he shakes his head and then walks to the front hallway where he keeps his wallet and keys. I see my purse sitting on the kitchen counter. I only have a few minutes before he's gone.

I force myself to stand.

He's bent over, pulling his shoe on when I sing his name. It comes out with a slight whistle, as I've lost more teeth. I turn my head to spit blood onto the floor. The swelling is distorting my voice, and it sounds like I'm speaking through a mouth full of marbles. He looks up, and before he can register surprise, I shoot him. My aim is good. I've been practicing at the range in town every day for weeks. A single hole appears in the center of his forehead, and a thin trail of blood runs down his face. It's quite clean, considering what it's done to the back of his head where the bullet has exited and exploded his skull. He falls forward. Blood, skull fragments, and brain matter have splattered across the wall. That will be a nightmare to clean. I want to check for a pulse to ensure he's gone. But that wouldn't fit with the story I'm about to tell the police. I don't have much time, so I pray my bullet took his awful, evil life.

I get to work.

I start by checking my wounds. In order for this to work, my blood can't be found anywhere but in the kitchen. I wrap the ones still oozing with toilet paper; thankfully, they aren't too bad. It feels like most of the damage is internal. I then systematically destroy my house. Furniture turned over, drawers opened with the contents pulled out.

Tobin's phone has been going off the entire time. In between the crashing of furniture, I hear it buzzing against the tile next to his body. Annoyed, I put on gloves and carefully lean over to pick up the phone to answer it. The caller refuses to identify herself. Fucking Eloise, suddenly a coward.

It's in the bedroom when I break. I know what I have to do, and it almost brings me to my knees. I walk to my jewelry box and pull out the small pieces, including my parents' wedding bands and grandmother's pearls. I don't have much from them, and now I'll have nothing. I have to do it. I can't leave anything to chance. I watch them twirl down the toilet and silently weep. The rings, earrings, bracelets, and necklaces from Tobin are much easier to say goodbye to. I grab the Lava soap I've hidden beneath the sink and scrub my hands until they're red and raw.

Once the house is successfully wrecked, I put on a pair of cleaning gloves and go into my backyard. I silently thank Tobin for the large fence and trees surrounding our backyard, affording me the privacy I need to dig a hole and bury the gun, gloves, and soap beneath my garden. Satisfied I've completed everything necessary, I dial 9-1-1.

"Help me!" I scream. "Someone broke into my house! I'm dying, and I need an ambulance!" I cry and wail, and they must think it's because of the terrible thing that's just happened, but, really, it's tears of joy. I am free. I am finally free.

"Are you safe now? Is the intruder gone?"

"I don't know," I drop my voice to a whisper. "Oh my God, they could be here, I didn't think—I just woke up on my kitchen floor; I don't know how long I've been knocked out. Tobin!" I scream. "Oh God, my husband, where is my husband?"

"Help is on the way, ma'am. I need you to try to calm down. Who else was home when you were attacked?"

"It was just me and my husband. I don't know, I think he was here. I can't remember. I don't hear anyone else in the house. Maybe they're gone. I'm going to look for my husband." I pause for effect, then collapse. "I can't walk, everything hurts. Hurry, please. I'm dying."

"They are five minutes away. Help will be there soon."

"I need to find Tobin." I crawl out of the kitchen, holding the phone, and see my husband for what the emergency operator thinks is the first time. The scream of a grieving widow reverberates through my home.

"There's blood everywhere. He's not breathing. Tobin, no. Don't leave me, Tobin wakes up." I end the call and smile. I have a few minutes before I need to play the part of a grieving wife.

When I hear a distant siren, I crawl to the front door, open it, and collapse on my front porch.

Chapter 59

BEATRIX

I'm walking back to my car, and my phone rings. My hope deflates when I see Poppy's name.

"Hello." I try not to sound annoyed.

Poppy's hysterics pierce my eardrum, and I have to hold the phone away from my head. Whatever crisis she's having can wait. I'm not in the mood. She's probably broken a nail or found out her favorite stylist is moving. I hear her scream, "Dead!" and quickly slam the phone back to my ear.

"Dead? What did you just say?"

"Tobin is dead!" she screams. "Suzanne is in the hospital—I'm on my way there. I don't even know what happened. Suzanne called me and told me she's been taken to Fairfax Hospital."

My phone crashes to the ground.

I pick the phone back up. "Beatrix, are you there? I think I've lost her. Beatrix, hello?"

"I'm here. Are you driving?"

"No, I called Eloise, I'm in her car. I was too much of a wreck to drive."
Bile burns my throat at the sound of Eloise's name. "Can you meet us
there? Suzanne will need us. Oh my God, she must be traumatized." A
fresh round of crying.

"Okay, Poppy, I'm hanging up. I'll meet you at the hospital. Text me
the room number when you get there."

Somehow, I drive myself to the hospital, though I don't remember a
second of it. There are too many emotions surging through my body.
Grief, confusion, terror. I can't grasp onto one for longer than a second,
and the constant chaos brings with it an overwhelming exhaustion. My
limbs feel like no matter how hard I try, I'm moving in slow motion. I
pull into a parking spot and dig my phone from my purse. Poppy has
sent me Suzanne's room number. I'm not ready to go in. I tilt my head
back to lean on the headrest, and I squeeze my eyes shut. I don't know
who I am more afraid of seeing, Eloise or Suzanne. Will Eloise have told
her? Is this why Tobin is dead?

I finally convince my legs to carry me through the main entrance. The
doors swish open, and I glance around the vast lobby, unsure where to
go. A woman sits behind a large, rounded desk and asks if she can help
me. I walk up and give her Suzanne's room number. Tears stream down
my face and she offers a sympathetic smile, pointing me in the right
direction. This kind woman is showing concern for me, thinking what
a good friend I am. If she only knew the true depth of my tears. I thank
her and walk toward the elevator.

As the elevator takes me up the building, my stomach plummets in
the opposite direction. By the time the digital numbers indicate I've
reached my destination, my entire body has numbed. I step into a hushed

hallway, and my sneakers make no sound on the linoleum as I make my way to Suzanne's room.

Her appearance makes my hands fly to my mouth. The swelling on her face has transformed it into an almost unrecognizable state. She's tethered to blinking and beeping machines.

Poppy runs over and hugs me. "Beatrix, you made it."

I walk to the side of Suzanne's bed and grip the railing to hide the tremor in my hands. Her head lolls to the side and she looks at me through half-opened eyes. Her hand lifts, and she manages a smile.

"Suzanne," I gasp. "I'm so—" I turn to Poppy. "What happened?" I notice Eloise standing off to the side. She looks, I don't know how she looks, almost amused. It sends a shiver down my spine, and I look away quickly.

"Someone broke into their home," Poppy exclaims. "Look what they did to our poor Suzanne, and they..." Her voice catches, fresh tears stream down her face. "They killed Tobin—he's been shot."

I look down at Suzanne, and she closes her eyes. She almost looks like she's smiling. However, it's hard to tell with the swelling. My words are stuck in my throat as if they've been glued there. I take two shaky steps to one of the chairs. The only place to sit is closer to Eloise, but I'm afraid if I don't, I'll pass out. The guilt and grief make spots dance in front of my vision.

"Does she have any idea who it was?" I ask.

"I'm right here; you can ask me yourself," Suzanne mumbles, not opening her eyes. "I'm not dead; I just look it." She tries to laugh and starts coughing. Poppy runs over and asks if she's okay. When the coughing subsides, she continues, "They were wearing all black, including a mask. Hood pulled up so I couldn't see their face or hair, or anything really. It looked like a man, tall, built like one. But it's all fuzzy. Hard to remember."

Poppy cries out and looks at Eloise. "That sounds exactly like the person who attacked you on your run. You don't think someone is targeting us, do you?"

I hate hospitals and doctors. I suppose that's a strange thing to say, being a surgeon's wife. Everything about them is so sterile, cold, and they all have the same strange smell. I guess no one would say they love a hospital, seeing as you only go to them when you are sick, or when someone you know is sick. You're supposed to go to the hospital to feel better, but every time I step foot in one, I have a physical reaction. I would have to be on my death bed to agree to go. Despite the cold air, I'm starting to sweat. The fluorescent lights are making my head hurt, and the urge to run is making my knees bounce.

"No one is targeting us. We aren't that interesting," Eloise says. Only ... she's staring at me. Her eyes are like X-rays, boring beneath my skin and uncovering all my secrets. "And yet—there have been a lot of strange things happening lately. My attacker, but there's more. My car and house have been vandalized, and I caught someone in my driveway the other day. And Robert mentioned Suzanne, that you went to him recently. You said that the person who broke into your house was a man, but the more I've thought about it, the more I'm convinced my attacker, and now this stalker, is most definitely a woman. Beatrix, Suzanne, what do you ladies think of that?"

Suzanne's eyes open despite the swelling. "You can leave now, Eloise."

"Suzanne, she didn't mean any—" Poppy tries to interject.

"I said, get the fuck out."

I'm completely jealous and proud. I look at Suzanne and can't believe what I'm hearing.

Eloise pushes herself off the wall. "I never stay where I'm not welcome. Suzanne, best of luck with your recovery. Do text me when you're released. The two of us have much to discuss."

A thick silence is left in Eloise's wake. Suzanne is the first to break it. "Stay away from her, she's dangerous."

"Oh, Suzanne, I know it's been a terrible day, but Eloise is harmless. All bark," Poppy says.

"She had a woman threaten me the other day, and now look what happened. Tobin is dead and I'm sure I'm supposed to be. If she got her wish." Suzanne's words are slurred, and her breathing is labored. Talking is taking a lot out of her.

"Who threatened you?" I ask.

"She didn't give me her name, but she walked up to me in a coffee shop and confirmed everything, then she said she'd kill me."

We both stare at her with our jaws unhinged. It's hard to tell if this is some false memory her mind has concocted. She's been through a lot today.

A knock at the door sends all our heads turning. Two uniformed police officers stand at the elbow of a woman in an ill-fitting business suit. She's built out of triangles. All sharp angles. A triangle nose, a triangle chin. Even her voice is sharp and cutting.

She asks us to leave, and I don't hesitate. Jumping out of my seat, I wave my goodbyes and mumble that I'll text later. I get to my car, and the tears come before I can slam my door shut. I don't think I've fully processed Tobin's death. It doesn't feel real; instead, it feels like my favorite character in a book has been killed off. It's not like I was in love with him. I'm not even sure I liked him very much. He was an egotistical asshole. Not to mention, he was cheating on his wife. But we did have *something,* and it feels almost wrong not to mourn him.

Chapter 60

Eloise

Poor, sweet Becca. She had such high hopes that night she followed me into the woods. She looked at the contents of the box and then back at me with her widened eyes.

"Go ahead, you can pick them up. Feel free to take your time looking through them," I said.

With surprisingly steady hands, she reached in and picked up a Polaroid before looking up, confused. She continued to reach in and pick up a different photo, studying each image, eyes frantically searching the group, finding each girl in the photos among the crowd surrounding us.

Tears streamed down her face, and her head shook slightly. She knew what was coming next, and now she understood it *was* worse than the brand.

A hand reached out and handed me my backpack. I rummaged around and found what I was looking for. The alcohol helped, but Becca needed something stronger to release her from the pain of the branding, something that would make what comes next more authentic. She winced as I rubbed the lidocaine over the fresh wound, already bubbling, her skin an angry red.

"Shh, this will make it feel better, I promise. There now, it will be numb in a few moments."

She nodded while the tears silently traced lines down her cheeks. I cupped her face in my hands and licked each cheek, enjoying the delicious saltwater. I took my thumb and gently swept under each eye to clean the mascara that had smudged below them.

After standing, I took the Polaroid camera and held it to my face. "Move your arms. I need to see your body. Cooperate, Becca, we don't have all night." My voice was stern and commanding. She didn't move, so two girls did it for her. She didn't fight them. I smiled; they would do anything I told them. My obedient soldiers. The camera button clicked, and a fresh image slid from the camera's mouth. One of the girls took it from me and shook it slowly, revealing a naked, branded Becca.

She was crying again because of the shame and humiliation. Every cell in my body vibrated.

I placed the Polaroids in the box with the new ones of Becca and locked it. No one ever questioned why the box of naked girls didn't include a single photograph of me. I walked over to Becca and sat beside her. After I brushed her hair from her face, I leaned my forehead into hers and closed my eyes. Her fear and shame fed me.

The rest of the girls erupted in squeals and cheers. When I stood and stepped back from her, the girls swarmed around her. Someone pulled her to her feet and into a hug, and someone else helped her re-dress. I sat on a fallen log, smiling at the scene, while the girls passed Becca around, welcoming her with hugs and more kisses. Becca managed to smile, but her eyes looked glassy, the fire that lit them so brilliantly earlier was now gone. She hovered between horror and self-hate.

The girls went back to gossiping and drinking. They'd been through this all before. They were fully under my spell, no longer shocked by the ritual. I pulled Becca to the side.

"If you tell, these photos will go to everyone you know. They will follow you around for the rest of your life. If you don't, we will show you things you didn't know were possible; the choice is yours."

Two weeks later, Becca's mother found her hanging in her bedroom closet. No note. No warning signs. Her parents left for work, she pretended to go to school, found a rope, tied a noose, put all the clothes on the bed, pushed her pink desk chair into the closet, stepped off, and after some convulsing, died. I know all this because I was there. Becca was my first Darling. And for that reason, she will always be very special to me.

Chapter 61

THE WATCHER

Bryony blocked my fake profile. A tiny part of me, the paranoid part, wonders if she suspects. The rational part knows that's not possible. Why would she suspect me—her violin-playing friend from California—of having anything to do with roofies being slipped into her beer during a bonfire party?

I finish the last gulp of my martini and slide the glass forward. The bartender walks over and I acknowledge, yes, I would like another. It's early and a weekday, and the only other people in the dim bar are me and a few small groups of people at high tops dressed in business attire eating lunch. A few have glanced my way, likely judging what a middle-aged woman dressed in leggings and a tank top is doing sitting in a bar drinking in the middle of the day. Let them stare, as their opinions of me can't be any lower than my own self-loathing.

I've always blamed Eloise for the lost life I've been grieving. It was her actions that created the first fissure in my mind. But she didn't fracture it, and I'm starting to recognize that. It's taken thirty long years, but I know now that I'm to blame.

"You look like you're going through some things. Need to get something off your chest?"

I look at the fresh drink the bartender has placed in front of me.

My eyes slowly rise to meet his. "What if that something involved people dying? Not just one person but multiple. Would the offer still stand?"

A frown replaces his friendly smile. He pulls the drink back. "I think that's enough for today. Need me to call a cab?"

I ignore the fact that I'm being thrown out, politely, but still, it's clear I've overstayed my welcome in his establishment. "Have you ever felt like no matter how hard you try to do the right thing, you just make things worse and worse and worse? I just wanted them to see who she was. I didn't mean to push Suzanne into killing him. It's not over either. There's more to come, all because of my meddling. And the fire. Oh my God, the fire. I don't even know why..." My head is in my hands, and I'm gripping my hair, pulling.

"Are you on drugs?" the bartender asks.

I stand and lunge over the bar. Gripping the edge, my nose inches from his. "Drugs? That's what you think? I wish it was drugs." I fall back into the stool and cackle. "Drugs. I could use some of those right about now." I look around the room, nodding, laughing, looking for comradery or someone to agree and laugh along with me. Because what else can I do. This is a madhouse. The world is a madhouse. I'm met with frowns and confusion.

The bartender is gripping me by the arm, dragging me to the exit.

I pull myself free. "Alright, yes, I get it. I'm leaving."

It's not the first time my mental health has been blamed for my ramblings.

Maybe if people had believed me back then, Eloise would have been stopped, and lives would have been saved.

Chapter 62

Eloise

While the police are searching for Tobin's killer and Suzanne's attacker, I'm on my own hunt. I must find a way to kill Alyssa. The need for her blood is all-consuming. My skin is too tight, my mind is unable to grasp any other thought. She. Must. Die. Until I can watch her eyes glaze over, feel her last breath on my cheek, my urges will be too strong, too close to the surface. I'll do something rash. I don't even care about Robert that much, but I don't like to share or to lose.

Or perhaps I am no longer two people: the Eloise who is able to charm anyone into bending to my will and the demon driven by bloodlust. It never occurred to me that I'd one day have to choose. I quite like my life the way it is. Adoration is just as, and often times more, fulfilling as killing. There has been a shift, though, and I'm certain the demon will win this battle. She's always been the stronger of the two.

"You seem distracted. Is what happened to Tobin and Suzanne bothering you?" Robert asks. Robert and I are sitting in the living room with Bryony. The television is on, but no one is paying attention to it.

"Yes, it's so—there are no words really," I say. "Poor Suzanne. I don't know how she'll ever recover. Mentally, I mean."

"Do they know who did it?" Bryony speaks for the first time all evening. The sound of her voice almost startles me. I keep forgetting she's here. She's become a ghost wandering our halls. It reminds me I need to deal with her as well.

"No," I say with an exaggerated frown. "But I don't think we have anything to worry about. A random crime, a burglar taken by surprise, I'm sure."

"Why wouldn't you be worried?" She's now sitting forward, and her eyes look crazed. "This entire town is fucked. Crazy people are taking over, killing, drugging kids. And you just sit there, so ... un-fucking-fazed."

Robert glances at me, no help at all, as usual.

"None of this makes sense unless..." she says, more to herself. Her eyes are moving back and forth in their sockets. She's thinking too much.

"Oh, Bryony." I stand, take a seat closer to her, and wrap my arm around her shoulders. She tenses. I sneak my other hand beneath the table to give her a quick but painful pinch in the side. "I'm sorry this has you so upset. There's nothing to be afraid of. We'll," I look at her father and back to her, "take care of you. Don't worry."

She jerks her face away when I try to caress her cheek with the back of my hand. With a concerned look still stitched to my face, I give her side another pinch, the angles of our bodies hiding my action from Robert. She knows better than to make a sound, and silent tears form in the corners of her eyes. If they fall, he'll believe them to be caused by fear of the faceless killer, not of me.

I lean in and kiss her on the cheek, then whisper in her ear, "Time for bed, my darling."

Bryony opens her mouth to say something, then stands and retreats, chin tucked to her chest, shoulders slumped. I want to dole out a lecture on her posture, but the entire scene pleases me. She is so strong-willed by nature; it has taken years to break her. I'd been so concerned all my work was unraveling. It seems this last incident may have been just the help I needed. I take such pleasure in killing, but there are so many other delightful ways to take someone's life, even while keeping them very much alive.

Chapter 63

Eloise

I lean on my car in the parking lot behind Alyssa's office. She's been working late most nights. At first, I assumed this was where she and Robert were having their secret rendezvous. I pictured her sitting on the edge of her desk, skirt hiked up, his pants around his ankles, pounding against her with her head thrown back in ecstasy. To most women, this image of their partner with someone else would send them into a jealous rage, but I'm not most women.

"Hello, Alyssa."

She doesn't startle, a perplexing reaction. Her outstretched hand is frozen with her keys out, the button to unlock her car not yet pressed. "Can I help you, Eloise?"

"You know my name, how lovely. We find ourselves acquainted without ever being introduced."

"I was at the party you threw and spoke with your husband. You know all this; let's not play dumb."

I release a piercing laugh. "Oh, darling, we both know who's playing dumb here."

Her hand falls to her side, and she releases a sigh. Still confident. Still unafraid. It usually doesn't take me this long to penetrate people's defenses. But Alyssa is a unique one, with her skin of steel. I'm struggling to understand her: what makes her tick, what she's after. It's making my pulse quicken with excitement. It's a challenge, and I like it.

"Is that all? It's been a day, and I'm not playing guessing games with you. Wonderful to see you again, it is pleasure to properly meet you. Have a nice evening." She unlocks her car and reaches toward the handle.

"Lovely evening, isn't it? Would you like to get a drink? Robert did tell me all about your conversation. Mentioned you were new here, looking for friends. My treat." I've turned up the charm. I don't know Alyssa well yet, but I have a feeling she'll accept my invitation. The curiosity of this strange encounter is too irresistible.

She returns my smile. "You're a peculiar woman, Eloise, but I *am* intrigued. There's a wine bar right there." She points across the street. I already know this. I've spent a significant amount of time there lately. The question is, does she know I've been there, watching, waiting?

I straighten and walk to her, then trace her spine with my fingertips before looping my arm with hers. "I can already tell we're going to be very good friends, Alyssa." I'm so close when I say this, that my lips graze her ear lobe. She doesn't so much as flinch. And I know she *is* going to be different; this is going to be some of my greatest work. Our dance begins.

The wine bar is full of men and women drinking away their stressful workdays. Alyssa and I slide into a booth in a dark corner. A flustered server welcomes us and takes our orders. Two glasses of chardonnay. Alyssa slips off her jacket, and at some point, she unbuttoned the top two buttons of her silk blouse. Her surgically enhanced breasts turn a few heads of the men closest to us. Once our wine is delivered, she traces the rim of her glass with a delicate, manicured fingernail.

"Are you ready to tell me the real reason you've asked me here?" she asks.

I sip my wine without breaking eye contact. My lips curve into a smile. "No hidden agenda. I am a very good judge of people, and you were someone I knew I wanted to meet."

She leans forward, elbow on the table, her fingers under her chin. "I'm flattered. But what kind of friend are you looking for, Eloise? That's the million-dollar question now, isn't it?"

Alyssa oozes sex. She's the type of woman used to having men and women trip over themselves for her affection. I'm still unsure why she would be interested in Robert. He's okay in bed, but she can thank me for that. It's taken years of training to get him to where he is today. It has to be the money. There's no other logical explanation. Regardless, this evening is going better than anticipated, as she's exactly who I expected her to be. A user of people. She believes herself to be the cleverer of the two of us, the more charming. I'll let her continue with this belief. It only benefits me in the end.

A few more glasses of wine and our conversation settles into safer territory. After an hour, we're interacting as if we've known each other for years.

"It's getting late, but we should do this again sometime," Alyssa suggests.

I nod.

We settle the bill and stand to leave. "I'm just going to run to the bathroom," I say.

The room stands at the end of a dark hall at the back of the bar. I push open the door and smile when I hear the hinges creak behind me. I smell her musky perfume before I see her. Alyssa grabs me and spins me around, pushing my back against the door, reaching down and locking it. With my face held in her hands, she looks into my eyes and presses her body against mine. Our lips part and connect, a hungry, animalistic kiss, our tongues desperately exploring the insides of each other's mouths. Her hands run down my body. I let out a moan that I know will excite her, allowing her to believe she's once again getting exactly what she wants. She bites my bottom lip and speaks, breathing each word into my mouth. "That was nice."

"Better than my husband?"

She releases a throaty laugh. "That's what this was about? Revenge?" she leans in and kisses me, "I much prefer you to your husband. Why don't we go back to my house?"

I push her back gently and put a finger to her lips. "Our secret?"

She nods, and we separate. I move to the mirror to reapply my lipstick.

"I have a confession to make." She's leaning on the stall.

I pause, and my reflection meets her gaze. "Go on," I say.

"You must be wondering ... why Robert?"

I stare, waiting for her to continue.

"I mean, look at me." She traces her body with her hands and laughs. "It must have crossed your mind that he's nowhere near my standards."

I close the lid on my lipstick, drop it in my purse, and turn so we're facing each other. My head tilts in a half nod.

"It was the strangest thing. It started with letters hinting at some 'big mission,' all very ripped from the movies. Then I received the letter with a request. Never one to pass on an adventure, I decided what the hell, I'll see where this goes."

"What request?"

"It simply had Robert's name and instructed me to seduce him. The letter included a five-thousand-dollar money order and said that if I completed the request, I'd receive ten more." She shrugs and checks her reflection. "Seems like you have an enemy out there, Eloise."

"Yes. So, it would seem."

"Anyway, let's not let that ruin our fun. Still in for my place?"

My smile warms. "Yes, darling. It will be a night to remember."

Alyssa's townhouse is the only predictable thing about her. Decorated in cool grays, it's minimal and modern. The second the door shuts behind us, she's reaching to unbutton my slacks. I slap her hand away.

"No. Go to your bedroom and wait for me there. I have a surprise for you."

Her eyes widen, and a knowing grin splits her face. "Mmm, okay. If that's how you like to play."

"What is this?" Alyssa laughs as I appear in the doorway. "Some sort of role-playing? I know you're using me to get back at your husband, but this may be a bit much."

"A game, yes. That's exactly what we've been playing, darling." I walk into the room; she's lying on the bed on her back. I stand over her. Robert's suits hangs off me, but I've rolled the pant legs and arms so my mobility isn't restricted. For the first time this evening, Alyssa's confidence falters and her lips purse.

"Seriously, what the fuck is this?"

She never gets the answer to that very important question. I'm on top of her, knife plunging into her chest. When I'm sure she's dead, I step back, breathing heavily. A full-length mirror stands in the corner of the room, and my reflection catches my eye. I turn my head to take a good look at myself and watch my head tilt to the side. I look so beautiful, covered in blood. Robert's gray suit is now soaked in it, making it look black and wet.

I turn my attention back to her mangled, lifeless body. I'm not ready for it to be over. I take off Robert's suit and lie down next to her, caressing her face and tracing her body with my fingers. Her eyes stare at the ceiling, two glass marbles, and I'm whispering for her unhearing ears. I should be worried about DNA, the police, of getting caught. But I can't think over the euphoria coursing through me. Tears slip from my eyes down to the pillow. It's so beautiful, too much to bear.

When my heart has stopped racing and I've caught my breath, I know it's time to leave. I clean Alyssa's body and room as best I can, removing any traces of my DNA. I don't think it will be an issue, not with what I have planned. First, the condoms filled with Robert's semen. 'A condom?' he had asked last night. I forgot to take my pill, I explained, blaming my forgetfulness on Tobin and Suzanne, the attack, and everything going on. I promised to do better, but we should be careful, just for a few weeks, just to be sure. He didn't look fully convinced, but what could he do? A man will do anything for sex. Next, the hairs, though fragments of him probably covered this room already. I take off his suit and stuff it into a trash bag, along with his knife, and put my own clothes back on. One more quick glance around the room, and I nod in approval. I drive home to my adoring husband. It won't be long before he learns what an incredibly stupid mistake he's made. And mistakes are always punished.

Chapter 64

Eloise

I wait a few days after Alyssa's death.

"Melanie, could you come in here for a moment?" I call for her to join me in our bedroom.

"Something you nee—" Her face drains of color, and for a moment, I'm struck by the beauty of her pale and shocked expression. It's the same effect human irises have in the moments of one's last breath.

"Do you have any clue what happened here?" I motion to the suit I've laid on our bed, crusted with dried blood. "Did Robert have some sort of accident?"

She shakes her head, wringing her hands by her heart. "No," she whispers. "I've never seen that suit. At least not like—that."

With my elbow propped by my hand, arm across my chest, I tap my lips with my index finger, deep in thought—a farce. "Hmm. Interesting. I wonder what happened."

"Could it be animal blood? He helped a wounded deer, perhaps? They are everywhere this season, bounding out in front of cars left and right." I can picture her mind racing, attempting to find an innocent, plausible explanation for the bloody blazer and slacks. There is none, and the uncertainty in her voice tells me she knows very well this was no wounded deer or animal of any sort.

"You're probably right; nothing to worry ourselves over." I shift my attention from the bed to Melanie. "But ... it is troubling, don't you think?"

She hangs her head. "Yes, a bit."

A curt nod. "All right. I think that will be all for today. I need some space to contemplate this situation. I can trust your discretion on the matter until it's resolved?"

"Oh, yes. Of course." She's nodding enthusiastically, eager to escape my home, I'm sure.

After Melanie has packed her things and left for the day, I find the card the kind officer left with me the day of my attack and dial his number. I explain my unusual yet concerning situation, and if he could please clear time in his schedule, I'd appreciate his assistance in the matter. No more than thirty minutes later, he's knocking on my door with a gentleman I've never met.

"Mrs. Williams, this is Detective Starling." Officer Donaley introduces his plain-clothed companion. "Why don't you show us what you've found."

I lead them upstairs to our bedroom, but before I can say a word, Detective Starling is on his phone calling someone, speaking in a hushed tone. The officer grips my elbow and turns me around.

Bryony pokes her head out of her room down the hall. "Mom, what's going on?"

"Are you two the only people in the home?" he asks.

"Yes, just me and my daughter Bryony."

He indicates with his hand that she should come with us. "I need both of you ladies out of the house. This is a crime scene."

"Crime scene," I declare. "I'm sure this is all a misunderstanding. No crime has been committed here," I say, feigning shock.

"Did he just say crime?" Bryony's panicked voice carries down the hallway.

I clasp my hand to my neck. "Could the blood not be from—"

"Blood!" Bryony interrupts. "What blood?" Her eyes are panicked. They shift between the three of us.

"Bryony, come here, sweetie. It's okay; it will all be okay." I hold out my arms, ready to embrace her. A flash of suspicion flashes across her features. She knows this is all an act. She also knows if she doesn't play along, there will be consequences. She shuffles to me, and I wrap my arms around her tense body.

"It's not Daddy, is it? Is he okay?" she asks.

"Your father is fine. Let's go outside and let these gentlemen do their job." I escort her downstairs and outside with my arm around her shoulder. Once he's sure we are out of their way, the officer disappears back into the house leaving Bryony and I standing on our front porch.

"What the fuck is going on, Mother?"

"Language!"

"There are two police officers in our house, and we were just kicked out. I have a right to know."

"This is going to be quite upsetting for you. But if you must know, I found your father's suit covered in blood."

Her eyes grow wide, and she looks like she is choking on her words.

"He's at work, and he's fine. But the police are interested in determining why I've found blood-soaked clothing stuffed in a garbage bag in the back of our closet."

Bryony purses her lips and shakes her head. I can't even begin to guess what stories she's spinning in her mind. She doesn't dare accuse me of anything, though. She knows better.

Detective Starling steps through the front door and requests a word with me. I follow him into our entryway.

"Can you tell me where you found the suit?" He's an older gentleman, nearing retirement if I had to guess, but in good shape for his age. Everything about him is nondescript, from his plain slacks and white button-up shirt, to his features and his demeanor.

"I was organizing his closet and noticed a trash bag behind the spot where he hangs his pants. I found it an odd place for a trash bag and thought perhaps it was clothing he had put to the side for donation. Imagine my surprise at what I found inside."

"Did anyone else witness this discovery?"

"Yes. Well, no, not exactly. Melanie, our house manager, was in another room. I called her in and showed her what I found. I thought she might know the origin of the blood. She takes care of our laundry, you see, so I thought if Robert had some sort of accident, he may have informed her."

"And?"

"She was as shocked as I was," I exclaim.

"Hmm." He nods and gazes off to the side as if he's thinking, but I know these tricks. He's offering me silence, hoping I'll serve him what he needs, like the typical blubbering housewives he deals with. He doesn't realize I'm not who he thinks I am. I patiently wait for him to continue.

"Do you know Ms. Alyssa McDaniels?"

I pause, pretending to think. "Yes, I actually mentioned her to Officer Donaley just the other day, in fact. Alyssa came to a charity event I recently threw—uninvited, I might add. That alone is highly unusual. These are exclusive events I throw. Robert was off to the side talking to her. I asked who she was, and he explained that she and her husband had just moved here and were interested in meeting new people." I knit my eyebrows and shake my head. "I have been married to my husband for many years, and it just—oh, how do I explain this? It didn't feel right. You know what I mean? It felt like he was lying, and there was more to this Alyssa character. With all the recent attacks, I'm on high alert for anyone out of the ordinary. She stuck out as someone out of the ordinary."

"Alyssa was found murdered two days ago. Brutal affair. I can't divulge any details, but officers are on the way to your husband's office to bring him in for questioning."

I stumble toward the couch and collapse onto it. "I'm sorry, I need a minute. This is—as I'm sure you can imagine... a lot to process." I pause, breathing, allowing the tears to pool in my eyes. "Robert would never hurt a fly. Surely you don't suspect he's had anything to do with this? He didn't even know this woman."

"I've put in a request for a warrant, which we should be receiving any minute. Unfortunately, we're going to need you and your daughter off the premises when my forensics team gets here."

"This is quite the inconvenience. But Bryony and I will manage. Are we permitted to pack some personal items? Certainly, we can't be expected to leave without any clothing or toiletries."

"Yes, one of the officers will escort you to gather a few belongings. Are you sure your husband hasn't had any other interactions with the deceased before the night of that event?"

"I suppose you can't be sure what anyone does when they aren't with you, can you?"

"No, you most certainly can't."

With our suitcases packed, Bryony and I are on our way to a hotel room for the evening, possibly for the foreseeable future.

I pull out of the driveway, Bryony sitting next to me, stunned into silence.

One down.

Chapter 65

Eloise

I'm sitting in Poppy's kitchen; it's been two days since the police have ransacked our home, and Robert has since been arrested for Alyssa's murder. His bail hearing is set for tomorrow.

"I don't understand why you and Bryony don't stay here. You know we have plenty of space, and you are both more than welcome," Poppy says.

"I don't want to impose. We are fine, absolutely fine," I assure her. "Even if Robert makes bail, he'll be staying elsewhere. I'm not worried about him."

She looks unconvinced. "It's just that with everything happening. First Tobin murdered, and now Robert arrested for murder. It's—unbearable. All of it." She's working herself up, and I don't have the patience to talk Poppy off her typical ledge. I'm too happy. We should be celebrating. Things are going exactly as planned. There is the pesky matter of who is behind the letters to Alyssa, but that's future Eloise's problem.

"Have you talked to Suzanne? She was released from the hospital yesterday. I went to see her, and she seemed to be doing well. I can't believe she's staying in that house after what happened. And with the killer still on the loose. I'd be terrified. She wasn't even scared."

She slides into a seat, placing two steaming cups of tea on the table. I take a sip and consider this.

"I have not. She was running around telling everyone Tobin and I were having an affair. I think it's time to cut ties with her. I have enough to deal with. Robert's upcoming trial will be an absolute embarrassment to not only me but Bryony as well. Bryony is still not fully healed, mentally at least. I don't have the time nor the desire to convince Suzanne her accusations were ludicrous."

"Beatrix feels basically the same way. She said that Suzanne is crazy now, and she wants nothing to do with her or her shit. That's how she put it anyway." Poppy shrugs and blows on her tea. "It's all so sad. I feel like...I don't know... I guess I just feel helpless."

I place my hand on her wrist. "There's nothing you could do. I'm sure we'll all be fine. Well, obviously, not Robert, and definitely not Tobin." I laugh.

"Oh! You think Robert is guilty?"

"As sin."

Bryony is watching TV and eating a bowl of ice cream when I get home from Poppy's.

"Must you, Bryony?"

She rolls her eyes and scoops a large spoonful into her mouth. Ever since her father was arrested, she's been unruly. A matter I'll have to deal with soon.

"Is Melanie here?" I ask.

"She just left, and said dinner is in the oven. There's a note on the counter with instructions on how to warm it up."

I'm about to ask what she's done with her day when a loud pounding on the front door interrupts me.

"Now, who could that be?"

"Probably more cops," Bryony replies flatly.

"Can you get it for me, please? I just walked in, and I'd like to put my stuff away."

I'd like to smack the look she gives me off her face, but if it is the cops, a handprint on her cheek may raise some eyebrows. She slams her dish on the side table and stomps to the front door. Annoyed, I look around for a paper towel or napkin to place under the bowl. I can't leave it like this. I walk briskly toward the kitchen.

"Mom." The shake in Bryony's voice makes me freeze. "Mom, please."

My back stiffens, and I turn around. From where I'm standing, I can see our entryway. Bryony has her back to me, but the fear convulsing through her is evident.

"Suzanne," I say calmly yet firmly. "Put the gun down."

"I don't want to hurt you, Bryony; I'm here for your mother." She's not looking at me. Her pistol gleams, held in front of her in extended arms, pointed at Bryony's chest. They are three feet apart. I'm contemplating how I'd feel if a bullet were to explode through her heart. The sympathy I'd receive, a husband going to jail for killing his mistress, a daughter murdered in front of my very eyes. It's almost enough for me to let her do it. I decide I'm not ready for Bryony to die.

"Suzanne, she's a child. Whatever issue you have is with me, not my daughter. Why don't we let Bryony go upstairs, and you and I can talk?" I step next to my side table where my purse sits.

She lowers the gun slightly like she's having second thoughts. Her chin dips, and her eyes are on the floor, not us. I take the opportunity to slide my hand into my purse and retrieve my own gun. When she looks up again, I raise it and pull the trigger. A perfect shot through her forehead. Bryony jerks when the blood splatters across her face, but she doesn't move. She looks at Suzanne's body sprawled on our foyer floor, and her head slowly turns to look over her shoulder at me. Still in shock, her mouth is outstretched in a mute scream. My ears are ringing from the gunshot. I make my way to Suzanne and stand over her body.

"Now we'll have to get the marble changed. That blood will stain. Shame, it's very rare. I doubt I'll be able to match it. The entire room will have to be redone."

Bryony finds her voice and releases a blood-curdling scream.

Chapter 66

Eloise

S uzanne dying in my foyer is enough for me to schedule an emergency trip to the spa.

"Bryony, you must move faster. The car is here, and we're going to be late."

I walk to the bottom of the stairs and grip the rail, glaring. We've had all morning to get ready, so I don't understand why it's taking so long. Finally, Bryony emerges, unbrushed hair pulled in a ponytail, sweatpants, hoodie, sunglasses, and Converse sneakers. She looks like trash. The entire point of booking appointments for us at my usual location was to demonstrate how completely fine we were. To remind the ladies that no matter what, I am who they strive to be but will never be.

She walks past me and snaps with more attitude than is appropriate, "I'm ready, happy?" I purse my lips and follow her with my glare. She turns her head and looks away from the dark stain in front of the door.

It will be taken care of while we are gone for the day. Suzanne and her memory will be left in the past, where it belongs.

Based on her attempted murder, I can only assume Suzanne was the one behind the prior attacks and stalking. So many problems resolved. I didn't even have to break a sweat.

We've settled into the back seat, and I ask Bryony if she's excited about our special day.

"It's time to get back to normal. Chins up. Smiles on. It will take more than a few inconvenient deaths to break us."

"Aren't you worried about your *husband*?"

I look over my sunglasses at her. "Why should I be worried about Robert? It's not as if I'm the one standing trial for murdering my lover."

"It's not fair he didn't get bail; I thought that was just a thing everyone got."

"Not if you're accused of murder and considered a flight risk. Though I'm not sure where the judge got that idea from." I turn and look out the window to hide my smile.

"There's been a whole lot of people dying around you lately. I'd hate to see you end up in the same spot. Doubt they have *spas* in jail."

My eyes remain looking out the window. My darling girl thinks she's so clever. She's forgotten who she learned from. It will take a lot more than her weak, veiled threats to get my attention. Bryony huffs and shifts in her seat. My smirk curves higher.

The rest of the drive is silent. I don't mind. I like the quiet.

The driver slowly approaches the historic mansion converted into a relaxation oasis, follows the circular drive, and stops to let us out at the front entrance. I instruct him to wait for us in the parking lot and remind him he's not to leave the property. The last time he made the mistake of running off to get himself lunch. I was forced to wait for him in the lobby for almost twenty minutes.

Bryony and I walk up the stairs leading to the front porch, marked by four massive two-story columns. The wooden planks creak under our weight. Inside, the entire space has been gutted. Each room is designed for a different treatment, so our bodies can be soaked, steamed, massaged, wrapped, rubbed, and polished.

An older woman and a smoother, younger version of her are pushing through the large wooden doors, laughing, talking, and not paying attention. I tried to sidestep, but the older woman barrels into me.

She squeals like a child and apologizes.

I lose control of my hands, and they reach toward her neck. Her smile turns to panic.

"Eloise?"

I've forgotten myself. This has never happened before. Bryony grabs the door before it shuts, holding it open. The two people I want to see least in the world are looking at me. I brush a particle of dust off the clumsy woman's shoulder and slip my mask back on.

"Something on your shirt," I say.

My warm expression has clearly fooled her, and her head nods enthusiastically in appreciation. The daughter doesn't look so convinced. I smile at her retreating back then turn and approach Poppy and Beatrix with my arms outspread.

"Darlings! What a wonderful surprise."

Poppy returns my warm welcome, but Beatrix remains aloof with her arms crossed and her eyes narrowed.

"Are you ladies coming or going?" I ask, looking between the two.

Beatrix, choosing to remain stubborn in her rudeness, walks toward the exit.

"We just finished!" Poppy says.

Internally, I sigh with relief. I'm here to relax, not listen to Beatrix and Poppy's nonsense. "Such a shame. We'll have to plan better next time." I indicate for Bryony to follow me. "Let's get ourselves checked in."

Bryony doesn't move. Her head tilts, and she gazes at me with a curious expression. I'd like to tell her it will give her wrinkles.

Her head turns, and she watches as the door shuts on Poppy's back.

I could stand here for hours waiting for her to work out whatever it is she's trying to work out, but I'm aware the girl behind the front desk is feet away, observing us.

"Bryony," I demand.

She slowly returns my stare, shakes her head, and walks past me to the front desk.

Chapter 69

BEATRIX

T he second Poppy gets in the car I'm asking, "Did you see it?"

She's digging in her purse for something. I smack it off her lap, and the contents scatter around her feet. Her head snaps up. "What the hell, Beatrix."

"Eloise almost choked that woman!"

"What woman? What are you talking about?"

I shift in my seat and slam my back into it with unnecessary, exaggerated aggression. She missed it. *Damn it, Poppy.*

"Never mind," I mutter.

Poppy shrugs and opens the door. She throws everything back in her purse and then slides back into the driver's seat. "Want to grab something to eat? I'm starving." She turns on the car and uses the backup camera screen to ease out of the parking spot.

I'm disgusted by her. By Eloise. By myself.

"No, Poppy, I don't want to 'grab something to eat.'"

My mockery makes her face fall, and she looks like she's choking back tears.

I can't possibly bring a child into this mess. This baby deserves so much better. I resolve to do everything in my power to protect this baby from the chaos which I've surrounded myself.

The only way to keep this baby safe is to eliminate Eloise.

Chapter 68

BRYONY

I logged into my socials before we left for the spa, for the first time in forever. Everyone has moved on. No one has shared the video in weeks and my DMs are empty. I'm not naïve enough to think that just because they aren't talking about the images of me naked and dancing like an idiot that it's suddenly erased from their memories, but at least it's in their heads and not in front of my face. Teenagers get bored easily; a scandal is only entertaining for so long. Then, they are desperate for the next person's misery to revel in. But judgment, that lasts forever.

I stare at my mom through the steam in the sauna. Her eyes are closed, and her head is leaned back. Not a care in the world.

Eloise's hands are full of blood, mine filled with time, enough time to know she hasn't used even a second of hers to check on my dad. She's convinced he's guilty and has found ways to annoyingly remind me of her opinion whenever she has the chance.

I know my dad. He doesn't even kill animals.

"Do you remember when we first moved into the house?"

Eloise sighs a ridiculously dramatic sigh.

I ignore it and continue, "Those mice that got in, do you remember?"

She visibly shudders. "Filthy things. Those contractors should have cleaned up after themselves. What kind of professional leaves a multi-million-dollar home crawling with mice? I hope those poor reviews I left them put them out of business. I should check."

"Yeah. Anyways. Dad spent *hours* searching the internet for a humane way to get rid of them."

"A complete waste of time." She resumes her position, head leaned back, eyes closed.

"My point is, how can the same person who couldn't even kill a mouse kill a woman? It makes no sense." I only look away for a second.

Her hand wraps around my neck, but my skin is slick from sweat, and it slips, sending her falling on top of me. I slide so my back is on the bench, and I'm able to get my feet between us and kick her off.

She sprawls on the floor, glaring when the door opens. A woman rushes to my mother's side, helping her adjust her towel and assisting her to her feet, asking if she's okay.

The back of her hand is at her forehead, and she's shaking her head. "The heat has really gotten to me. I stood to leave, and it was all too fast. I'm sure I've given my daughter quite the scare." Her green eyes seem to glow as they glare at me. "Don't worry, Bryony, Mommy's alright."

I swallow. Nod once. Then gather myself. I jump off the bench and wrap an arm around her shoulders. "I tried to grab for you. I'm so sorry. I wasn't fast enough. I thought..." I manage a sniffle and a tear. "I don't know what I thought."

The women are looking at us with sympathetic frowns.

"Ladies." Mother nods to the women. "I do appreciate your help, but if I don't leave, I fear you may be picking me up off the floor again." We all chuckle. Old friends they've become. A month from now, they'll see each other in the massage parlor lobby and share a laugh about the incident.

We're in the locker room gathering our things and I check my phone. I've picked it up a hundred times, ready to tell the police exactly what I think of Eloise's convenient find. The suit that will be sending my dad to jail for the rest of his life.

To tell them that and to tell them everything.

Yet, something stops me every time.

I'm not sure what will happen next, but I do know I can't be the keeper of her secrets anymore.

The seams in my skin are starting to tear.

We've run out of room.

I love her.

I hate her.

Chapter 69

Eloise

I've invited Beatrix and Poppy to brunch. After Beatrix's chilly interaction at the spa, I felt it important to put her back in her place. They saw what happened to the last person who made the mistake of throwing me out of a room and ending a friendship: she ended up dead in my foyer. I hope that was enough to remind them who decides when my relationships have reached their conclusion.

"You're looking happy and well for someone whose husband is sitting in jail," Beatrix says.

"And you're looking—not well, Beatrix, if I'm being honest." I actually mean it too. Dark circles ring her eyes, and her cheekbones protrude, but not in a nice way.

Poppy and I both gasp when she bursts into tears. I really thought she was stronger than this. The unbridled display of emotions is unbecoming, especially for her.

"Beatrix! What's wrong?" Poppy exclaims.

"I'm pregnant," she confesses flatly.

I smirk, and Poppy grins like an idiot, standing with her arms open, ready to pull Beatrix into an embrace.

The server approaches our table and sets down our drinks.

"Sit down," Beatrix hisses at Poppy. "This isn't a fucking celebration."

Poppy's face drops as quickly as her body does into her seat. "I don't understand. This is wonderful news. With everything going on, we could use some happiness."

Beatrix dabs her eyes dry with her napkin. She's left some mascara smudged under her left eye, but I'm not going to be the one to tell her. Let her look like a mess.

She sucks in a deep breath and lets it leak out through her pursed lips slowly. "It's Tobin's."

"What?" Poppy gasps loudly.

"Poppy, enough with the dramatics," I scold. "We're in public, really. Contain yourself."

"Tobin, as in Suzanne's Tobin?" Poppy lowers her voice.

"Well, the good thing is, Suzanne is dead," I say. "I suppose you should thank me for taking care of that problem for you." I hold my wine glass up in Beatrix's direction.

Poppy stares at me, jaw hinged open.

Beatrix narrows her eyes. "This isn't a fucking joke, Eloise. Two of our friends are dead. I'm pregnant with a dead man's baby, and my husband had a vasectomy years ago."

"Ah, I see your dilemma—can't pass the bastard off as his. Shame. It would have been an easy out for you. You certainly have gotten yourself in a predicament here, Beatrix."

"I mean, have you considered, you know—taking care of it?" Poppy asks.

"I'm keeping the baby, if that's what you're insinuating."

"If you have no desire to save your marriage, I'm sure Tobin had a healthy life insurance and a DNA test is all it would take for you to be financially stable at least. As far as mental stability goes, well, you seem to need some work in that area."

"You're such a bitch, Eloise. And frankly, I don't have the patience to deal with your shit right now. Do you really think money is what I'm concerned about right now? I'm pregnant. With a dead man's baby, whose wife *you* killed." The tears are back. So annoying. "I can't do this anymore. All of you, you're all so fucking messy. I'm done. Poppy, I'm sorry, I love you, but I just can't anymore. Don't call me; I'm moving on with my life. I have a child to think about now, and I can't play these games anymore."

She stands, throws her napkin on the table, and storms out. Internally, I'm groaning, wishing I could follow her out because now I have a crying Poppy to deal with. Her head is bowed, she's sniffling, and she's not even trying to hide the tears dropping off her face. At the same time, I want to put a bullet in Beatrix's retreating back. This brunch was scheduled to teach these ladies no one walks out on me.

Poppy composes herself and blows her nose. "What do we do?"

"Not a thing. None of this is our problem. Besides, now you know the kind of person Beatrix truly is. Do you really want her slinking around your husband? Good riddance."

"I suppose you're right. It's just ... Suzanne's dead, and now this." Her eyes bulge. "Not that her death was your fault," she rushes out. "She was *not* in her right mind, obviously. Bryony could have been killed, and you did what you had to, to protect your daughter."

"I have zero guilt over killing Suzanne. She made her choices, and now she has to live—well die with them."

"Yes. Unfortunately, that's exactly it."

I indicate to the server and she returns to our table. "We won't be eating today. A bill for the drinks, please, quickly. We've had an emergency come up."

Chapter 70

BEATRIX

I knew Poppy would be surprised when I called. I made it very clear at the lunch that I was done with her and Eloise. And I meant it. But what I'd found was too important not to share.

She opens the door with a wide smile. "Beatrix, come in! I'm so glad you called. I was worried about the way we left things. I wanted to respect your space, but also ... oh, I don't know." She steps aside and ushers me into the kitchen.

I throw the stack of papers on the island.

"Can I get you something to drink? Water, Tea, Coffee?"

"No, I'm fine. We need to talk about something," I say.

"Sounds serious." She stops fiddling with the coffeemaker and gives me her full attention.

"I need you to read these and keep an open mind with what I'm about to say."

"Okay," she replies, letting the "O" drag out.

She picks up the stack and starts flipping through the pages. They've been printed on standard letter-sized paper, but they contain newspaper articles.

She shifts her focus from the papers to me. "I don't understand. Why am I looking at these?"

"Don't just skim, *read* the articles." My hand rubs my belly. It does that a lot these days; I don't even realize it until it's too late to stop it. I'm sure I've noticed David catching me doing it. I'll have to tell him soon. I'm just not ready to say goodbye yet.

Poppy starts reading an article about the search for a missing woman. She then moves on to the next, an article about the same woman, her body found mutilated beyond recognition. Police had to use dental records to identify her.

"I remember this," Poppy whispers. She looks up from the article. "Wasn't she one of the first?"

I nod, then grab the papers from her hand and start laying them out page by page until her counter is covered.

Poppy stands and walks to the fridge to fill a glass of water from the door. "What's the point of all this? I'm sick of all the death and murder."

"Well, that's just too bad. Because these were left on my front porch ... with this."

I walk over to her and hold up the photo. Her glass shatters on the floor. She grabs it from my hand and holds it up to her face.

Taken from far away, we're sitting around a table at who knows which brunch. Suzanne's head has been scratched away, and Eloise's face is circled. The hand that held the pen that made these marks was angry, ripping through the ink. Above her head, in messy handwriting, is the word "Murderer."

"It's Eloise!" I scream.

Her head jerks back in confusion. "This must be about Suzanne." She hands the photo back and bends, picking up the larger pieces of glass and walking them to the trash can. Her eyes land on the articles. She pauses and bites her thumbnail. "There's no way Eloise could have done all that." She flicks her wrist over the articles. "Oh! Maybe this is the work of that stalker of hers."

"And maybe that stalker isn't a bad guy."

"No, this can't be true. Eloise is our *friend*. She's not a killer." Poppy laughs nervously.

I throw my hands up in exasperation. "She killed Suzanne—"

"That was self-defense; Suzanne was going to kill Bryony. And the entire situation would have never happened if you hadn't been sleeping with her husband. That's what drove Suzanne mad. Maybe this is guilt, Beatrix. Your poor decisions are what set these awful things in motion."

My words become sticky in my throat. Poppy's never been so blunt with me before. And maybe there was some guilt. For a split second, I wonder if I've gotten it all wrong. What if Eloise's stalker is just some jealous mom who's out for revenge because Eloise stole some PTO award or whatever it is they use to earn PTO status.

I shake my head. It's not like we all don't know something is off with Eloise. She hides it well, but those of us closest to her have always seen it. We've just never had the courage to speak the words out loud.

"There's something else." I shuffle the papers around until I find the one I'm looking for.

Poppy reads it out loud. "How well do you know your friend?"

"Doesn't it seem strange that she killed one of our friends, her husband is on trial for murder, and she's acting like nothing happened?

Brunch with her friends. Spa day with Bryony. Her behavior is not normal, Poppy. And it never really has been."

"Maybe she's still in shock. Everyone processes trauma differently. I have no idea what goes on in Eloise's mind. Yours either. But you can't go around accusing people of murder without proof. A few newspaper articles aren't enough."

"I'll just have to find proof, I guess." I gather the papers and turn to leave.

"Beatrix, you're pregnant. Think of your baby. Maybe it's best if you let it go. If Eloise is guilty, let the police do their job. Let them be the ones to figure it out."

I stop walking and turn around to face her. "She's way too good for that."

Chapter 71

THE WATCHER

I stand naked in front of the full-length mirror in my dark motel room. The curtains are pulled tight against the windows, but a single beam of sun sneaks through, illuminating me and the dust. I trace the circle on my hip with an index finger, round and round. The uneven skin is puckered and white. My entire body is marked with scars. Years of raking a razor blade over your skin will do that. But this is the only scar that matters to me; this is Eloise's scar, the only visible one, at least.

I knew something was wrong with Eloise ever since Billy's death. We all did, I'm sure. But no one dared speak the words out loud. We were alone with those feelings. And we were just kids. Adults don't get involved in the bickering of kids; they certainly don't take kids' opinions into account. So, we all went along with it. Every stupid game, every stupid idea. And then Layla.

I may have felt alone, but we always have choices. I chose to let Eloise morph my jealousy of Layla into hate. I chose to smash her head with a rock. And I chose to tell no one. I joined the search parties and helped hand out the missing person flyers. I watched my mom and aunt cry and beg for her to return, all while I knew exactly where her body lay. I had the closure they so desperately needed, and I kept that from them.

I let myself fall deeper into Eloise's sadistic world.

Then senior year came. One more year, and I would have been gone. Off to college, away from Eloise and her evil. I'd fooled myself into thinking once I'd gotten away from her, I'd be fine, healed, and able to move on with my life as if it was all a terrible dream.

During the day, I played along, followed her around with the rest of her lapdogs. At night, I chugged my mother's stolen wine and dragged a razor across my skin.

I had a great life, loving parents. But the same can be said about Eloise. Her parents raised her right—none of this is their fault. I guess some kids are just born evil, and there is nothing you can do about it.

"I have an idea," Eloise said on the night. All of us girls looked at each other. We knew that any idea of Eloise's wasn't a good thing.

"We're so close, like sisters. We should do something special. Something that bonds us forever. Because that's what sisters have, a forever bond."

"We're already sisters, Eloise," I said, Layla's face flickering behind my eyes, reminding me of the last bond we made. "Isn't loving each other enough?" I couldn't do it again. Whatever she had planned, I knew I wouldn't survive. My body might, but not my mind.

Eloise looked at me like I was a child, too young and dumb to possibly understand her enlightened view. "Oh, Cricket, we *are* sisters," she said and caressed the side of my face with the back of her hand. I could feel the trail of cold it left in its wake. The kind of cold that burns with pain.

She walked outside the circle we were sitting in around the fire pit at The Greasy Woman's shack, and without the glow from the flames, she disappeared into the shadows. When she returned, she was carrying some sort of metal rod.

"What is that?" I asked.

"This is our bond."

"What are you going to do with it?" One of the other girls asked. Her voice shook with the same fear, closing my throat.

Eloise pointed to the end, an iron circle. "This part gets heated by the fire, then I'll place it against your skin. Each of us will have the same mark. A permanent reminder of our sisterhood and love for each other."

"Absolutely not," I exclaimed. "We aren't cattle. Do you know how much that will hurt?"

She smiled at me, the fire lighting her from below, casting shadows on her face, making her look like the demon she truly is. "Physical pain is temporary, but there are other types of pain that are not."

She was outnumbered, and we shouldn't have taken her threats seriously. But Eloise has a way with people that's impossible to explain. She gets into your head, and her thoughts become yours.

"Cricket, why don't you go first? Show the girls it's not so bad."

Determined not to let her feast on my fear, I stood and made my way over to her.

"A few more things," Eloise said. "Secrecy and loyalty are the foundation of every bond. Wouldn't you all agree?" She gazed around the circle at each of the girls to ensure everyone was nodding their heads in agreement. "Each of us will carry this circle with us for the rest of our lives. With that, we will also carry the bond and trust of everyone here. To ensure that trust, I will be keeping something from each of you, something you would do anything to protect. And that will keep our secrets safe and our trust unbreakable. Please remove your clothes, Cricket." A few of the girls giggled, and a few gasped.

"Just do it and hurry up so we can drink." I couldn't tell who had spoken, but I knew I had no other choice. I stripped and stood naked in front of these girls who were supposed to be my friends. My eyes squeezed shut, waiting for the pain. When it didn't come, I looked around and saw Eloise had retrieved something else. A Polaroid camera. My breathing became raspy, and my heart felt like it was working too hard; I just knew I'd collapse dead at any moment.

"First things first. Down on your hands and knees Cricket."

Tears started streaming down my face, and I shook my head. Inside, I was screaming, "No!" I looked around the group to see if anyone was going to save me. They all refused to meet my eyes.

I slowly lowered myself to the ground, and Eloise began taking photos. A photo was forever, and I knew not only was the physical copy permanent, but the shame would be tattooed on my bones for the remainder of my life. She continued to position me, each pose more humiliating than the last. None of my friends, my 'sisters,' demanded she stop, and no one stepped in to help me.

I didn't step in and help Layla years before, and she was family. This was my penance. Until I died and went to hell, hell would come to join me in the living world.

Back on my hands and knees, she held the brand over the fire until the iron glowed as bright as the fire's flames. I'm sure there was pain, but I felt nothing. My mind had already left me, and there was nothing left inside my body to register my burning flesh. With my skin permanently sealed to Eloise's demented idea of friendship, she leaned down and kissed me on the cheek. Her lips seared more painfully than the brand.

"You did so good, my darling. So, so good. Now, let's get you dressed."

The rest of the girls suffered the same humiliation. Stripped naked, branded, photographed. None of them in as many poses as me, though.

After that night, I searched everywhere for a means to numb my pain: drugs, alcohol, sex, self-harm. No matter what I tried, I couldn't close my eyes or be alone without Layla and Eloise joining me.

Finally, one day, my parents, not knowing what else to do, sent me away to a mental health facility where I lived for seven years. I've never told anyone what Eloise did to me, Layla, or to those girls.

I kept her secrets. How could I not? They weren't just hers.

Like my life, my words were stolen from me. Eloise stuffed them so far down my throat, I choked on them and have been suffocating ever since.

When I was released from the mental health hospital, Eloise didn't force me to hunt her down. It wasn't Eloise who walked away from my family, my friends, from everything and everyone I'd known. I did that all on my own. And each step I took down the path leading farther away from a safe and normal life caused the fractures in my mind to splinter and split. It's gone now, shattered beyond repair.

My scar suddenly feels on fire; it does that sometimes, especially when the memories float through my mind. I reach down and lay my palm on it.

I'm no longer a person. I'm a capsule of hate, regret, and revenge.

Chapter 72

Eloise

The letters began arriving two days ago. No return address, simply a piece of paper, each with a single name written on it, starting with Alyssa's. Each letter had a different name, each name one of My Darlings.

The predator has become the prey.

"I'm sorry to do this, Melanie. You've served our family well, but with all that's going on, I'm going to have to dismiss you. You'll receive six months' pay and a glowing recommendation, of course, anything I can do to help you land on your feet. I do hope you understand."

She sheds a few tears, says she understands, and I walk her to the door. My next stop is the hardware store. I have a new plan, one I've been forced into. I need some time to think. I'll have to leave the country. I know this for certain, but when and how, I haven't figured out yet.

Bryony and I enjoy a nice meal, takeout from one of our favorite Italian restaurants. I even allow Bryony a glass of wine. We've been through so much; we deserve a bit of indulgence.

She takes a sip and scrunches her nose. "This tastes funny. Are you sure it's not gone bad?"

"That's just your immature palate, dear. You're not used to finer wines. This isn't a beer pumped from a keg or wine from a box. Keep drinking, your taste buds will acclimate."

She does as she's told.

The Rohypnol works wonders. I silently thank my foreign contact, as Bryony is soon face down, drooling into her chicken parmesan. Not about to ruin my dinner, I finish with Bryony snoring across from me. I glance around the table of dirty dishes and am dismayed by Melanie's absence. When I find out who has been sending me those letters, I will cut off their fingers and toes one by one. Then I'll make them lick my dishes clean.

After dabbing my mouth with my napkin, I test Bryony's weight. She can't be more than 125 pounds, but she feels three times that size. I hoist her up, so I'm carrying her like a baby. Thankfully, our panic room is located on the first floor, so there will be no stairs to struggle up. My back aches remembering the last time I had to carry a body up a flight of stairs. I toss her on the bed and close the door behind me. This is where she'll be spending the rest of her life. A day, a year, ten years; I haven't yet decided. This was another decision yet to be made.

I pour myself a glass of wine and make myself comfortable on my couch. My phone to my ear, Poppy's phone only rings once.

"Eloise, hello. How are you doing?"

"Poppy, I've called with the best news. Bryony has been accepted into a very exclusive music school in Switzerland. One of the scouts I invited to her concert just called. They had a spot open, and she leaves the day after tomorrow. It's all very last minute, and we have so much to do, but I'm—we're both ecstatic, as you can imagine."

I look at my phone, and another call comes in. I roll my eyes. This is the fourth time Grace has called; you'd think she'd get the hint. I reject the call.

"That's wonderful. A fresh start is just what she needs. And you both could use some good news. If there's anything I can do to help, please let me know. Tell Bryony congrats from me!"

"I will make sure to pass on your message. I hate to run, but as I said, there is much to do and not a lot of time."

"Yes, yes, of course. Chat soon!"

I hang up and click Grace's contact.

"Grace, so sorry, I was just on the other line with Poppy."

"Eloise, so glad I've finally gotten you. I've been trying to call you for days. First, how are you doing?"

"I'm wonderful. In fact, we've just received the best news about Bryony."

"Bryony is actually why I'm calling. Annabelle received a strange text from her the other day, and she's been very worried."

"What sort of text?" My fingers grip my phone a bit tighter.

"It said. "I'll miss you.""

I wait. Sure, there's more to this supposedly strange text.

"Eloise, are you still there?"

"I'm here. I was waiting for you to get to the strange part."

"You don't find it a bit ... foreboding?"

I huff a laugh. "Not at all. She's been accepted into a prestigious music school in Switzerland. Isn't that wonderful news? I'm sure that was Bryony's way of telling Annabelle. Maybe she didn't want to hurt her feelings, what with her music career about to take off, and Annabelle's ... not."

I can hear Grace breathing, so I know she hasn't hung up. However, she doesn't react quickly enough with her congratulations.

"That sounds wonderful," Grace says without sounding like she means it. "What's the name of the school?"

I'm suddenly craving a razor to drag across my arm. How could I have been so careless not to have a school name ready? Of course, this would be a question I'd be asked. However, anyone in my situation would have fared much worse. I've outsmarted them all, and one small mistake won't ruin that.

"I want to tell you so bad. We've signed an NDA. It's all very exclusive. Very hush-hush."

"I—that seems all very wonderful for Bryony. I just have never heard of a situation like that."

"Perhaps if Annabelle practiced a bit more, she'd be in the position to receive a similar offer."

Her heavy breath on the phone disgusts me. "Speaking of Annabelle, could you let Bryony know she'd like to see her before she leaves? I know she'll be crushed if she doesn't get to see her off."

"I'll be sure to pass on the message. She leaves in just two days, though, so I'm not sure if she'll be able to fit it in."

We say our goodbyes. It's now abundantly clear that leaving the country will have to happen sooner rather than later. With my necessary calls out of the way, all that's left is to decide whether anyone else needs to die prior to my departure.

Chapter 73

THE WATCHER

It's been three days since anyone has come to or left Eloise's house. The forest lining her property has made for a convenient hiding place. With nothing but a sleeping bag and backpack filled with power bars and water, I've sat watching and waiting. By now, everyone has received my letters. Eloise knows I'm out here, maybe not here on her property, but she knows there is someone wandering this earth who knows her secrets. And I'm no longer bound by sisterhood to keep those secrets for her. I worry for Bryony. Her social media accounts have all been shut off, and there's been no movement in her bedroom window. The lights never turn on at night, and I haven't seen her since they went to the spa.

I have seen Eloise. She stands at her front window, curtain pulled to the side slightly, staring into her yard. She hasn't walked around the property yet. If she did, she may have found me, or at least traces of me. Is this her way of beckoning me?

Every time I consider calling the police, I trace the burn circle with my finger, and my resolve strengthens. This is my fight. My chance for revenge. I won't let the police or anyone else take that from me. I need to do this for Layla, Billy, and the rest of Eloise's victims.

The sound of a car engine startles me from my thoughts. I whip my head around to see a police cruiser slowly winding up her driveway.

"No, no, no," I cry to the trees. Has someone already called them? I've missed my chance.

Chapter 74

Eloise

I open the door to Detective Starling. "What a surprise, Detective. I wasn't expecting you. Do come in. Is this about Robert?"

"No, Mrs. Williams, I won't take up much of your time. I'm sorry to bother you what with all you're going through."

I huff a laugh. "It has been quite an eventful few weeks."

"We've had someone make a report. I'm sure it's all a misunderstanding. But procedure and all that. One of your friends stopped by the station today—"

"I don't know which friend this is about, but I have enough going on. I'm sure whatever this issue is can be resolved without me."

He sighs. Annoyance? Discomfort? I begin studying his body language.

"The problem is, this woman had a pretty wild theory. Claimed Robert is innocent, and you were the one who killed Alyssa."

"Absolutely ridiculous. I've heard enough. I think it's time for you to go."

He pulls out a notebook from his back pocket, and as he's flipping the pages, a name sticks out: Beatrix.

"Your cooperation would be much appreciated. I'd hate to have to ask you to come speak with me at the station."

I stare him down. "I know my rights, and you've overstayed your welcome. Unless I'm under arrest or you have a warrant, this conversation is over."

"Roger that. This friend of yours also accused you of being a serial killer responsible for several women's deaths. Do you know why anyone would accuse you of something like that?"

I laugh. "I don't know who this person is, but they are clearly no friend of mine. A serial killer? Do I look like a serial killer?"

He scribbles something in his notebook, but he flips it shut and slides it in his back pocket before I can see what he's written.

"Well, that's all I have. I'll be out of your hair now." I gladly escort him the few steps back to the front door and open it for him.

He turns on the front porch to face me. "Have a nice evening."

I offer him a pinched smile and shut the door, standing at the front window peeking out the curtains.

His cruiser makes its way down the driveway. I let the curtain drop. With my eyes closed, I rub my temples, sucking in deep breaths. The motion does nothing to calm the fury tightening my chest.

I make my way to the panic room and unlock the door. Bryony scrambles off the bed and into a corner. She's dropped the book she was reading on the floor. I pick it up and flip through a couple of pages.

"Are you enjoying this?"

She nods.

With the book raised above my head I lunge at her, beating her in the head with the hardcover. Her hands fly over her head to protect her face from the blows. Her weak attempts are no match for the rage driving me. I toss the book back on the bed and pull her up by her hair, dragging her across the room, where I throw her onto the small twin bed as well. She tucks her knees to her chest and silently cries.

Straightening, I smooth my hair and inform her there will be no more meals today.

"Why?" she croaks.

"Because I'm not in the mood to cook."

"Not the food. Why? Why are you doing this to me?"

My head tilts. I'd answer, but I'm not even sure myself.

As I close the door, I can hear her beg, "Just kill me."

Which is exactly what I may have to do.

Chapter 75

THE WATCHER

T he police officer leaves alone; maybe he came because of Robert?
Lies, lies, lies. I try so hard to lie to myself, and I'm terrible at
it. I shouldn't have left those articles for Beatrix. It was compulsive. I
just wanted her to know it wasn't her fault. To try to alleviate her guilt.
Suzanne didn't die because of her affair with Tobin; she died because she
breathed Eloise's poisonous air for too long.

I rock back and forth, chewing my nails. It's time.

The only weapon I have is a knife. She's a skilled killer, and I'm positive
I won't live through the night. That's okay. I've left enough evidence
to convict Eloise if I don't. I open my phone and send the email to
Beatrix and Poppy with instructions on where to find the key to the
safety deposit box, and the bank it's located in. There's no turning back
now.

I stand and take a deep breath. My mind flashes once again to what my life could have been, what it should have been. I picture Layla's green lawn and white picket fence and her beautiful, freckle-faced kids.

I'm not afraid to die, but the thoughts flow over me like a wave of sadness. There's been plenty of time for regret, for what-ifs. I've made my choices, and I always knew they would bring me here to this night.

As I'm walking toward her front door, the garage opens and Eloise's car is backing out. I watch her leave with tears blurring my vision.

Chapter 76

Eloise

It took some prodding from the hospital staff, but finally, David comes to the phone. I'm on my way to his house, but as expected he's at the hospital. Thankfully, I've caught him between surgeries.

"David, hello, Eloise here. I know you're a busy man, so I'll make this quick. I have some alarming news to share with you. Your wife is pregnant—"

"Eloise, I'm at work. Beatrix isn't pregnant. This is none of your business, but I've had a vasectomy. We can't get pregnant."

For a doctor, he's not the brightest. "It's Tobin's. Tobin and Beatrix were having an affair. She's now carrying his bastard child. Surely, you've noticed she hasn't been drinking lately. Do you really think Beatrix would voluntarily give up her nightly wine that we all know she's so fond of? Anywho, I thought you deserved to know. I'll let you go now."

He's saying something, but I've hung up too quickly to hear. I can picture his stunned face staring at the phone, wanting to deny what I've just told him but knowing damn well it's the truth. I depress the gas pedal and watch the speedometer climb. I'm soon pulling into Beatrix's driveway.

Beatrix opens the door cautiously. She wraps her cardigan tighter around herself as if it can protect her from me.

"What are you doing here?"

"Can I come in?"

She begins to shut the door, and I throw my hand up to stop it from closing. Her eyes widen, and her mouth opens to say something, but I cut her off before she has the chance. "Had an interesting visitor today. The police came by. He told me a friend of mine paid them a visit. Know anything about that, darling."

"I have no idea what you're talking about."

I chuckle and shake my head. "Enough with the lies. I know what you've been doing. Attacking me in the woods, drugging my daughter, throwing bricks through my window, and now the letters."

Her fear turns to confusion. "Bricks, letters, *Bryony*. What are you talking about? I had nothing to do with any of that."

She's not that good of an actress. She must be telling the truth. If it wasn't Suzanne or Beatrix, who could it be? I don't have time to think about this now. I pull out my gun and shoot Beatrix in the head. Her body crumbles to the floor. I look around to see if the gunshot has lured any nosey neighbors from their homes. The street is silent and empty. I kick Beatrix's body far enough into her house so I can shut the door. Poor David will have quite the surprise to come home to. I hope he doesn't have a heart attack.

He'll call the police, and my house will be the first place they come. My time has run out—at least here.

Chapter 77

THE WATCHER

E loise isn't gone long. She comes flying down the driveway like she's on a highway. Something has happened. It's now or never.

She opens the door after I've knocked three times.

"Who are you?" She looks genuinely confused. It's been many years, but her forgetting me so easily still stings. My entire world has centered around her. Her voice in my head is so familiar it's indistinguishable from my own. And she doesn't even recognize me. *Fucking bitch.*

"I thought sisters were forever. Isn't that what you told us? An unbreakable bond."

Her eyes narrow and she begins to shut the door. I throw my body against it. The door swings open, and she stumbles back.

She looks like a robot. Feet together, hands at her sides, the only thing moving is her mouth. "Thank you for stopping by; I'm busy and not able to take guests today. Let me show you to the door."

I start laughing, shut the door behind me, and take two steps so we're inches from each other. "I think I'll stay."

"Who are you?" she demands. Her green eyes have the same cold, unfeeling glare I remember. The face surrounding it has changed over the years, but her soulless eyes haven't.

I frown and cluck my tongue. "I guess it was all lies. Sisters forever. Loyalty. Bonded for life."

Her eyes flit around the room; she's looking for a weapon. She doesn't know how well I know her mind.

"It's Cricket." I step back and hold out my arms. This leaves me vulnerable, but I'm willing to risk it for the sake of theatrics.

Recognition lights up her face, and she lunges toward me, hands reaching for my neck. I'm quick, as I've been practicing for this my whole life. I evade her grasp, grab the knife from my back pocket, and plunge it into her stomach. Her eyes bulge and she takes three shaky steps back, holding the knife handle.

I've made a mistake. I shouldn't have released my grip. Eloise pulls the knife from her abdomen and smiles at me. She waves the bloody knife in front of her face. "You forgot something, darling."

I scramble back toward the wall. A vase with lilies sits on a table, and I reach to my right and grab it with both hands. Eloise runs toward me and slips on her own blood; this is my chance. Before she's able to regain her footing, I swing the vase and hit her across the side of the face. She crashes to the floor, and the knife slides across the marble.

She's down, bloody, bruised, but she's still awake, still fighting. I run past her to reach for the knife. Her arm reaches out and grabs my leg, and I crash to the floor. My face smacks the hardwood, and black spots float in front of my vision. I'm screaming at myself to stay awake in my head and crawl toward the knife. It gives Eloise time to grip my other leg with her free hand. The floor is slick with blood—hers, mine, I don't know. We're now face to face, and her hands grasp for my neck, but she misses. I bite down until I taste metal, and she screams as my teeth tear through her skin. Her grip on me with her other hand loosens, and I kick her in the stomach where the open stab wound is.

I'm free, my fingers inches from the knife. Her hands grab me one more time, but she's weakening. With the knife in my hand, I flip on top of her and plunge the knife into her back. Not making the same mistake again, I continue stabbing her forty, fifty, one hundred times. There's so much blood, a river of red.

I won. It's over.

I have to find Bryony and save her. I hope it's not too late.

<hr />

I'm fading. I want to lie down and go to sleep. My eyelids are so heavy, and every step is like walking through quicksand. I've searched the entire house, every room, every closet. I lean my back on the wall and slide down. If I could rest my eyes, just for a moment. Maybe Bryony is already dead. Buried in the backyard. My search is in vain. I should leave. Call the police. After a few minutes, just a few minutes of rest.

My head snaps up, suddenly alert. I'm sitting in front of a closet. Someone is screaming at me inside my head. It doesn't sound like my voice, but who else could it be? It's pulling me to that door. Telling me to open it. To keep going, that Bryony is still alive, that it's my duty to find her and save her. Maybe the two of us can run away. She can be my family. I'll adopt her. She can be my daughter. We'll have a white picket fence, picnics, and vacations. It will be a beautiful life. The life we both deserve.

I struggle to push myself up. I need a break. Still leaning on the wall, I take a step, testing my legs to see if I can trust them to hold me. I stumble on the two steps it takes to reach the door and grip the handle with my hand, still slick from blood and sweat. My head leans against the door. I take several ragged breaths before turning the knob. It's just a closet. I step inside and flip on the light, pushing the jackets hanging in front of me to the side. Several fall and I see it, another door.

Chapter 78

BRYONY

The room Eloise locked me in is windowless and soundproof. I have no idea how many days I've been in here or what is happening beyond my prison's door. This room was built for our protection. A place to hide if there were intruders. If my dad knew the only time it would be used was to keep me captive, he would be devastated. I think about my dad a lot, as I have a lot of time to think these days. I'm fully convinced Eloise set him up. I know he couldn't kill that woman. If I get out of here, I'll find a way to clear his name. I've begged for her to kill me, end this pain. I take it all back. I don't want to die. I need to save my dad.

The door is opening; she's back.

She's made a mistake. The infallible Eloise is not so perfect after all.

I stand where I know the door will hide me when it opens, gripping her mistake so hard it slices my palm open.

She's walking in. I summon every ounce of strength left in me and lunge, plunging the shard of broken plate in her neck.

As my arm comes down, I realize I've made a mistake, too.

"You're not my mother."

This stranger of a woman is lying on her back, grasping at her neck, blood pumping from the wound with each beat of her heart.

She's trying to talk.

I bend and place my ear near her lips.

She's saying something. Repeating it.

"She's. Dead."

I straighten and look at my hand, still holding the shard of glass, then slowly release my grip and let it fall to the floor.

My eyes meet hers. She's no longer trying to talk. Her body convulses, then stills, then repeats the process. A tingling begins beneath my skin. It dances. I squat and look closer into her eyes. The walls and bed and entire house fade. It's just me and this woman.

And I understand.

I fill my lungs with air. The kind of breath you take before diving deep, deep, deep underwater.

I sense the exact moment she shifts from living to dead. It's a beautiful sight. Magical almost.

I place my lips next to her ear and whisper, "Good night, My Darling."

The End

Acknowledgments

First a giant virtual hug to all the OG readers who I met when I debuted last year and who have stuck by me through book three. You keep me going when the words are stuck and the doubt sinks in.

Alex and Tina, what a long, strange trip it's been. Thank you for continuing to push me to be better, knowing when to tell me to knock it off and put on my big girl pants, and most importantly knowing when I just need a shoulder to cry on. Here we are on book three, and here I am once again saying cheers to the many more books and the many more years to come.

Jacinda, thank you for catching every missed word, missed comma, wrong word choice, and all the other things I can't help but do; the readers, thank you for your meticulous attention to detail as well.

Katrina Escudero and Alyssa Weinberger, you have worked tirelessly to bring my characters to life in a way I never thought possible. I couldn't ask for a better team. A million thank yous wouldn't suffice.

Leo Richardson, you are so damn talented. But more importantly, your energy and enthusiasm for life is contagious. How I got so lucky to have you as part of this journey, I will never know ... but see you in L.A., first round's on me!

Justin W. Lo, Kelly Ripa, Mark Consuelos, James Griffiths, Michael Halpern, Lindsay Maizel, and everyone at Milojo Productions and Fee-Fi-Fo Films; thank you for loving these characters as much as I do. I couldn't imagine them being in anyone else's hands.

And finally, a massive thanks to the unsung heroes behind the scenes, my writer friends especially Arden and Maggie, my critique group, David, Susan, Melissa, Alexa, Tony, and Rick, my first and still biggest fans, Mom and Dad, my husband, and a new inclusion, my little (not named yet, but will be when this book is released, but I had to turn this in before he's due, so sorry bud I'll get your name in the next one) nephew and my baby sister Laura, who is going to be the best mom ever.

About the Author

You can find Marie Still heavily caffeinated reading and writing books in the Tampa area, while balancing time with her husband and four kids who are slowly getting older and moving out ... they have been replaced by cats. Marie's debut *We're All Lying* received several awards and was named one of Buzzfeed's most anticipated thrillers of 2023. She also writes under Kristen Seeley (*Beverly Bonnefinche is Dead*), where she focuses less on murder and more on unconventional women and the lives they lead.

Upcoming Thriller from Rising Action

Bree knew that life married to a beat cop would be tough, especially in the crime-infested city of East Bernheim, but she believes they will be fine living in "the Burner" even after she has their first child. Family life is manageable until one day crime follows them home, threatening their safety.

At a loss of how to keep his family safe and keep his job, Jake agrees to stretch their finances and move an hour away, to a bigger house in a somewhat better neighborhood. Their life seems to improve until Bree, heavily pregnant with their second child, begins to hear voices and suffer strange dreams. And then when tragedy strikes on the job, Jake enters a spiral of guilt and grief that degrades his grip on reality.

Bree, isolated and struggling, must protect her children from the one person she thought would always keep them safe. She and Jake are haunted in every way, and not just by whatever is lurking inside the house. A thriller that tackles toxic masculinity in police culture and trauma, Every Fall will have you on the edge of your seat.

Releasing January 28, 2025